RULES *for a* BORN AGAIN BACHELOR

RULES *for a* BORN AGAIN BACHELOR

NELSON BROOKS

Copyright © 2016 by Nelson Brooks.

Library of Congress Control Number: 2016905947
ISBN: Hardcover 978-1-5144-4828-1
Softcover 978-1-5144-4827-4
eBook 978-1-5144-4826-7

All rights reserved. No part of this book may be reproduced or transmitted in any form or by any means, electronic or mechanical, including photocopying, recording, or by any information storage and retrieval system, without permission in writing from the copyright owner.

This is a work of fiction. Names, characters, places and incidents either are the product of the author's imagination or are used fictitiously, and any resemblance to any actual persons, living or dead, events, or locales is entirely coincidental.

Any people depicted in stock imagery provided by Thinkstock are models, and such images are being used for illustrative purposes only.
Certain stock imagery © Thinkstock.

Print information available on the last page.

Rev. date: 04/21/2016

To order additional copies of this book, contact:
Xlibris
800-056-3182
www.Xlibrispublishing.co.uk
Orders@Xlibrispublishing.co.uk
733294

I am a creative well, bubbling with ideas and gushing words. However, that is not the way that books come to life. Yes there has to be a draft, but just as importantly there has to be the person who makes sense of the babble of words I initially scrawl across the electronic page. The person who sees that it all make sense is my wife, friend and editor Elaine. She diligently marks up by hand each printed word. When it doesn't always gel, she adds the glue. When the point is not clear, she challenges me for clarity. She also allows me the anti-social moments of total concentration that every writing endeavour invariably needs. This book would not be here without her support and for that I thank her.

Suffolk Libraries	
30127 08418370 1	
Askews & Holts	Jul-2016
AF	£10.99

Chapter 1

One of These Nights
10 December 2010

Hanging by my fingertips from a first-floor balcony in Pimlico is as good a place as any to consider the state of my life. My perception is sharpened by being naked, with my clothes lying fifteen feet below in a puddle. Standing next to them is a large salivating dog of mixed parentage. By that I mean he looks like a big nasty bastard who appears to have anger management issues. To complete the picture, this is not my flat, it is nearly midnight and we are in the Christmas party season. All around me is the silence of a night when the rest of London has headed towards their beds. The only sound is that of the distant sigh of bus and taxi brakes as they speed the weary home. I am beginning to wish I'd headed back to my own bed. My fingers ache and want to let go, while my brain is screaming to the contrary. My heart is pumping with adrenalin and at the same time heavy with disappointment as another promising liaison has gone wrong. I thought it was only men that lied about being married.

I know that seems a little naive, but I only re-entered the dating market fairly recently due to an unforeseen hiccup in my married life—divorce. I have now reached the point where I doubt my judgements about anybody, male or female. I mean I should have seen the signs when Annie, my ex-wife, started spending a lot more time at the office and in her Pilates class with her instructor. I never really considered how affectionately they hugged when they met, just pupil-teacher bonding, I told myself. Trust me when I say that nothing knocks a guy's confidence more than when, after eight years of marriage, his wife runs off with her sports teacher, it is almost a cliché. The split was amicable enough and to be honest I didn't miss the sex life as that had been non-existent for some time, but I did miss the company. My best mate Gerry and his wife Charlie have told me since that if company was all there was to it, then I should get a dog. My parents and my siblings, Paul and Beth, have since also shared their views on the suitability of Annie and my original coupling, information which might have been helpful far earlier, like when we met and before I married her. What this means is that I am back on the dating scene at just over 40 years of age, with no idea how it now works anymore (not that I was any good at it the first time around). The damned world went and changed and didn't have the decency to tell me.

This short period of suspension allows me to reflect on all of the things that have happened since Annie and I split as some of them have been rather bizarre. With the obvious confidence knock I got after the divorce, I have started to blame myself. Well, I am the single common denominator in all these occurrences; could it simply be me at fault? Maybe I didn't read the signs; I certainly know that I need to become a little more observant. So while I hang here contemplating letting go, injuring myself in the fall, and being savaged by the slavering hound below, I think it would be a good idea to consider how to avoid getting into these situations in the future. There have been some learning points that I could share with other guys who find themselves in my position. By this I mean newly back on the dating market of course, not hanging stark bollock naked from a balcony in London in mid-winter.

'Oi, Raffles,' came a disembodied voice from below. I tried to see the source but the particular configuration of my arms was not really allowing this. At least that dog had stopped barking.

'Who's there?' spoken in the world's worst stage whisper. I was very aware that just one double-glazed pane away from me was potentially a very good pasting.

'You're a burglar, I'm guessing? Is this some sort of way of not leaving any forensic evidence? Or maybe you're one of those Parkour guys, free runners, or in your case, very free runners. Well if you want your clothes back, monsieur, I suggest you drop down before Misty here makes even more of a mess of them.'

It was surprising enough to find a female voice attached to the beast below and even better still that she sounded friendly. I thought the best idea was to let go with one hand and twist around to take a look at her. As I took one hand off, the other failed to take the strain, gravity then did the rest. I slipped and let out a fairly noisy expletive. Let's be honest, the ground is hard from two feet when you hit it as a child. In winter, from fifteen feet, when naked, it is bloody hard—cold and hard. Coming out of the darkness into the pool of a streetlight came first the mutt, then the lead, which was very taut. Finally into the light appeared a rather attractive brunette. I did my best to cover up my obvious embarrassment with my hands.

'I would either get dressed or grab your clothes and go if I was you.'

'Your dog; are you going to set it on me?'

'It? SHE, Misty, she's a bloody girl. Anyway with what I can see from here you haven't got enough of anything to satisfy her. No, I was referring to getting away before he catches you,' at which she pointed upwards sharply.

Above my head I could see the light from the window brighter than before and a rather large man looking to see what the noise was. I was beginning to wonder if he had noticed my attire or the lack of it, when he started to shout.

'You're right', I agreed with her, 'time for a tactical withdrawal.' Pulling on my boxers and grabbing the jeans, shirt, and leather jacket, I started to run down off down the alley. God knows where my shoes were, I thought, until one went whistling past my ear. Ah, I think I left them in her hall.

As we reached the end of the street, the girl with the dog turned to the left while I went to make off in the other direction. I was freezing and figured out the best idea was jump into a cab back to my place since I still had my wallet in my jacket.

'Raffles', she yelled, 'you are going to catch your death like that. My place is just around the corner, why don't you come and get a drink. No funny business; just a drink.'

'Are you insane, you don't know me from Adam'—the irony of that statement never fails to escaped me—'I could be an axe-wielding maniac with a huge blade.'

'It's okay, having seen you naked, I know that's not true. I'm perfectly safe as I have Misty here and I would love to know what you were doing up there. I enjoy a good story and I have some Scotch that would warm the cockles. Then you can grab a cab home afterwards. I don't want you dying of hypothermia on my conscience. Come on, it's five minutes up the road and I know more about you than you realise. Besides, I think that man over there may be looking for you.'

I looked over my shoulder and noticed a veritable gorilla emerging from the doorway I had entered thirty minutes before. I mentioned he was big, but did I also say wide and angry-looking? I conceded she might have a point and decided to follow her, half out of curiosity and half out of fear of getting a beating from the bruiser. The thing is, I really like dogs, but I don't like girls with dogs. But right now I could feel the pull of a whisky bottle and I had all the strength of will of a compass needle. Once we rounded the corner and were out of obvious danger, I stopped.

'Can I take a rain check on that drink? I'm tempted I admit, but I have rules, you see.'

'You have rules? What, like Housebreaking 101?' Contempt or sarcasm cascaded from her mouth with each syllable.

'No, to stop myself getting into trouble with women, I have devised some rules; it's a work in progress as you can see. Meet me for a drink next week and I will tell you more. Oh, I'm Adam by the way.' I pulled a card out of my wallet, thrust it into her hand, and ran off to find a cab.

From the distance I heard her call back, 'In case you're interested, it's Sarah.'

Half an hour later and a hell of a lot poorer due to the cost of late-night taxis at Christmas, I was back in my own flat in the East End and wondering about the lovely lady with the dog. But there are rules, you see; rules that are there for a purpose, which should be followed and not ignored.

Chapter 2

Lyin' Eyes
10 December 2010

So I admit it; I have lied in the past. Well when I say lie, I really mean embellish. Let's not be picky, I am not an MP in an expenses scandal or some celebrity love rat. But I have occasionally told the odd white lie about my life. I have stretched the truth to within an inch of its breaking point and possibly beyond on occasions. But I guess that you want specifics; well let's talk about the scar on my forehead; that's a prime example. As a child I went looking for explosives and fell off my bike. To be less cryptic, at my school some guy from the police had come and told us that they were looking for stolen explosives from the railway depot. The ones they put on the track when they want to stop a train. You know that bit on *Scooby-Doo* or in a modern horror film where you are supposed to walk away when you know danger is lurking, but in the end you walk towards it? What this means in reality is that my mate John and I went looking for them. We cycled around our kingdom; that equated to about a mile every side of the house (well I was only 9 years old), and then we came to the big hill. Suffice to say it didn't end in a good way. I came off and skidded down the street using my face as a brake. I was not a pretty sight, but after a few days in bed, I was just left with the scar; however that is not what I tell people.

To be honest, *I fell off my bike as a kid* sounds particularly weak. So I have embellished. I have been a lifeguard who got into trouble in a sea rescue and then there was the time I smashed it on a concrete edge on a construction site when working as a Brickie. One time I even stated I got caught in an earthquake in the Philippines; mind you, I had been drinking at the time when I told that one. I think to a certain extent I just get bored with the mundane. I never deliberately lie outright, but I have a good imagination and love to spin a yarn (hopefully you can tell).

Why is this important? Well you can get into a ton of trouble if you say things you can't back up. There are a whole bunch of examples where I may have exaggerated for effect. Mentioning instruments I played (yes, I have been in a band), books I have allegedly read, and even holidays I said I had been on. This is wrong, let's be clear. However in all these instances bar one, apart from a red face, there was no real penalty for me. I created the *no lie* rule (rule 2) after a piece of embellishment that finally dropped me in it, almost literally. The lie was made to a girl called Sandy.

Alisande, or Sandy for short, was a stunning lady. She had some Turkish in her family line and that explains both her name and her striking looks. She was exotic in a way that English men lust after. It was the old Fry's Turkish Delight advert all over again, a touch of Eastern promise. Well anyway, I came across Sandy one day when I met up for a pint with Greg, an old friend from university. One of the things I found when I split with Annie was that suddenly at least fifty per cent of my friends no longer wanted to know me either because they didn't want to take sides, or because they were embarrassed by the whole thing. This meant that eventually I had reached out to old friends from my time at uni in Nottingham and from previous jobs that I had lost touch with. Facebook does have its advantages, but also its failings (see rule on internet dating).

I hadn't seen Greg for a few years as he had been out of the country teaching but then we started having a beer every couple of weeks and we were getting back into the old banter. On that particular evening, Greg wandered into the pub with his usual rolling gait. If you remember the Hofmeister Bear, you have pretty much hit the nail on the head. Following him was Sandy, catching the eye of almost every man in the room. The ones who didn't have partners who would have noticed; you get the point?

'Greg, I didn't know you had a good-looking sister,' I opened, thinking I could check out her situation.

'Back off, bozo, she's out of your league,' replied Greg.

'Hi, I'm Adam, and you are?'

'As he said, out of your league,' but that did not match the smile she flashed me. I held out my hand to this gorgeous creature and then realised something was odd. It wasn't the handshake but the grip that got me. It was that 'boy outdoing boy' deal that you used to get in the city. She had a grip like a python.

'Where the hell did you get a grip like that? You work out?'

'What's the matter, not used to strong women?'

'Strong women are great but I often draw the line where they can use my hands for origami. Come on, spill the beans, what's the trick? Weights, yachting, martial arts?'

'Rock climbing; well actually free climbing. Ever tried it?'

'I've done a bit.' And there it was, the little white lie was out. What I should have said was that when I was 17 I had one afternoon of rock climbing at the local outdoor pursuit centre. This was around twenty years ago when I was a lot lighter and a hell of a lot fitter. But being a bloke, I thought how hard can this be? She will probably have all the gear with the right labels on it. Then she would climb one wall and be off for a skinny goat's milk mochaccino. I should be able to do this standing on my head.

'Okay, then we should climb a face sometime.' At this my heart not so much dropped as repelled off the side of a cliff. I was going to have to dance pretty deftly if I was going to get out of this one without ending up flat on my back or being made to look a fool. But I am always someone who will give it a go. I agreed to meet up with her the following Saturday; she was gorgeous, how could I not? Frankly I also liked the obvious brooding intelligence that lurked just below the water line like a shark on the prowl. I thought my combination of quick-wittedness and dumb luck would see me through; it usually did.

Well Saturday came and with it a dull grey sky that Dulux would only match with a battleship or an accountant. I looked hopefully out of the balcony of my flat for the odd spot of rain, flake of snow, or a monsoon—nothing. It was like a mill pond out there, not a leaf stirring, not a crisp packet drifting across the street (this was the East End, remember). No, it looked like I was going to have to go through with this. I checked my phone on the off chance all hell had broken loose at work and I was required to go in. The BBC News showed no alien invasion or particularly virulent air-born toxin to avoid. Time to show Sandy whether I was a man or a mouse, at which point I had a strange urge to get a piece of cheese from the fridge.

Dressed in my most sporty casual clothes, I headed to the outdoor pursuit centre down at High Rocks in Tunbridge Wells. It is a strange irony that this is where I last climbed, all those years ago. My car being neither sexy or a total old banger looked odd in the car park, which seemed to be split between beamers at one end and hippie campers at the other. I parked in the middle feeling like the automobile ascent of man and went off in search of the inevitable pain that was to come.

'Ah, you made it at last. I thought I was going to have to start without you.' She was ribbing me, but to be honest for the smile it was probably worth it. 'Shall we start with me climbing and you belaying? I don't want to tire you out too early.' With that this beautiful creature turned into something half mountain goat and half contortionist. Her fingers were strong enough to hold her entire body and her back could almost bend double. I remembered my climbing experience; you only moved one hold at a time. It took care and attention. She moved with the speed and precision of a panther, reaching the top in less than three minutes, I was a little concerned. Then of course it was my turn. I climbed the first wall slowly and carefully and did not do too badly. When I had landed back at the bottom after abseiling down, she assessed my performance.

'Okay, you can do an easy climb. Let's see if you can handle something a little harder.' This time it was my turn to go first and Sandy prepared to belay. I reached the first three levels fairly quickly.

'You're better than I thought you were going to be. Your mate assured me that you would cry off. Greg suggested either a work excuse or feigning an injury.'

'Do I really look like a guy who would stand you up?' With this I reached up over my head for a stretch hand hold I should never have attempted. That's when I heard the almighty crack. 'That isn't supposed to happen I'm guessing,' I whined. I must have increased my pitch much more than intended as she told me to let go and slowly lowered me down, without help I may add.

'Not as fit as you think, are you?'

'Not as fit as I remember, sorry.'

It took about five weeks for my dislocated shoulder to return to normal and I am a lot more wary these days as I am told once it pops out, it is likely to happen again. Frankly, *Lethal Weapon II* is just not as funny as it used to be. When Mel Gibson pops his shoulder joint out at will, it looks cool; it is surprising how painful it can be in reality. The caveat to the story is I try to keep the embellishment within the bounds of possibility these days.

This tale and the rule that goes with it are meant to be an example of me learning from my past mistakes so that I don't put myself in these situations going forward. But as you can tell from my recent balcony escapades, other people can still lie to me, so the rules only go so far. The state of my shoulder also probably explains why I couldn't hang on for long that evening.

Chapter 3

Working Nine to Five
15 December 2010

Now I should make a couple of things clear. Firstly, I am not a misogynist, I had to use the spell-checker to even get that right. I do not spend my time finding fault with women or playing some kind of East London Lothario with delusions of grandeur. I am just a normal guy looking for a normal woman, whatever that is, and having no end of issues making this happen. Secondly, I do not have independent means to spend my life as a lotus eater waiting until Miss Right comes along (again) and hence I have a day job. During the hours of light and quite a few of the hours of darkness in the shorter months, as we are currently in December, I can be found in the offices of a major Swiss bank (you will have to excuse me if I am not more obvious about which one, but as I say, I do need to keep my day job).

No, don't go all high and mighty on me, there are some very nice people who work in banks, we are not all a bunch of insensitive money-grabbing bastards. In fact, I would generalise here and say there are two types of people that work in banking: bankers, those who must shout buy buy, sell sell, etc., and the rest of us. We are not by profession spending our time buying and selling shares, stocks, bonds, or any of a thousand financial instruments. No, we pass our days doing all the little bits in the background that make those things happen. We are IT geeks and lawyers, compliance experts and personal assistants. We eat, drink, exercise, chat, gossip, and occasionally knuckle down to a bit of hard work for our dull European masters. Generally we don't go around in pin-stripe attire but we usually wear suits, except on Friday for dress-down. Then it is just a fashion parade of loud shirts and designer jeans (and that is just the girls).

One of the hardest parts about being single in the workplace is that you are faced every day with that uphill battle to compete with your peers, both professionally and sometimes physically. These fall into three rival groups: the Party Animals, the Cuffed Couples, and the Duffers. The Party Animals are only a group through a mutual love of thrill-seeking, alcohol abuse, and sometimes less legal substances. There is a lot of banter about the level of drunkenness, the lateness of the party hour, and the state in which people return to the office in this 'live fast, play hard, burn out' culture. Now don't get me wrong, I'm not looking down my nose at them, I have been out with them many times and certainly will do again, but I am neither a twenty-something with a death wish nor a 55-year-old hanger-on who does not know when to quit. Occasionally I can chime in something useful about a band I've seen or a club I've visited, and generally they are harmless when taken in small doses. Being single again, I do have a certain amount of empathy for them.

It's the second group that probably causes me a bit more angst. The very nineties idea of the 'smug married' has moved on. There are a lot of couples out there, some married (they are the Manacled Married) and some just bound together (Cuffed Couples), but I tend to refer to them all as 'Cuffs'. They drone on about their own lives, but you get the feeling that deep down they would rather be with anybody but their partner. They have equity and probably a couple of kids, but they live almost separate lives. They can't split without losing it all, so they cover it up with a display of blissful bravado and relationship sleight of hand that would make Harry Houdini or Mata Hari proud.

I don't think even when I was married that I banged on about it the whole time. Do you know I don't need to hear about Tarquin's school or Jemima's first poo? I really don't care if you have upgraded from a

Saab to an Audi estate so that you can drive down to the Algarve this year. The winter is not too bad, so we are in the quiet season in relation to the continual one-upmanship, which would become as loud and annoying as a braying ass in the run up to Christmas and the New Year. Come February I will need to hear interminable tales of woe as they fail to secure sallopettes for Oliver and Olivia as they whisk the family off to somewhere in the Alps for half term. The height of the season for these materialistic mind games is when we hit the summer and the English weather threatens to offer a warm weekend. Then we will have the attack of the barbecue baristas; you have all met them. They have the gas-powered kit that they roll out of the shed which is the equivalent of an industrial furnace. The other half will have spent the previous day marinating or drizzling something that oik Jamie Oliver mentions in his book or that Tom Kerridge highlighted on the cookery channel (Sky whatever). I like food and I like alfresco eating, please don't misunderstand me, but whatever happened to a barbecue being something that just involved charcoal, burgers, and sausages? Sometimes it feels like every social occasion is an excuse to see how far ahead of the Joneses each Cuff can position themselves.

What I am saying is that all of this need to prove what you have simply appears to cover up what you are missing. The relationships just come across as dead. Unfortunately, in hindsight I now guess that it must have been this way for Annie, or she would not have left. How could I not have noticed? I keep thinking. I sometimes fantasise about myself in the witness box, being cross-examined. On a good day, I come out on top, but most days I am just left sitting waiting for the prosecution to push the knife in a little deeper.

The final group are the 'Duffers'. They are dyed in the wool bores who only stay to earn what they can and do the nine-to-five. They are typically men of 50 or above who are waiting for that magic pay-out of redundancy, while their partners at home are probably hoping for a heart attack and an insurance cheque. I try not to have anything to do with them as it is just too depressing. Cynical, me? Surely not.

I drifted a bit there, sorry, I'm back now. So these are the people I get to work with, in excess of ten hours most days and you wonder why I get a little cranky. A typical Monday morning will be a case of dealing with the weekend and early emails from Asia and then having a set of searching questions from the troops as they walk in the door. My response from the Party Animals is generally pitying because I am seen to be boring or from the Cuffs feeling sorry for me because they imply I am past it, whatever they privately think. The Duffers just grunt and get on with their internet surfing. You know sometimes you just can't win.

I should at this point introduce the team. Yes, it is a huge multinational bank with a home in the land of chocolate and cuckoo clocks and in London we have several thousand staff. However, like most places I do not work with thousands of people directly, but a floor of about three to four hundred and an immediate team of nine including myself. They split very comfortably into four Party Animals and four Cuffs and (pretty predictably in banking) only two of them are female—Angie in the former group and Jennie in the latter. Let's start with Angie who is 23, a graduate of some dubious poly come university up north and drinks pints like I drink water. She is a huge lover of heavy metal and would not be seen dead without the scars of battle from the latest gig or festival. Whereas the lovely Jennie (as I enjoy calling her, though she does not appreciate it) is 35 and has two under 5, which generally means a lot of nine-to-four working days and inflexible holidays. Although she does not come to the pub, she does a lovely hog roast on a hot summer's day I have heard, (and try not to overthink that one).

In my head I hear the trumpet fanfare from the film *Rocky* when I introduce the other three Party Animals, the first of which is Ricky (too cool for Richard, definitely not a Dick) aged 27 and a business analyst, vodka Red Bull drinker and a chain smoker. Ricky can often be seen in a club on a Friday night doing the infamous big fish, little fish, cardboard box while dancing to something with more bass than treble. Our second contestant is Andrew, a.k.a. Drew, who is 25, a strong proponent of a red wine diet and the front man for a rock band at the weekend. Drew has a degree in fine arts from Keele and frankly your guess is as good as mine as to what he is doing in banking. It is apparently something to do with diversity, but he is a hell of a tough act to follow on a Monday. He is as skinny as a rake, just under six foot tall and wears a ponytail like an ageing hippy. Even in a suit, he seems to sport an amazing amount of black in his attire. My final member of the singletons is Ralph (pronounce how you will) who is 47, has a righteously earned beer gut, and probably has a tattoo somewhere on his body for CAMRA, although I'll be damned if I'm ever going to ask where.

Now switch musical veins (and slash them if you feel the need) to the remaining members of team Cuffs. The music is unfortunately the theme from the *Good Life*, the 1970's Richard Briers, Felicity Kendall, and Penelope Keith comedy; Keith played the amazingly stuck-up Margot Leadbetter, a more appropriate name I cannot think of. We begin with Malcolm, a 37-year-old testing engineer who is teetotal based on the ruling of his harridan of a wife Patricia. I am not sure how he got so overweight when he does not drink; I think he may be comfort eating. When he is not doing that, he is boring for Surrey (although I believe he has the potential to go to national level at this discipline). Next we meet Steven (oh god, never call him Steve), who could send you to sleep on the merits of merlot for the Appellation Controlle of several French wine regions. He is physically fit, as he runs half marathons for charity, but he is an easy shot for those of us sniping, as at 41 he is thinning quicker than a Headingley test wicket. Finally the last to make an appearance, as this is more appropriate than you realise, we have Bernard (emphasis on the '*ard*). He is another business analyst who loves his heavy reds, but he has an aversion to an alarm clock and a massively impressive flexible working policy adherence; yes, he doesn't get in early or often. His 44 years have not been kind and now the spiders are starting to make his face look like crazy paving. Bernard is also known to the office as Rudolf due to his often bright red nose from the copiously well-observed liquid lunches.

A typical Monday in December, you already know the Friday night I had, so after arriving first I get down to the busy task of making my boss look good and await the slow dribble of my peers' arrival.

'Would you Adam and Eve it, looks who's 'ere first,' warbles Drew in a mockney accent. I fail to turn and look at him deliberately as I didn't want to encourage him.

'I hadn't realised it was national be a Cockney tosser day, you should have warned me, I would have got cakes in and everything,' I said and went back to looking at my mails.

'Oi, no need for that. You have a good one? We had a gig in a pub in Putney, what a shit hole.' He slopped his coffee on the desk and clumped down on his seat as he liked to make a real theatrical entrance.

'Do you know what I miss about you when you are not here?' I asked him.

'My sparkling wit and repartee?' He smirked.

'No, five eights of fuck all, now shut up and let me get on.'

'I am guessing that lovely lady from the party did not turn out as expected? That was quite some dancing there. Almost dad dancing I would say.'

'Nodding your head like the Quo until you need an osteopath does not make you a world expert. Anyway, mind your own.'

'Thought so; you got blown out, as opposed to blown, right?'

'Whatever, jog on, you loser.'

'Just making conversation, man.'

This was a pretty typical post-weekend exchange, although the party followed by my balcony antics had made it slightly more embarrassing than most. The problem was Christmas was a week or so away and I was without any form of date. It would be the second year on the spin that I would be at my parents' house alone and frankly my sister's Bridget Jones references were starting to get on my tits. I needed a plan and needed one fast.

Chapter 4

Man Eater
15 December 2010

After the initial high-brow banter of Monday morning, the office calmed down into the normal humdrum of answering emails, screaming managing directors, and insane fire drills for information from hung-over bosses. Lunch was the usual sandwich at the desk while juggling a conference call, mostly on mute, and filing away spurious missives from well-intentioned idiots. It was about two thirty when I saw something odd come into my inbox. I was actually surprised it got through the spam filter but then again that is one of the things that appear to be in the lap of the gods. One day I won't get that urgent email from a vendor but I will get an email for penis enlargement. Anyway I digress; an email appears in my box from Misty.she.wolf@gmail.com, which piqued my interest.

As has been suggested already, I have picked up a trick or two from this period of being back in the dating game. A Gmail account is pretty much something you can set up anonymously and so is a great way to contact someone with no comeback. By this, I mean you cannot be traced back if it turns out you are talking to a nutter. Misty.she.wolf@gmail.com looked playful and the title was specific enough for me to open the email without too much of a risk of it being a virus. When I mention the title being specific, I think you will see the point:

From: *Misty.she.wolf@gmail.com*
Subject: What Ho Raffles

Watcha, Raffles, how are you doing? Are you real, or is this just some bogus scam card that cat burglars, even naked cat burglars, give out to their intended victims, or innocent bystander witnesses. . . . I thought about catching up with you over the weekend as you intrigue me. It is not every day that a man says no to a nightcap when offered one. That reason you gave about 'The Rules' got me interested and it sounded like either a bloke speaking the usual drunken rubbish or something worth finding out more about. Fancy a drink sometime, on neutral ground, and with your clothes on this time? BTW, this is not a date . . . let me know, I am free on Wednesday. In case you are wondering, I am using Misty's email; she says hi or rather woof.

Well okay, the lovely lady with the hound from hell decided to get back to me. This could be an interesting diversion if nothing else. Now Wednesday nights are typically a do-nothing, middle-of-the-week type of thing and so a bit of a jolly over to the West End sounds like a bit of fun. I did however need to bait the hook for the evening or she might not fancy turning up. She had been cheeky, playful, and slightly flirty so I needed a good response.

To: *Misty.she.wolf@gmail.com*
Subject: Mistress of the hound

Greetings, Sarah (I am guessing that is what you shouted at me the other night), I see your acerbic wit does not diminish during the hours of daylight. I also thought about our meeting over the weekend, although admittedly part of the reason was the fear of Misty (How clever of her to have her own email address, does she has a pawsport too?). Do I assume we are not off to Battersea for a meet-up with her mates? If we can agree a pub, I would love to meet up and chat as I did say I would explain my position. I know you are around Pimlico, so what about 8 p.m. in the Marquis of Westminster? I am hoping you have a dog-sitter booked for the night?

Please bear in mind the Marquis is a busy pub with both tourists and locals and most importantly it is not dog friendly (according to the internet, so you can never be sure). I figured as I knew she lived in the Pimlico area somewhere, she would be fine with a place like that. In all first meetings of men and women, a public place is wise (rule 9). So with this, I got back to work and did not spend the day watching for further emails from the crazy dog woman. Okay, this is a lie. I know I said I don't but this is between you and me. Let's face it; I was just as intrigued by her. It takes quite a lot of gumption for a lady to mail a guy she has met on the street at midnight, especially when hanging naked from a balcony. I knew the next two days were going to drag on a bit. Fortunately work was busy enough and the children in the office were up to their usual games. Office politics is rather like war and unfortunately there are more foot soldiers in life than generals.

On Wednesday evening, I walked into the bar and had a look around for a familiar face, while all the time trying not to look like a date that had been potentially stood up. I saw her standing on the far side of the bar and she did look rather good. She was wearing a tight blue pair of jeans, a chunky jumper, and a rather heavy biker's jacket (I had to admit when I got closer to her that she had a nice arse, but that's just between you and me). As I crossed the bar, she turned and gave me a big smile, and I think I could guess the first line.

'You're going to say it, aren't you?'

'Oh yes,' she said nodding her head. As I drew near she smiled at the bar man who started to approach, and as he got within earshot, she enunciated very clearly, 'I didn't recognise you with your clothes on.' Well obviously this got the required look of horror from the bar man who then gave me a rather charitable glance up and down.

'What can I get you?' I thought I would get things off on the right foot. I looked down the bar and did a little mental juggling; beer, wine, or spirits, what gives the right signal?

'A glass of New Zealand Sauvignon Blanc please. Make it a large one if you wouldn't mind.'

'Perfect, make that two of those please, mate.' I grabbed the drinks after paying and gestured toward a free table in the corner.

'So let me get this straight, you have a set of rules by which you date girls?'

'Not strictly . . .'

'Now you are being cagey.'

'No, seriously, the rules are not about dating, they are more about rules for a relationship.'

'Isn't that a point of pedantry? How are dating or relationships different? Give me an example, how did it begin?'

'You know that's a bloody good question. I think, no, I know, I sat down one night with my best mate Gerry over a beer or six, and as we discussed my run of particularly bad luck over the years since my separation and divorce, it was decided I needed a plan. Gerry was and still is a big fan of the US cop show *NCIS* and in particular the character Leroy Jethro Gibbs. Gibbs has a set of rules that all his staff seemed to be aware of and that help him live his life. Well over the next hour we came up with the first ten rules. We started by writing them up on the score area of the dartboard in chalk, until the bloody darts team came in and started to rub them off. I remembered most of them the following morning sufficiently to write them up, as I had in my possession four beer mats with spider scrawled writing on them.'

'Okay, I will buy that, so the most important question is . . .'

'What is rule number 1?'

'How did you guess?'

'People who hear about the rules always ask. I suppose it is the logical question. The trouble is, people think that it is therefore the most important, but it is just the order in which we came up with them. I suppose related to the significance they had at the time.'

'So . . .'

'Tick-tock, tick-tock, tick-tock.'

'Bad timekeeping? Excessive use of onomatopoeia? Never date a terrorist?'

'Body clocks, you smart arse. Women that wake up in the middle of the night and hear that ticking sound while they see their chance of motherhood slipping away. Those that are simply so desperate to have a child that their voice of reason seems to have deserted them. Don't get me wrong, I love kids, generally other people's kids, but I am fairly ambivalent about having my own and I most certainly don't want to be rushed into it by a thirty-something holding a calendar in one hand and a thermometer in the other. Ovulation is not a topic I choose to discuss over the evening meal.'

'So you never dated women who are in this category?'

'No, that's the point of the rules. I won't date women in this category AGAIN.'

'Oh how wonderful, I have a new name for you. Now I know you are no cat burglar, I think I will call you Captain Hook. Tick-tock, tick-tock. How do you feel about crocodiles?'

'Oh very droll. Pretty and intelligent with a literary bent.'

'Flattery will not work on me, Captain; you are still in the dog house, at least as far as Misty is concerned.'

'Oh how is the darling little she-wolf?'

'Sitting at home sulking and waiting for a rematch. I most definitely saw her eyeing up your leg for a good bite last time we met.' With this I almost spat out the wine that I was drinking.

'I am sure that can be arranged the next time I find myself hanging around in the area.' With this I went off to the bar to replenish the drinks.

Chapter 5

My Lucky Number
18 December 2010

I am not by nature a judgemental person (and I can see you expecting there is a '*but*' coming here), so I would not like you to think that I simply have a single bad experience and that instantly forms an opinion. When Gerry and I first drafted the rules, it was after a couple of years of a variety of painful and comic moments that solidified into the first ten. The one that was the simplest to codify however was rule 1. There had been three girls, not serially I may add, but with something in common and that something was a desire to have a child. We shall call them Alice, Belinda, and Carrie to protect their identity, and because I have a maths degree, we always start with A, B, and C.

Alice was a friend of a friend, we were introduced at a party and she was a very nice-looking lady in her mid-thirties. She had long brown hair, brown eyes that sparkled when she talked and that seemed to scan the room in the way that the lights did on the front of Michael Knight's car Kit. I saw this as charming and not at all predatory, possibly something to note for later. The party was an afternoon barbecue being held at the house of Steven, one of the Cuffs from the office (actually a Manacled Married in this case) and they were trying to wow their guests with the usual bollocks. It seemed important to tell us where they got the wine from and how they marinated the meat in the tears of an angel and paprika; I am sure you have heard something like this before many times. I had arrived my customary twenty-five minutes late and had got the train over so that a drink was going to make the day better however it turned out. Steven acting as the alpha male Cuff was glued to the brick grill like a wannabe Michelin chef, while his wife Siobhan was greeting the guests and passing them on as soon as possible to start the conveyer belt once again.

'Adam, I would like you to meet Alice,' my host twisted me round by my shoulders and pointed at her like a Cruise missile. Alice and I smiled at each other and I walked over to her while our host beat such a hasty retreat that she would not have looked out of place at the siege of Mafeking.

'So are you one of the sad singles like me or one of a hip-joined pair who has forgotten his tagalong,' she opened with. Now that is quite an opening line from a girl I had never met before, this looked promising. I had to admit next to intelligence, I do find sarcasm a great quality in a woman.

'Ex Manacled Married, now sad single, I am afraid to say, yourself?'

'Yup, sad single, you must excuse my cynicism but you do get a feeling of cattle markets at these things. How do you know the hosts, work?'

'Don't tell me I have the same "banker at work" logo tattooed on my forehead?'

'No, it's the bank's logo on your tee shirt.' Well that told me.

'Fair play, I had forgotten that, I was some charity thing we did and I just grabbed the first clean thing from the drawer before coming here. Drink?'

'While they still have some, let's empty the European champagne lake that our host keeps banging on about.'

'Now you are talking. I see you too find him a bit of a wine bore. What is it you do when you are not undermining the landed gentry?'

'Primary school teacher.' Okay, should I have read something into this or not. Would you have done?

We went off to the pretentious makeshift bar they had set up in a corner of the garden to break into the bubbles while leaving the two bottles of Marlborough I had brought untouched. She was very funny and very sarcastic. Also, she seemed to be able to hold her drink which was a bonus. As the afternoon wore on, there were a few interactions with other people and the inevitable war stories that go on at these eventss. Who had done what at work, with whom, and what it had cost. The Cuffs were starting to compare their stories of parenting from potty training to the older ones who had future Pulitzer and Nobel Prize–winning 6-year-olds with so much 'potential darling'. The singles generally drifted into groups to discuss anything else—sport, music, and very often movies (nobody seems to mention books anymore). While all this was going on, Alice and I were getting physically closer to each other until the inevitable cheap shot from one of the other singles suggesting we 'got a room'. With this Alice whispered in my ear that it was not such a bad idea and she wondered who was closest, as she was only twenty minutes away by cab. I was astounded as this sort of thing does not happen to me. But after, if not emptying, at least dredging the wine lake, my sense of fun took over my common sense. They say that man only has blood enough for one head at a time and mine was not on my shoulders. We subtly made our goodbyes and I shelled out for a cab.

Now whilst we were not on a 'first date' as such (so no rules broken there, just stretched), she did start to get very frisky even in the cab. My mind turned to protection even after several drinks. I suggested we stopped somewhere on the way, but she said she had it covered so we got back to her place and almost crashed through the front door. It was a nice little two up, two down in immaculate condition but that was about to change. As we started to bump into bookcases and tables, I was reminded of the scene from the *Tall Guy* where they trash the flat when they jump each other. Although she was physically shorter and slighter than me, she ended up almost throwing me on to the couch. I bounced down, and as I turned back towards her, her shirt was already halfway over her head and she revealed a sexy bra with a generous filling. I am not backwards at coming forwards so I lost my tee shirt and went to reach up for her. She pushed me back down on the couch and proceeded to straddle me while she removed the only thing containing her breasts. And there they were, pert and inviting, this was unbelievable and going through my mind was that American tactic of shock and awe (I wasn't shocked, but I was in awe by this point). These sorts of things don't normally happen to me.

There was some very heavy petting as my parents would have called it for the next ten minutes as bits of her anatomy above the waist connected with my mouth and hands. It was then she got off and almost ripped the rest of the clothes off her body and off mine. This girl was either a fast worker or she had a train to catch; I was not sure which and finally ended up ignoring the question. Suddenly she went to climb back on top of me and to euphemistically make a connection. It was at this point when my blood rushed from one head back to the other and realised there was something wrong.

'Hold on, hold on, we need to use something.' The last thing I wanted right now was any accidents or any other lasting consequences.

'It's okay', she said, 'don't worry, it's all under control.'

'What do you mean? Pill? Coil?'

'No, you are going to be my baby father as they say in Jamaica.' Thank god that I have only so much blood in my system as previously mentioned, for my brain needed it all now and the thing that had almost come between us suddenly started to sulk.

'Oh no you don't,' and with that I partly rolled and partly lifted her off me. 'That's not the sort of thing I want right now and certainly not the first time I meet someone.' I was now looking for my clothes and way out.

'Oh come on, I want one and you can give it to me. What's the harm, you get to have me as much as you want and I get to have what I really want, in about nine months.' She got up and stared to put her arms around me as I was pulling on my jeans. I pushed her off and grabbed my stuff before heading for the door.

'Sorry, luv, that's not the way things work in my world. If I have children, I want to be there for them and not at the other end of a

CSA cheque.' With this I headed to the door while she screamed obscenities at the back of me. Once outside I tried to get my bearings and oriented myself to a railway station from which I could get home. Going through my mind was the question, did my hostess know what she was like, and if so, how much stick was I going to get come Monday morning?

◈

Belinda was a very different kettle of fish, not quite so mad, much more subtle, and a huge deal more patient. When we first met through an online dating agency (see rule 8), she initially appeared to be very nice. I know 'nice' is not a great word, but neither is 'normal'. She was fairly plain and physically a few pounds overweight, but she had a good brain and a good job that was not too demanding. She seemed to have a lot of friends that she did things with and so the initial scheduling of dates had been quite fraught. However, after meeting up for our first drink, we realised we got on and had a particular love of the cinema through both sci-fi and fantasy films. We began to see each other a couple of times a week and the inevitable flood of what I like to call initial interest texts (IIT). That would be 30–40 texts a day. This is a number that looks horrific in hindsight, but when you are getting one or two an hour you don't really notice the build-up.

The concerns only started to grow when we began to see each other more than not. Her friends very much took a backseat and she was always available. She also lost a few pounds going to the gym and started to take vitamin supplements. I thought this was very healthy and encouraging until I noticed that one of the supplements was folic acid. Now I may not know much about women's bodies, like most blokes I am more likely to find a lost golf ball than a clitoris, but I do know what folic acid is used for. It's one of the many facts you pick up from over-exposure to Cuffs in the office.

When I queried her over it, she took the entire thing in her stride and simply said that having a baby would be the next logical step and so she was getting prepared for it. You needed to be taking the supplement for at least six months for it to have an effect. When I queried that we had only been going out a month and that maybe she might want to mention it to me first as it did impact me rather, the argument started. It was not pretty and I will not bore you with the details, but after one hour, three emails, forty-seven texts, and a very public insulting session on Facebook, we agreed to spend more time seeing other people as opposed to each other.

Carrie had none of the aggressiveness of Alice and none of the subtlety of Belinda, she just seemed to have an obsessive desire for reading baby magazines. She was reading one on the day I met her. We had got chatting in a pub one lunchtime while I was waiting for Gerry to go to the match. She was short and petite with closed cropped blond hair (apparently this is very practical when you have babies) and the most beautiful blue eyes. She looked after herself and dressed elegantly without being stuffy. She was a PA at one of the banks on the Wharf and spent a lot of time looking for Mr Right. I got the feeling that many frogs had been kissed on her journey. However we hit it off and when Gerry turned up I gave her my details and said to call me if she fancied a drink later.

As you are requested in theatres and cinemas, Gerry and I are considerate punters at the football and always turn off our phones (much to Charlie's annoyance). When the match had finished and Gerry and I were heading for our post-match constitutional in the Birkbeck Tavern, I turned my phone on to find seven missed calls all from the same unrecognised number. As I was checking this, a text came in, it was from the lovely Carrie. As I was reading it, the phone went off (I guessed later she tracked message delivery so knew when my phone was back on. I learned this trick from another unfortunately overly passionate lady with a penchant for bunnies). Apparently she was free for a drink and wondered how soon I could meet up with her. I said I could get over to the pub she mentioned in about an hour and agreed to meet there then. I finished my beer with Gerry and commented on the fact she was a bit keen before finally heading off.

When I arrived, Carrie was sitting at the bar, in a different set of clothes (she did not appear to have been drinking all afternoon, another good sign) but still reading a magazine. In fact it looked suspiciously like another baby magazine.

'Hello, I got here as quickly as possible, what can I get you?'

'Oh just a Coke please, I am trying to I keep my body in good condition and alcohol is bad for it.'

'You know this is a pub, right?'

'Of course, but I don't have to drink, do I?'

'Are you in training, a marathon or triathlon, maybe?' I scanned her up and down and I could really see her doing this, she was fairly pneumatic as Aldus Huxley would say. At this point, she started to go a little red.

'No, I am just trying to get my body in the correct state for a girl of my age.'

'Am I missing something, or are you saying that some nights you are woken by the sound of a clock ticking?'

'Is that some sort of sexist putdown?' Now I think she believed the she had the upper hand at least morally.

'No, but if I am right, you are after a baby as soon as possible and that would not fit into my plans in the near future. If this is the case, I think I will skip the drink and let you get back to your magazine.' With this I drank my pint down in one and walked to the door. She was not fazed and continued to peruse her magazine as I watched in the barroom mirror on the way out. The trap was being laid for the next guy.

I should be clear, meeting a lady in a pub and hitting it off is rare. I think sometimes when it happens, flattery can undermine logic. Did I say I am a slow learner?

Chapter 6

To Cut a Long Story Short
15 December 2010

When I had finished relaying the story, Sarah sat there open-mouthed. She had smiled a couple of times as I explained the history of rule 1, but looked horrified as I mentioned going back to Alice's place. I just got the impression she thought I was some sort of tart and I suppose it may have sounded that way but they were very isolated incidents. This was not the point at which I was going to get away with saying I've changed, but frankly I have and I owe a lot of it to the creation of the rules. It is not just about other people, it is about my reaction to them, and before you say anything, I am not trying to pull the wool over your eyes either.

'Do you want another?' I offered as a way to cut through the iceberg that seemed to be emerging. I never really saw myself as Leo and certainly she was never going to be Kate, but that's a good thing, right? Nobody needs to die in freezing water.

'I am gonna pass, thanks, I need to get back for Misty. But I need to ask you something.'

'Books don't get a lot more open than me.'

'How did you see this evening going? What did you think would happen?'

'Not sure I follow you; explain?'

'Well, did you see me as your next big conquest? Am I another story to be added to the rule book? Will you go down the pub and have a chuckle with your mates?'

'Whoa, someone is a touch sensitive. I wanted to buy you a drink to say thanks for the other night and also to explain my behaviour, which would have seemed a bit odd to anyone. According to rule 12 I always have a month in between any relationships, but no, I was not up for a date. I just thought you seemed like the sort of person I could have a laugh with and possibly the occasional drink? Is that of any interest? I could always make you smile and tell you how some of the other rules came into being, they don't all put me in a bad light. Some of them actually show I can be a gentleman, if that is even allowed these days.' She got up from her chair and pulled her biker's jacket back over her shoulders.

'Well I am sure Misty and I would appreciate the odd email every now and then if only for the sake of protecting the rest of the female race from the likes of you. Reach out if you fancy another drink next week. If you don't screw this up, I might even give you a phone number. But just remember, fella, there is only room for one mongrel in my life and that's Misty!' With this she flounced off (yes, flounced) out of the bar with an emphasised wiggle that would have made Mae West think twice. At the door she turned and blew me a huge theatrical kiss. The entire pub then turned and looked at me; she had done her job well. The barman who had heard the dubious naked joke early simply looked at me with pity as if I was a dog being trained.

'You got ya hands full there, mate.'

'Chance would be a fine thing. Can I get a pint of lager please?'

'You sure you're allowed? What will madam say if she finds out?' The smile was breaking across his face's attempt at seriousness.

'Oh, hang on, let me see'—I looked down at my crotch—'I seem to have grown a pair, so can I now please get the bloody pint of lager.'

'All right mate, just having a laugh.' With this he waltzed off down the bar and got me my drink. I sat there and nursed it for only as long as it would take for the stares to go away and then necked it so I could sneak out and get back home without any more grief. I walked across to the door and the barman called out.

'Oi, Romeo, see you soon,' and with this he repeated the gesture that Sarah had performed on her way out. I slammed the door behind me. Note to self, let's not meet there again.

Getting into work the following morning I was not expecting to see anything in my inbox, so once I had gone through the overnights and responded to anything pressing, it was a pleasure to see not one but two emails from the lovely Sarah.

>From : *Misty.she.wolf@gmail.com*
>Subject: A bit harsh
>
>Morning, Captain, just thought I would drop you a quick line, I know you city blokes start early, to say that I had a surprisingly nice time chatting to you last night. I was also going to say that I may have been a little rough on you when I left as I was tired. You are probably not an axe murderer or cat burglar and I think it would be fun to keep up the dialogue. You could bring a bit of enjoyment into my day with your weird and wonderful stories and odd rules.

Suddenly this looked a lot more promising. Ignoring the fact she has ritually humiliated me in a pub full of strangers, she did seem to want to meet again, or was it to have another chance to make fun? Oh what the hell, I like having new drinking partners if nothing else. I thought I had better just check on the other one. When I went to open it, I realised that it had no content just the subject line, 'But this does not mean it is a date'. I think I had been well and truly made aware of that.

Well for once I thought the appropriate response was to play it cool, and to be honest with you, I was a little bit busy for banter. Hong Kong had issues that needed sorting out and with the eight-hour time difference, you don't have much of a window to deal in. With one thing and another I looked up and five hours had passed. Two of the party animals, Angie and Drew, had popped down the pub for a 'technical project meeting', probably discussing viscosity, flow rates, and specific gravity. I thought the best move now was a sandwich at my desk from the staff restaurant and maybe catch up on some technical reading for a while. As I returned to my desk, the new mail indicator was flashing the number 35 (no rest for the wicked), but most interestingly there was another one liner from Sarah, asking if I was screening my mail, however this time it included a mobile number in the text. Going through my mind was one thought: Game on!

I quickly sent a message to her mobile, from a website that hides my ID (I am not stupid and I have learned to be cautious), saying I had not had a chance to reply because of work but was really pleased to see her mail. I would reply to her in detail a bit later. A bit later actually turned out to be gone six due to a problem with New York, it never rains but it pours. I thought about what I could say to keep the banter at the right level.

To: *Misty.she.wolf@gmail.com*
Subject: New acquaintances and friends

It was a surprise and real pleasure to see your mail this morning, Sarah. Yes, apart from the stick I got after you left the pub, I had a really nice time. Don't panic, I am not after another conquest or friend with benefits (I have rule 22 for that), but a drinking buddy is always fun. If you want to catch up soon, just let me know, and if YOU are good, I may repay the gesture and give you my number. As Clint Eastwood would probably say in this situation, *Pat Misty for me*.

Adam.

Well, you know what they say—nothing ventured, nothing gained. With that I shut off my screen, gathered my stuff, and headed for home. I was however smiling, which made a nice change after a day like that.

Chapter 7

He Ain't Heavy
18 December 2010

You may have gathered by now that Gerry is the closest thing I have to a best mate. We have known each other for so many years; in fact we started senior school together on the same day. I had not gone to the local rough secondary modern school after concerns from my parents (the weak and feeble wallflower that I was) and so through a series of letters to the local education authority I arrived at Bleasdale Comprehensive. It was a large and very new school, some seven years old and had lots of *right-on* teachers who still wanted to make a difference. On the first day, I was met by a sea of faces mostly in groups as they had all come up from one of three local schools and then there was Gerry. He was standing at the edge of the hall on his own, he was a chunky chap even then, rather like me trying to figure out which group looked the most promising and which looked least likely to beat him up. When he noticed I too was on my own, we sidled up to each other and did the usual *aright* that adolescent boys do in acknowledgement. We quickly fell into an easy and fully unspoken partnership.

During this time we shared a lot of things—homework, dubious magazines, and on numerous occasions, detentions. I am not a rebel or not particularly bad, but I did at this time have a bit of a mouth on me and was cleverer than the average kid there and so got bored with the pace. Gerry just loved to wind people up (and he still does). We were, in the end, the lovable pair of rogues that the teachers knew would survive but who needed the odd helping hand along the way. Gerry is the only school friend I still keep in touch with as the rest seemed to have nothing in common with me as time went by. We even tried a couple of school reunions (not using Friends Reunited is definitely a rule—rule 20 in fact), but they always seemed to go the same way. Each time we met anyone from the old school, they simply seemed to have expanded or bloated from the last time. They still hung around in the same groups they had done almost on that first day of school and bragged about what they had achieved. For Gerry and I, it was fun to see how little had happened to the bullies and the less mentally robust inmates. We tried not to gloat, but it is nice to leapfrog your foes sometimes. There were a few jailbirds, small-time Hitlers in offices and corner stores, but generally they had not kept up with Gerry's craft or my earning potential.

In all this time Gerry and I had shared everything except one—girlfriends. We had a rule even back then that we would not go out with someone that the other one was either interested in or had gone out with in the past. It wasn't really a problem except when it came to Sally Pascoe. In our fifth year we had been busy with exams and revision and just for once we had been seeing a bit less of each other outside school. Suddenly one day when Gerry turned up at my house, he shared the little titbit with me that he had seen a new girl that he was interested in. I also had my eye on a new lady, but with me at the time, this was the usual pie in the sky (some things just don't seem to change). I was having no luck with anything in a skirt due to a painful shyness whenever the opposite sex appeared on the horizon. Gerry on the other hand was the man. He was confident and fearless, some would now say foolhardy. He would rush into a situation with the opposite sex while there were queues of angels hanging around gingerly testing the ground with an outstretched toe. So even though I was not actually going to get around to doing anything about the now-contentious Sally, the fact that Gerry was moving in for the kill did somewhat put a dent in our friendship for a few weeks. This however is the only thing that has ever got in the way of our friendship.

Now here is the other shocker: Gerry and I got married. Of course I don't mean each other, but it was on the same day. He met Charlotte (now Charlie) a few months before I met Annie and for a while we all got on like a house on fire. We did a lot of things as a group of four, even a couple of weekends away. But after the weddings, back to back in the same church, things started to cool. I don't mean as soon as the reception was over, which was shared back in the village we both grew up in, but very soon after. Charlie found herself getting more and more wound up with Annie and this did at times put a bit of a strain on the Gerry-Adam pact (I know, it sounds like something out of Ulster, but I will try and steer clear of politics). When Charlie had her first and then subsequent two other children, it seemed that the link between Charlie and Annie was finally broken. In so many ways Charlie was more than a little triumphant when Annie was finally off the scene (not that she said it directly to me). I think Gerry mentioned she was pleased she never had to 'air kiss that brainless bimbo again' (that's bad, right?).

So now I see Gerry a couple of times a week and am occasionally called into play as an impromptu babysitter as I am godparent to all their fabulous offspring, Peter, Carly, and Ellie. It is an easy relationship and Charlie often insists on cooking me a dinner, because of course I am completely incapable of looking after myself now I am single. She did at one point offer to do my washing but I am not going down that road. I love Charlie, but I don't need another mother.

Charlie does still have two slightly irritating habits (no, Gerry, she has never made a pass at me; in case you are reading this). Firstly, as she was proved to have such good judgement when it came to Annie (well she tells me she knew all along), she now insists on *vetting* potential partners. I have gone as far as to tell Gerry he is not allowed to let her know I am seeing someone for a month just so I can prepare them for the ordeal myself. She has been known to *drop round* to borrow a cup of sugar knowing full well I am entertaining. I wouldn't mind but we live ten miles apart. I want to make this clear, I am not complaining. Charlie is just trying to be protective, but sometimes, I want to be able to make my own mistakes and not have to be told what is wrong with the latest one.

The second thing that Charlie does is related to another rule. She has a habit of trying to set me up with worthy friends who she thinks might be right for me. Now I am not being funny, but my mother stopped picking out my clothes when I was about 2. My ex-wife stopped picking out my ties after the first year of marriage. I am not having my best friend's wife picking out my partners in some form of new age Darwinian behaviour of the survival of the fittest; there, my friends, I draw the line. I know Charlie thinks she knows best, but relationships are about chemistry, not a networking opportunity.

You know the best thing about Gerry? He never judges me. Physically he is a bit like an ox. He has his own business as a cabinet maker and has expanded to have quite a few staff in the last few years. I never quite got over the fact that he has such an eye for intricate detail. When you look at him you might think gentle giant or possible thug, but he is the right guy to have at your back when the rubber hits the road (this may have happened a couple of times over the years). He has a tattoo on his forearm that is old school blue dye, none of this fancy coloured stuff. He even had Charlie embossed on his shoulder soon after they met. She thought at first it would keep them together. I know the fact that he is completely besotted with her means he would never look elsewhere. Do I sound jealous? I'm not, but I am really happy for him. He is a great father and a devoted husband. God, I sound like an estate agent selling a house (good fixer upper, structurally sound). Gerry and Charlie make a great team and they are bringing up my godchildren in a really nice way. They have made the best of their talents and now share that with the kids.

Gerry and I have a common love of football and have become season ticket holders at Leyton Orient since we were old enough to afford them; we try to get to all the home games. Leyton is one of the smaller clubs in the area and is good as we like to see a decent match without the bank-account-breaking cost of a premiership club. Leyton happened to be far enough away from home that we were not going to drink with the locals during the rest of the week but also pretty much equidistant from our homes (Mile End for me, Wanstead for Gerry), problem solved. We meet up at a bar close to the station and the ground for a couple of pints before the game and then one afterwards before wending our respective ways home. It gives us that perfect boy's catch-up time that the other guys in the office seem to do on a golf course. Trouble is neither Gerry nor I visit golf clubs much anymore after some issues from our youth (and a girl called Mad Mary, more of her later).

Chapter 8

Night Games
16 December 2010

I am running down the street and sweat is cascading off me. I am imploring my legs to move faster but they feel like lead. I jump a puddle, gate vault over a fence, and head towards the forest. I can almost feel them close behind me. I figure if I can just reach the tree line I can lose them. I am trying not to look back as then I know I will lose my footing and trip. Finally I reach the trees and my lungs are on fire. The lactic acid is burning in my calves and my thighs. I can hear feet coming behind me maybe fifty yards off. I turn to look and all I see are faceless women approaching me. They are all shapes and sizes; each is wearing a running vest, some very inappropriately, and on each vest is a number. The numbers refer to the rules. I make out rule 11, and I see that the girl is unbelievably skinny; as she turns she almost disappears as she is paper thin. I look again and I see number 7, she is being followed by hundreds of smaller runners behind her all wearing small number 7s. I turn and kick off back into a run and break through the trees. The trees are getting thicker and thicker and the branches start to scratch against my arms and skin. The branches feel like they are trying to hold me back and catch me. The pack is falling back and I can hear the noise level dropping down as the trees absorb the sound. I break out of the forest and find myself in open space. It is dark in front of me, too dark. I come to a halt and find a massive cliff edge. There is steam rising from my body as the cold night sucks the heat from my body. I realise I am trapped. Do I go back to the mob, which is now getting louder again, or do I jump? I look below but cannot see the bottom. I drop a stone from my hand but do not hear it land. I am Gandalf standing on the bridge knowing that falling is

Rules for a Born Again Bachelor

my only option. I jump and I hear nothing, my throat will not scream, the noise is simply in my head.

I awake on the floor of my bedroom. I am now literally covered in sweat from head to foot and there is banging coming through the wall from my next-door neighbours. I guess I have been screaming again. My heart has now stopped trying to leap out of my mouth and is returning to its normal resting position in my chest. Its rhythm slowing, calming; the adrenaline seeping out of my pores. The fight or flight response has ended in flight again and I have survived.

I don't get nightmares every night, don't get me wrong. It is more like once every few months. Generally when I am between partners and often when I have added a new rule to the list. It is one fifteen in the morning and I am wide awake. What the hell do I do now? I could do the parental thing, you know, go make a milky drink (what am I, 3?). I could be a real man and go and get a beer or a whisky to calm me down. I am a serious fan of Rebus, Ian Rankin's brash Scots copper, and I am always amazed just how much Scotch that man can put away in a single evening with almost zero sleep and still function; but no, not this time. I go for the only option which does not involve porn or disturbing other people and that is the PlayStation. Nothing like mindless violence for taking your mind off your troubles and so aid restful sleep. I pull some shorts on; it is too hot for a tee shirt and plonk myself on the sofa. Within five minutes I am embedded in a high-octane slugfest with random players online and I am as usual scoring well but getting toasted occasionally by the semi-pros that haunt these events in the middle of the night.

I play for about half an hour getting stuck into a four-way game and suddenly start dying a lot more frequently than I had before. Something is very odd, then I twig; they are all using headsets. I pause and wander off to the cabinet to find mine and check that it has batteries. Yup, blue light, check. I connect up and head back into the game. You can't normally tell much about people from their handles (game names) as most of the time they lie on the internet (see rule 8). I was intrigued to hear the chatter and after a while I realised that Artful Dodger was most definitely female. Well don't get your hopes up, she's a geek who likes games and is nocturnal, but that does not mean she is either in my city or even in the same country. It also does not mean that she is single, above the age of consent, and interested in chatting to other game players. However, after a couple of rounds of slightly more cooperative play, we both seemed to regularly be the only two surviving.

'This is getting too easy, fancy something harder?' she messaged me. Well now, I am most definitely intrigued. I say yes back to her and we both duck out of the game. I am now receiving a friend request and from that I can tell she is UK-based. I accept and we start chatting. Play it cool, she might just want a game.

'Fight or flirt?' comes back the next message. I am concerned and start to literally pinch myself in case I did not actually wake up the first time. I respond in the way that every red-blooded male should do.

'How old are you?'

'Twenty-nine, why how old are you?'

'Well I have a few years on you. Where are you based?'

'Catford.'

'Not that far away then, I'm in the East End. Why ArtfulDodger?'

'Really, with a handle of EastEndBoy69 I would never have guessed. Oh about the name, I used to live up there and I really liked Oliver when I was younger.'

'Makes sense I suppose. So what do you want to play?'

'Something seriously bloody, I am in the mood.'

'Done. What about Bulletstorm? We can pick off some other freaks if we work as a team.'

So it is now four in the morning (no sign of Faron Young, yet!) and we have been sneakily obliterating all newcomers in the network rooms of Bulletstorm. We have run up more trick-shot points that you can wave a shitty stick at and I am starting to finally flag. My alarm is going to go off in one hour and I have a pretty full day in the office.

'I gotta go, the real world is calling.'

'Really, it was just getting fun.'

'The words "day" and "job" come to mind.'
'And . . . ?'
'Another time?'
'Okay, send me an invite.' And with that the line went dead and her player went offline. I switched off and crawled back to the bed. It was still damp; bugger.

※

I got into work a mere twenty minutes late after grabbing just over an hour's worth of sleep. I looked like I had slept in my face and the entire office commented as they came in as to how rubbish I looked. It was going to be a challenge to get through the day and I fell back on the standard approach of strong coffee and excessive carbohydrates. I was due to drop in on Gerry for my weekly bite to eat and to see the kids but I have to say I was not feeling like it. I got my head down and battled on through the day until six and then sloped off.

Gerry rang on the way and suggested a swift sharpener in his local before we got to the house and to be honest I thought it was a damned good idea. It was going to be tricky to stay awake and so a pint was just what I needed. He was there already when I walked in and was hovering around the pool table with a pint in each hand. I wandered over, took a mouthful, and fished in my pocket for a quid for the table. The cues had tips that were more war-torn than Sarajevo and the chalk only recently relegated from the darts tally board.

'Jesus, Gerry, you know how to spoil a girl!'

'It's local, all right; the clue is in the name. Anyway what's up with you, you look like crap, man. Did you spend the night drinking or making the beast with two backs?'

'A bloody nightmare, no literally, you know the one with the women wearing rule numbers chasing me; then I couldn't get back to sleep.'

'So?'

'So I went online and started playing.'

'And drinking? Come on there is more to it than that. I would give you an hour max and then you would head off to bed.'

'Okay, now it gets a bit weird. I got chatting with this other player online and then she suggested a new game. We played that for a while and then she got a bit, well, flirty.'

'Hang on; I thought you had a specific rule for internet dating, God, though for the life of me I cannot remember the number.'

'Well this is not exactly internet dating'—it's rule number 8, by the way—'This was just chatting, but then she tells me where she lives, roughly, it's Catford by the way and that she's 29.'

'Okay, so what are you going to do?'

'Well I think that all depends on her for a start. I might not ever hear from her again. I might get home and find there is an invitation to play, no pun intended, waiting for me in the inbox.'

'Bloody hell, it's like pulling teeth, man. So if there is . . . what will you do?'

'Play of course.' With that we got on with the game and finished our pints. In respect to Gerry's family (particularly Charlie who still scares me a wee bit), we just stuck to the one pint and went for dinner. I ended up as I always do playing with the kids and reading the normal bedtime story involving bears and dragons, you know the sort of things. Apart from being tired, my mind had sort of drifted off the thought of my little game buddy. I caught the tube home and got in just to see the end of the news. Was it worth checking the box to see if there were any messages? What if there were; I really needed bed. Just in case, as I didn't want to appear rude, I booted up the machine and flicked over the box. With a great deal of disappointment, I saw no flashing message indicator. Maybe it was too early for my nocturnal friend. Maybe it was a narrow escape for me or maybe I was just too tired to care at this point. I switched off and headed for the bedroom.

As I plugged my phone in and checked my alarm, I saw a new message alert. The lovely Sarah had dropped me a hello world message. I decided that enough was enough and I am pretty sure my eyes closed before my body hit the sheets.

Chapter 9

A Walk in the Park
18 December 2010

'How come you never mentioned this before?' The glare from Sarah as she spoke these words reminded me both to wear sunscreen and not to gaze directly at a gorgon, especially when enraged. We had met up for a walk across Hyde Park, now just a week before Christmas. A walk of course meant Misty was in tow or rather towing, so she had been let off the lead to gambol in the leaves. It was Saturday; hence me seeing daylight when not in the office and it was one of those days that make you glad to feel alive. Blue sky and a sharp wind across the city blowing the cobwebs away and just enough heat from the midday sun that the wind chill was not unpleasant. The park was still full of fallen leaves from the late autumn which had been piled into drifts by the wind, meaning that every now and then we literally lost Misty to a leave avalanche (would that be a leafalanche?). Eventually the call of her mistress (not mine I hasten to add, voice or mistress) or the lure of a ball would have her bounding back. It was wonderful to watch.

You probably won't have realised this yet, but I love dogs. I had one for a while growing up and I like to think I have a naturally affinity for them. No, I don't drink from the toilet bowl or sniff crotches, but I do seem to get on with them and love nothing more than to take one for walk. This of course leads to the obvious question, why would you not have one yourself then? Come on, with work I am out of the house 12–13 hours a day and I live in a second-floor flat, which is hardly practical. I have been known to dog-sit at weekends for friends as I kind of get the best of both worlds, but I draw the line at girlfriends who have dogs, which is where we came in.

'I was just getting to like you and now you turn out to be a dog hater.'

'I am not a bloody dog hater; you are such a drama queen. I simply said that I don't date girls with dogs. There are very good practical reasons and that was the final rule that Gerry and I came up with that night.'

'What practical reasons?' At this point Misty chose the most inappropriate time to act as some sort of fifth columnist and came sidling up to me (well I did have the ball thrower, she is not stupid). 'Oi, Misty, you little turncoat, come away from the nasty dog hater.'

'Again with the dog hater, Jesus.' With this obvious change in tone, Misty slunk off back to her mistress in an attempt to curry favour. 'Misty, frankly I am shocked at you, don't listen to her.' I did admittedly bend down at this point and try to encourage her back, the dog that is, not Sarah (apparently I am not stupid either).

'There's no point trying to win her affection back, she knows a wrong'un when she sniffs one.' Sarah was now down making a fuss out of Misty and giving me an evil stare. 'So if are not a dog hater, explain to me why you don't date girls with dogs.'

'There is no mystery about it, it is mostly a case of hygiene and the experience of one particular young lady, who in many ways turned out to be a bit of a bitch herself.'

'Hygiene, really, hygiene. Do you know the expression, *when in hole, try digging up not down*? How can you say dogs aren't hygienic, they have been man's best friend and companion for centuries.' With this she stuck on Misty's lead and started to stomp off towards the exit. I scampered (okay, don't take the Mickey) after her in an attempt to keep up.

'Come on, behave, let me have a chance to explain. What about a coffee and a bun for your wonderful hound?' With this she turned and gave me one of those smiles and I knew I had been played. 'Oh, were you getting cold? Was this just a way of getting a free coffee?'

'You know I am not cheap, coffee, come on, you can do better than that?'

'What about hot chocolate and a shot of Baileys for you and a muffin for Misty, oh that's good, I like alliteration.'

'Done. Then maybe you can start to get yourself out of that huge hygiene hole; see two can play at that game.' With this we walked off to find a pub on the edge of the park for something warming.

※ ※

With a little circuitous walk we found ourselves in the Horse and Groom in Belgravia, not too shabby and providing a rather fine Bloody Mary for me while Sarah settled for the aforementioned turbo-charged hot chocolate. Misty seemed okay with water and the ubiquitous bar snacks (although with the speed she consumes them, she might be developing a chorizo addiction).

'So come on then, dogs and hygiene, Misty is mystified.'

'You've been working on that one for a while, right? Probably the entire way here, I am guessing? Or did you outsource? What Puns are Us? Pun U like?'

'Okay, smartarse, just get on with the story.'

'Okay, well this is something Gerry and I came up with late on in the pub that night and only because this girl walked in and reminded me. I went out with this girl for a couple of months and after the first date I knew that her life was not her own. We had to get her home straight after the film, due to the fact that Harold, her bulldog—who calls a dog Harold?—needed to be let out for his evening constitutional. Well that night I let her out of the car at her house and gave her a quick peck on the cheek. As usual I waited to drive away from a partner's house to make sure they were safely inside. What I witnessed was the thing that dog owners do. As she opened the door, I saw the dog leap up and lick her face and kiss her pursed lips. That is so gross. My lips had been there a few seconds before and I was not keen on where the dog's mouth had been previously. As I drove away I was having serious misgivings about the next date.'

'Is that it? Is that all I have to do to put you off? Dog garlic, my little Lothario vampire friend.' Sarah reached down to give Misty a kiss, but Misty just looked at her and then panted heavy Paprika breath on her at which even she pulled back and gave her a worried look.

'Hang on; let me get to the end. I told you, none of these rules are a single issue. They are a combination of either recurring issues or multiple-related problems.'

'So what else then.'

'Well, okay, after a few dates, things move on and eventually I got to go to her place. We had a nice takeaway meal and a glass of wine followed by some getting-to-know-you time, although I have to say I was not comfortable with the way she had been feeding Harold at the table and making a fuss over him. I really wanted her to wash her hands.'

'Okay, so maybe I agree with you there. Misty never eats from the table.'

'Come the end of the evening I got myself off home, see I'm not that much of a Lothario. When I got home I took off my shirt and jeans and I realised quite how disgusting they were. Every inch of them was covered with hairs from Harold. So now I am stuck with the idea of going to her house and getting covered in crap or her coming to my place and disappearing early before any fun occurs. Then there was the issue with the kissing, I just can't get my head around that.'

'You're saying that due to your issues with one girl who was very unclean with her dog that you won't ever go near a girl with a dog again?'

'It's not just one girl. As I said, the night with Gerry in the pub, what got this in the top ten list was the girl that walked in. She sat her handbag dog on the bar and started feeding him bar snacks from her mouth and then the dog licked her face afterwards. Come on, that's really quite revolting. Gerry was making incredible retching noises, well he was until her boyfriend started to give us a really nasty look. At that point, we necked our pints, picked up the beer mats on which the lists were written, and then headed out towards the door. As we passed the leering bloke and the dog lady, Gerry turned to the mutt, pointed at the girl, and said, "You've missed a bit," and then we left before he punched us.'

'Oh you really are a pair of charmers. I must meet this Gerry sometime if only to see if you are as full of crap as you sound. He is probably a lovely man who enjoys needlepoint and is teetotal.'

'Boy, are you in for a surprise. You're gonna love Gerry! You might even survive Charlie.'

Chapter 10

Mistletoe and Wine
20 December 2010

'Hello, Mum,' it had been a week or so since I had phoned and I knew I was in trouble. Don't get the wrong idea, I love my mum and dad and I am very lucky that in their early seventies they seem to be in pretty much rude health. They still live in the family home that we all grew up in down in rural Kent. It's a place called Hothfield just outside Ashford, one of those rural idles that is all winding lanes. It's beautiful during fruit-picking season but treacherous when the snow starts to fall or the river levels rise; I think you get the picture. As I say, the place is nice; the people are daft but nice, so why am I struggling with the phone call? Well it is now five days before Christmas and I have been putting off accepting the invitation to stay there for the holidays in case I got another offer. I know this sounds heartily uncharitable, but come on, I'm 40 and I am going home alone to Mum's. I may as well buy my own unstylish Christmas jumper and get the word 'Saddo' tattooed on my forehead. It does not exactly signal that life is going well for someone in my position, does it? To make matters worse, this is the second year in a row this has happened.

'Hello, sorry, who is this? The voice is familiar, sounds like somebody I used to know.'

'Okay, Mum, I think you might have pressed the sarcasm button on your hearing aid. I called you just last week.'

'Sorry obviously my memory is going, along with my weak limbs.'

'Jesus, the sympathy shop must be having a closing down sale there in Kent. Shall we try this conversation again? Hello, Mum, how are you?'

'You always were a cheeky little beggar. So are you finally going to tell me you're coming for Christmas or by some minor miracle have you found another gullible female to latch on to?'

'Bit harsh, Mum; easy. Yes, I would be delighted to accept your wonderful invitation to come for Christmas this year. I will get there in the early evening on Christmas Eve if that's okay with you?'

'And then you will bugger off again first thing Boxing Day? Or will you actually stay to meet people in the village this year?'

'I was planning to stay and spend a bit of time with you and Dad and leave on the twenty-seventh.'

'Wow, I must get a bit more food in then. I assumed you would scarper again like last year. Oh, I did say your sister was coming, didn't I?'

'No, and just when were you going to let me know I had to buy her a present? I will have to find something suitably recycled. Is madam eating meat this year, or is it still murder?' I always liked to get that line in. My sister Beth is a 33-year-old singleton ex-hippie, tree-hugging friend of the earth (with the mind-set of a 60-something spinster without the cats—yet). She cannot see a cause without throwing her weight behind it. I make it sound like she is some kind of caricature or parody, but honestly the truth is stranger than fiction in her case. Last I knew she was working for one of those eco-charities somewhere on the outskirts of North London. The only time I really ever hear from her is when one of her charities polishes a new begging bowl. I am sure they are all good causes, but I strongly believe some are more deserving than others. I would rather provide clean water for underprivileged Africans than worry about sick cats, but that is just me I guess. 'So on the positive side, I guess Kangaroo Jack will not be joining us this year?'

'Why can't you be a little more pleasant about your family? Your brother is very content down in Oz and I know he's planning a trip back next year to bring my grandchild to see me at last. And for God's sake, call him Paul.'

'Okay, sorry, I will behave. You know this time of year makes me ratty. I actually miss the city when I am down there where the yokels grow thicker than the head on the beer. You need me to bring anything? Booze, food, a delightful sense of irony, and some kitsch clothing?'

'There you go again. All city high and mighty with your fancy flippant phrases; hang on, that's alliteration. Damn you, boy, I think you are rubbing off on your dear old ma.'

'You taught me that well over thirty years ago, Mum, and don't you forget it. Anyway, before I go, how is Goliath? Is he sleeping?' In my mind was the quote about the gimp from *Pulp Fiction*, 'Well you better go wake him up then'.

'Your father is well, and it wouldn't hurt you to say something nice about him. He is out in the garage pottering. I never know what he gets up to out there, but from the smell of it, I suspect it involves alcohol.'

'Just the normal winemaking, I guess? Or are you telling me he's set up a still for moonshine suddenly? Could we be the new Dukes of Hothfield? *Just a good ol' boys, never meanin' no harm.*'

'I thought we had a no karaoke rule with you, young man?'

'Mum, I'm 40, a bit too old for that line.'

'I know how old you are, I bloody bore you.'

'Okay, I've heard the story before, in fact I believe I was there at the time.'

'Try and cheer up before Christmas, Adam, or with your current level of cynicism, you are going to curdle the cream.'

'Bye, Mum,' and with that she was gone. Are you like me and start to interject movie quotes and song lyrics into your life? I am not sure if it is simply because I don't have a strong-enough grip on reality or more likely that I have a low boredom threshold. All that was left going through my head was *Here I go again on my own* (always nice to give White Snake a lyrical airing). Anyway, I am now left with the challenge of finding a present for my sister that she cannot complain about and to pick up some booze for the Christmas trip to see the folks. I might also get some breadcrumbs so I can leave a trail and find my way home.

Rules for a Born Again Bachelor

I got off the phone feeling a bit better for finally having bitten the bullet and now knowing my Christmas plans were sorted. It was still too early for bed even on a Monday night so I thought I would kill a virtual few soldiers. I had not been on the PlayStation since last week. When I turned it on and went online, I was surprised to see the number 3 flashing in the email box. My little nocturnal friend fancied a rematch. She had tried Friday, Saturday, and Sunday; let's hope she doesn't think I am ignoring her. I sent off a response to her but she appeared to be away so I got on and started to play a good little shoot 'em up to remove the evils of my world and the stress of having spoken to Mother. Honestly, most of the guys and quite a few of the girls in the office use this instead of recreational drugs or alcohol. It really does allow you to get rid of the stress of the day without hurting a single living soul, although many pixels may have been destroyed in the making of this fun (and it's not quite as bad for the eyesight as the available high-quality pornography).

About an hour in, and I got a ping in my ear from the curiously nocturnal Catford citizen. I dropped out of my game and pinged a response. A message box opens up.

'You been busy? You weren't around at the weekend.'

'Bit of work, bit of play. Just not a lot of time to get online. I am guessing you have been on here every night then? What do you do for a living?'

'Not a lot at the moment. I am between jobs.'

'Didn't you say you were 29? That must be tough on the bank balance.' Now are you like me, do you read between the lines? Do you start to get the hairs standing up on the back of your neck when things don't sound quite right? Or am I just paranoid? (It's time to play detective. I think a bit of CSI: Catford is in order).

'What do you do when you are in work?'

'You've got a bit nosey all of a sudden, what are you, a social worker?'

'No, but I have the odd suspicion of anyone I meet online and I'm never quite sure about anyone that answers a question with a question. Can you see what I mean?'

'Whatever. You wanna play something? You wanna play with me?'
'Not quite yet. I am allowed one more question?'
'Go on then, I am starting to think you are a bit more boring than I remember.'
'Are you married, or living with someone?'
'Why?'
'I have rules. I don't flirt or date people who are married or attached.'
'Tell you what, let's just forget it.'
'I take it that's a yes then?'
'Bye,' and with that she was gone. I am guessing I hit a nerve there and most definitely I was right. In case you are wondering, it's rule 7. I don't knowingly go near married women (or any Cuffs) as I would not want what happened to me to happen to someone else. I am still smarting from Annie leaving a little bit. I may be old fashioned, but if you want a new relationship, you finish the old one first. What do you think?

The final task of the evening was to go into my profile and remove the friend (and block). With that I think I had been put off killing any more pixels (or pixies for that matter), I switched the football on, vegged in front of the TV until time to hit the hay. Is it me or are Mondays just getting weird?

Chapter 11

Mr Postman
21 December 2010

I am afraid to say that I share something with the great Douglas Adams's down in the mouth hero Arthur Dent of Hitchhiker's Guide fame; I never could get the hang of Tuesdays. In the case of Arthur, it was a passing remark whilst clothed in a dressing gown (oddly enough) sitting in a pub drinking six pints before his house and indeed planet are destroyed to make way for a hyperspace by-pass. Mine may be a bit more run of the mill, but it is nevertheless just as real. However much we like our jobs (mine regularly varies from hero to zero), we still tend to fall into that predictable pattern of life whereby Monday is fairly depressing, Wednesday feels like the top of the rollercoaster, and Friday is the day we exhale before we have a two-day permit for rest and relaxation as they say in the army. Where do Tuesday and Thursday fit into this? Well Thursday is the night out in the city (forget Friday, nobody wants a hangover on their own time) so that kind of has an acceptable face. But we are left with Tuesday as the day when nothing really happens. So it was on this the last Tuesday before Christmas.

If you add to this the fact that it is December, a very tricky time in the city, then you find there was not a lot of work going on. How can I explain December in one of the large financial centres to a person who does not work there? Let's start with the workload. Firstly, at lot of the contract workers have been forced to have holidays as the amount of project work has dropped off. They put change freezes in place so people in a *holiday* mood don't break the systems after lunch. The level of business tends to tail off as well and so there are less support issues to address leaving people with a little extra time on their hands. In theory one should be using this time to do housekeeping and general paperwork that has been left to the bottom of the pile. In practice, the lunches tend to get longer and the starting times later. As the month goes on, there is a feeling of a slow growing hangover haunting the office. If you add to this the number of Christmas events, suppliers, clients, and staff based, you see that the level of office noise is down to a minimum. When one of the team, generally a Party Animal, says let's grab a quick beer after work tonight, we are meeting up with some people we used to work with, you know how unlikely it is to be just one beer. In fact it is not uncommon that four hours later you are standing putting money in the pint glass held menacingly in front of you by a scantily clad lady in a Shoreditch pub, who seems keen to get even less dressed for the duration of on one track on the jukebox. Actually, to be honest it is only generally evenings out with Ralph that end up that way and I think the less of those I get involved with the better.

As the morning progressed, I realised I had a few things to get sorted out before the Christmas bash at Mum and Dad's. Firstly, I needed to get my bloody eco-warrior sister a present. Having chatted to the Cuffs in the office, I got the idea that the most in vogue thing to do in these cases was purchase a goat. Come on, not a real one that they are given on Christmas morning (can you not see it nibbling the other presents and the tree?), but one of those Oxfam jobs that they purchase for less fortunate people. The best bit is that they provide you with a fridge magnet in exchange for your money and so I would have something very simple and small to wrap for Beth. Surely even she cannot complain about this.

Secondly, I needed to get the presents over to Gerry and Charlie. I may have come over a bit curmudgeonly about kids, but I do really rather like my godchildren and Gerry and Charlie (for all her interfering on occasions) are very good friends and help to keep me sane. Every year

I get better at this (you should have seen the presents in the first few years, at least now I read the ages on the toys; well how was I to know). This year I had got them sorted by the end of November and they were already wrapped. Charlie and Gerry were getting a pasta maker as she told me that was what *they* wanted; God only knows if she will use it, but I am very good at following instructions. The kids were getting spoiled as usual. I was due to drop them off there on Thursday, which would get me out of any work drinks so close to Christmas.

The final thing I wanted to do, as I figured that Sarah might actually end up being a good mate, was to get her a card and present (and maybe something sausage based for the mutt). For this I would need to know her address (I would courier it over to save missing the last posting day) and for me it was causing a certain amount of concern. I am struggling slightly to make sure she does not get the wrong impression about me and so I am not sure what her reaction will be when I ask her to tell me where she lives. It could go very well, it could go terribly wrong. Either way I needed to get on with it or I would miss the boat before disappearing down to Kent. I sat at my desk and pored over a few bits of work until I got the right sort of text for an email in my mind.

To: *Misty.she.wolf@gmail.com*
Subject: Christmas baubles

Greetings, Sarah, thanks for the walk at the weekend. I had a great time with you and the mutt. I am not sure what you guys are doing over the Christmas period, but I thought it might be nice to send you a card and a little something in the post as we appear to be moving towards the positive position of being mates, or at least dog walkers. Any chance you could let me have your address so I know where to send to? I am driving down to Kent on Friday after work to see the old folks, what you up to?

Well, I then had to wait for her to come back to me, so I thought I would take the opportunity to dash out and purchase the aforementioned card and present. Something smelly always seems to work (that's for the dog of course) and nothing says I am a man in touch with my sensitive side more than buying a woman a scarf and one of those chemical hand warmers. Come on, she walks a dog morning and night in the winter, I bet she gets cold hands; there is no point you sneering about it. By the time I had returned to the office, chilled to the bone from the fact the temperature seemed to have dropped ten degrees since I came in this morning, I saw I had a reply mixed in with all the other emails.

From: *Misty.she.wolf@gmail.com*
Subject: Hey Mr Postman

Captain, my Captain (you must have known that line was coming soon). Actually you look a bit like Robin Williams (but younger of course). Now, what's a girl to think? You want my address, are you a stalker as well as a cat burglar and philanderer? Tell you what, as I have an attack dog (that you keeping calling a mutt) and you seem to be a nice guy, why don't you pop round for a quick drink tomorrow after work. I will meet you at the Marquis as it's just around the corner and you can come back to mine and we can exchange cards, etc. Let me know soon as my telephone is literally burning me from the number of invites I am getting and my diary is filling up fast.

That I thought went better than I had expected. I now felt it was lucky I had managed to secure presents and a card. I would clear my evening tomorrow (there was meant to be a vendor catch up) and go to see the lovely Sarah in her lair. I sent her back a brief acceptance; I won't bore you with the details (I can assure you though, it was something suitably witty and pithy). Now the only thing left to do was get some wrapping paper and get on with what I laughably call my day job.

***

I walked into the Marquis and of course the first thing I caught sight of was the barman. He smiled at me in the way that made me feel like a lamb to the slaughter.

'Does she know you're out?' he proffered as I approached the bar. 'Usual, when you are on your own, or are you expecting company?'

'You know, I have only met you once before and I'm already starting to dislike you. I'll have a pint of lager please, something without too much of a kick.' I looked down the row of beers. 'Make it a Fosters please.' He poured my pint and I paid. I was expecting smartarse retort from him and was not sure why he had not come back at me, until I turned around and realised Sarah was standing behind me.

'What does a girl have to do to get a drink around here?'

'Make it clear she is here is always helpful. Wine?' At which she made a small mewing noise before bursting into laughter. 'Have you been drinking already?'

'Might have had a couple, my agency had its pre-Christmas lunch and it went on a bit. I am just a bit giggly and Misty has got the hump with me as she only got a five-minute walk due to me being late home.' You know I swear she was swaying slightly. 'If you want to get me a teensy gin and tonic, that would be lovely, and then you can come and give me my present.' This last bit she said one or two decibels too loud and I have to say that we did get some strange looks from the other drinkers close by.

'Tell you what, the lager is not up to much here, why don't I just take you home and we can grab a coffee there?'

'I am not a cheap date I will have you know.' Now this was the tricky bit. I needed to not ply her with more alcohol but I did want to get her home as I was now suspecting she had already consumed more than a few teensy drinks before meeting me. What I needed was a ploy to get her to leave without causing a scene (and I may add before you get the wrong idea, I am doing this for all the right reasons, not the wrong ones).

'I know, I know, it's just that I got something for Misty that is probably best consumed fresh or refrigerated so maybe we should let her have it sooner rather than later.' You have to at least give me marks for thinking on my feet.

'Well, that's okay then, why didn't you say. Finish your beer and I shall take you to see the old girl straightaway. Now I think you are only after me for my puppy. I am not operating a service for recalcitrant dog owners you know.' I necked my pint, smiled at the barman, and grabbed my jacket. With this she looped her arm through mine and we started to totter towards the door. The other drinkers were now giving a combination of relieved and knowing looks that were really starting to annoy me. But getting out of the pub was imperative. I turned on the way out and the barman's parting air kiss reminded me that we needed a new bar to meet in.

When she has said that her place was only ten minutes away, I think that would be without the use of the random walk that her increasing intoxication was causing. The air hit her like a sledgehammer. After about twenty minutes we got to what she informed me was her palace. A really nice-looking ground floor flat with a garden in a Victorian house overlooking a small park. There seemed to be the level of fumbling for keys that only happens in *Carry On* films and for the Chuckle Brothers, but eventually we got in the house with Misty barking up a storm. After a certain amount of coaxing and crotch sniffing, Misty calmed down and I went into the kitchen where I put the kettle on.

'Coffee?'

'Yes, please.' I looked around and it was spotless. So much for dog-based grime. There was not a sign of a stray hair or a dodgy dog toy. I waited for the kettle to click off and hunted for cups. I am pretty self-sufficient and can find my way around any ordered kitchen so I made coffee and then got to the difficult part, milk and sugar.

'Sarah, you want milk and sugar?' I waited for a response. 'Sarah, are you there, how do you want your coffee?' As they say, no response was normally a stern reply. I put my head back into the living room and she was slumped on the sofa spark out. It must have been a good party. I finished making my coffee and sipped it while I looked around the place. It was amazing how much you could fit into a room and still have it pristine. There were four bookcases, all ordered and tidy. On the wall were a series of very-high-quality pen and ink sketches and caricatures. In one corner, there was what I could only assume was a draughtsman's table and angle poise spot lamp. Next to the desk were a set of neatly stacked binders with what I presumed were pieces of work. Finally in the other corner was a rather large dog bed, containing one rather large Misty. She had her head balanced on the edge of the bed watching Sarah and completely ignoring me. Once I had finished looking and sipping, I washed up my cup and tipped her rapidly cooling coffee away. On the side in the kitchen, there was a card and present wrapped. Using my investigator skills, I assumed it was a bottle and book (I am good with shapes like that). I took my presents out and swapped them with hers; it was not quite what I had in mind for a present exchange.

I looked around the room and saw a throw blanket folded neatly on one of the chairs. I now had to do the gentlemanly thing and make my exit whilst leaving her in a reasonable state. I covered her with the throw and thought of all the times I had slumped into a chair after a boozy session. Easy to see when she was not being a stroppy little miss just how cute she was. Anyway, it was time I made my exit. I left a hand-scrawled note wishing her a great break and hoping to see her after my return. I propped it up against a large glass of water and placed it on the table next to the sofa. With this I picked up my bag and made for the door. Looked like an early night for me after all. Now all I had to do was figure out the best way to get to the tube. As I exited the flat I realised why the temperature had dropped so rapidly earlier. In the twenty minutes I had been inside, it had started to snow. When it began to settle in London, which is always warmer than outside the city, you know you had got problems coming. Is it wrong to say it crossed my mind how bad the weather might be in Kent?

Chapter 12

The Boys of Summer
23 December 2010

The countdown to Kent has started and I just had one last act to perform before I left—dropping the presents off at Gerry's. I popped over after work on Thursday night, which normally meant the promise of a good meal as well. Now I remember why Charlie wanted the pasta maker; the girl can actually produce some wonderful food. Tonight it was beef in red wine and it had been cooked until the meat just fell apart. I had made it over reasonably early so the children could open their presents before the younger two went to bed. They had already broken up for school but Charlie was a real disciplinarian, which I rather appreciated as the kids have always been very well behaved. Gerry makes sure they have enough fun along the way. The presents were opened with a great deal of gusto and much ripping of paper which almost managed to drown out the excessively loud Christmas music in the background. I know you are going to say Bah Humbug, but by Christmas week, I had been hearing this stuff for over a month and it was getting a little tedious. I don't even know what 'Stop the Cavalry' has to do with Christmas apart from Jona Lewie's incredible timing one year. I got the customary cuddle from each one and then went off to read a bedtime story, more for the benefit of Ellie now rather than the older two, who have been working on aloof pretty effectively recently.

The pre-bedtime godparent bit completed, I went downstairs to where Gerry had topped up my wine far higher than was warranted in a red wine glass. He seems to think that wine breathing before it is drunk is a mortal sin as this means some of it is evaporating. I tried telling him once that half the taste comes from the nose, but he just gave me that *Shut up, dictionary boy* look and we changed the subject. It is not worth annoying a friend over a piece of pedantry. I flopped into the chair and he turned the music down so that we could talk. Charlie was in the kitchen cleaning up and giving Gerry a hard time about not helping her.

'It's your job, woman,' was most definitely in jest, but even I knew he was pushing his luck.

'Oh, so brave when you have an audience. Let's see how brave you are later when Adam's gone.'

'Charlie, if you need help burying the body, just let me know. There are some quiet stretches of river nearby and frankly he won't need much weighing down.' With that a cushion came flying my way and nearly took the glass of wine out. 'Oi, careful, you don't wanna spill this red, do you, it will stain.'

'So I am all ears, what's the latest in the love life saga. If you keep the volume down, Charlie might not even hear.'

'I am not deaf or stupid. If he has a woman, I want the details, you know the rules. Adam, you provide such good value with your love life that I have stopped watching *EastEnders*. More weird things happen to you than in the whole of Albert Square.' Odd to hear this disembodied voice floating in from the kitchen accompanied by the Huron Carol on the stereo.

'What happened to the play girl?' Gerry now needed to regain the imperative in this conversation.

'What?' I was a bit slow on the uptake and I am sure my face showed it.

'You know, the girl online with the PlayStation?'

'Oh her, she was a bust.'

'Hang on, I know the rules. You don't do internet dating, are you going over old ground again,' Charlie interjected as she wandered into the room drying her hands on a tea towel.

'No, it was not internet dating, Charlie. I was chatting to this girl on the PlayStation. We were playing online and we got chatting, I was telling Gerry last week.' With this Charlie glared at Gerry. I am guessing he had kept this to himself and now he needed to backtrack.

'Anyhow; moving on,' I said in an attempt to lighten the mood. 'She turned out to be either married or a Cuff. She was just evasive online and when I called her on it she cut the connection. I have blocked her now, so it should not be a problem going forward.'

'So there is no love interest on the horizon?' Charlie was now engaged and was moving to sit on the sofa next to Gerry.

'Well I don't go to Mum's for Christmas just for the fun of it.'

'Oh don't forget your folks' present from us, Adam; it's on the side there with the card.'

'Chocs and booze?'

'Just something little; your folks are lovely and they were always nice to us.'

'I swear they think babies were swapped in the hospital, they prefer Gerry to me and I think they want your kids as grandchildren. Kangaroo Jack being in Oz is hard on Mum.'

'So no gossip then on women.' I have seen this before; Charlie now had the bit between her teeth.

'I may have a new friend. I would have said drinking buddy but after last night I am guessing it is not one of her strong points.' I swear Charlie's eyes went from forty to one hundred watts in about a millisecond.

'Really, do tell. I am all ears. Gerry, go make some coffees.' With this Gerry knew he was out of the loop for the next ten minutes. I explained about the balcony and meeting Sarah; about Misty, the emails, and the drink last night. Charlie sat transfixed, grinned a few times, and then when I had finished, turned to the kitchen door where Gerry was entering with a tray of coffee.

'How much of this did you know?'

'I knew he went dog walking with some bird but nothing else. I didn't realise it was serious or I would have told you, babe.' With this Gerry winked at me conspiratorially.

'It's not serious, she is just some girl I met and she seemed like good company and a bit of a laugh. She is not interested in me, but she finds the rules amusing.' I got up and started to pace the room. Honestly with these two it can feel like an interrogation. 'Surely I am allowed to have female friends?'

'We all know that does not really happen. We have all seen *When Harry Met Sally*, it might start off as one thing, but it always leads to another. You know that Gerry is not allowed female friends? I don't like the competition and he doesn't need the distraction, do you, Gerry?'

'Oh no, dear. I know who wears the trousers around here.' Gerry looked at the jeans that Charlie was wearing and unconsciously pulled on the belt of his.

'Don't "dear" me. Adam, he knows damned well that when he goes out, he leaves his dick in the fridge. He can have it back when he returns. He has no need of it elsewhere. And for that matter he has no need of other women. So now, ask yourself, is there more to this woman than you are letting on?' I believe at this point I could see a spotlight coming on and the chair turning into black leather while Magnus Magnusson started so he would finish. Talk about the bloody third degree.

'No, just mates. I'm not even sure she is going to talk to me after the episode last night.'

'Why, you said you were a gentleman. Are you being honest?'

'Yes, and not just because there was a bloody great dog there. Anyway, as nice as this little interrogation session is, I think I will depart before you get the thumb screws out and while my fingernails are still intact.' I bent down and gave her a peck on the cheek and gave Gerry a boy's handshake (white guys trying to be in the hood). Then I grabbed the bag of presents and headed for the door. When I opened it, the world was getting whiter by the moment as the snow was settling thicker. Maybe I needed to get away a bit earlier tomorrow.

Rules for a Born Again Bachelor

As it was, Christmas Eve was a great working day in the city. The markets closed early and you tended to leave between midday and three depending on workload, mostly straight to the pub unless there were any issues. In my case I had the drive to Kent so I managed a Coke and then slipped away to the flat at about two to get the car and bags for the weekend. Although there was about four inches of snow on the ground, it had been cleared off the main roads, but the sky did look fairly grey and pregnant with a large fall forecast. My mind slid to Kentish back roads, it would not be the M20 that was the problem but once I got off it.

With the car packed, I headed off towards Blackwall and tried to beat the queues through the tunnel which I did remarkably well. I think the other motorists were following the advice of the AA and staying off the roads. Just as I got off the A2 and onto the M20 at Swanley, my mobile beeped. I had an hour to go, but I make it a principle of not touching the damned thing while driving. Half an hour later it beeped again but I resisted the temptation. It was probably only Gerry checking on my progress.

By the time I came off the motorway just North of Ashford, I was seeing the difference between the city and southern Kent in terms of snowfall. Where there had been four inches at home, there was eight to ten here and the wind had started to cause it to drift ominously. The ploughs and gritting trucks had been out on the main roads but on the way in to the village, I was down to ten miles an hour as the car had slid twice already. Finally pulling up on Mum and Dad's drive, I turned the engine off and looked at the clock. That had taken nearly twice as long as usual as it was now seven and dark. I picked up my phone before going in to see three texts from Sarah. The first one simply said 'Sorry'. The second one was only slightly more verbose, 'Am I forgiven or is it my turn in the dog house?' I had not even heard the third text come in as I had obviously been concentrating so hard on the last part of the drive: 'Are you ignoring me now? I said sorry'. I needed to stop this getting any worse, before it escalated. I looked up and Mum had the door open, but I pushed it closed in order to keep the heat in and told her I would be there in a minute. I then sent a simple text back to Sarah to put the situation on hold.

TEXT: 'No need for sorry, we all do it. Not ignoring, I was driving. Chat later?' With that I pocketed my phone and unloaded the car.

'Hey, Mum.' I walked in, dumped my stuff down, and gave her a big hug, trying not to break her back as I am often accused. With the requisite peck on the cheek bestowed, I grabbed my things to go upstairs. 'My usual room? Has the rainbow warrior arrived yet?'

'Could you stick to one question at a time, remember my advancing years, young man. Yes, in your old room. Your sister is chaperoning your father to the pub.'

'You mean she is getting the old man to buy her a drink?'

'Can you at least for two days try to be a little bit more charitable? It is Christmas.'

'Okay, I will put my things away and then we can pop down there and join them.'

'No, you are all right, the Hare and Hounds on Christmas Eve is the last place I want to be.'

'Then I will stay here with you and we can catch up.' I smiled sweetly and I swear the old goat actually shuddered.

'We have two days for that, go and see your father and sister.' I dashed upstairs, dropped my things, and headed out towards the pub with Mum calling after me about dinner being in an hour.

The Hare and Hounds is the first pub I ever got drunk in. Mind you as a kid growing up around here, there was pretty much bugger all else to do. I was never going to be the young farmer type. Once I got my grades at school, I was out of there like the proverbial shot. First to university in Nottingham and then on to my first job in the city. I never looked back, well not until the divorce, when I may have crashed a few nights to get away from the lovely or not so lovely Annie at that point. The trouble with these places is that everybody knows me and they all know the story. As I mentioned we got married in the local church, in the slot after Gerry, and half the village had been at the one service or both. They all came to the reception, which was held in a marquee at the pub. Now as I walked in the door and looked around for Dad and Beth, I saw recognition tumble from a dozen faces around the room. Then of course they looked away after a weak smile as nobody still knows what to say at this point even after a few years.

I saw Beth and Dad huddled in a corner as far away from the music as possible, both with half-empty pints. There was a third person sitting with them, another girl who had her back to me and whom I did not recognise. I caught Dad's eye and indicated fresh drinks. He nodded. The girl turned to see who Dad was looking at and she smiled at me. It took a moment and then the penny dropped. Without missing a beat, I gestured to her if she wanted one and she nodded. It's not like I wouldn't know what she wanted as Mary was my first girlfriend over twenty years ago; snake bite and black it was to be then. I got the drinks and walked over to the table. I motioned to Dad to move up and squeezed in next to him even though Mary had made a space next to her. I think she had made her intentions plain when she squeezed my bum as I wriggled past.

'Mum's on the warpath over dinner,' I half shouted over the sound of the background music, which was more foreground if the truth be known.

'We have time to finish these, I am sure.' Dad was not getting the hint. I needed to be away from here as quickly as possible. Mary was saying something that I could not make out and my lip-reading skills are not what they should be. I leaned into her to hear what she had to say and she bent down to provide a floor show from the top half of her body.

'You always did have a nice arse from what I remember,' she slurred into my ear. This had all the hallmarks of a classically bad evening unless I got us out of here soon. I made small talk with Dad and Beth who was glaring at Mary and encouraged them to drink up as soon as possible. Fifteen minutes later we were making our apologies and were on our way to the exit. Mary wrapped her arms around my neck and was demanding a Christmas kiss. I gave her a peck on the cheek and made for the door.

'I'll be in here tomorrow morning. See you then?' was her parting blow. I smiled and waved on the way out. Now how can an ex-girlfriend be a problem? Well Mary breaks so many rules it is difficult to know where to start. She drinks like a fish, gets territorial and jealous, and is, after all that, honestly not that bright. But the one thing she has that makes her very special is her exhibitionist tendencies; she is most definitely a thrill seeker (rule number 6). When Gerry and I wrote the rules, it was without doubt Mary that we both thought of when it came to this one. When we were going out, she wanted to literally do it anywhere and everywhere, the more public the better. When I said that Gerry and I don't go to golf courses, that is not actually true, but we stopped going near golf courses from about 19 as I got banned from two in a week. It became apparent that Mary liked to have sex on the beach and I don't mean the cocktail. As we lived twenty-five miles from the coast, a bunker is the next best thing (which also explains rule 18, no golf courses). Look, I am not proud and I have learned my lesson, but it did seem like a good idea at the time.

As we traipsed back to the house through the snow, Beth and Dad took a fair amount of fun at my expense on Mary having been there. Mum had been talking in the butcher's about me coming back for Christmas and Mad Mary had actively sought out Dad and Beth in order to accidently bump into me. This was going to be two very long days.

Chapter 13

Lonely This Christmas
24 December 2010

As we entered the house, it became bedlam.

'You're back early,' started Mum. 'I said an hour to Adam, which meant I expected two at least.' She was sitting on the sofa, TV on, remote in one hand, drink in the other.

'Mad Mary's back on the scene and she's got the hots for our Adam, Mum,' squealed Beth with delight. Anything was fair game if it took the spotlight off her for a moment. She didn't like the limelight and physically squirmed if she ever got trapped in it. She ran off upstairs before I had a chance to retort.

'Mum, by any chance did you tell anybody I was coming back for Christmas?' I gave her my very best Paddington bear hard stare, as we would have said when we were kids. Isn't it amazing how being back at home for just one microsecond can bring childhood flooding back. All those games, all those rhymes and the names we used to call each other. It's just like someone has slipped off a cloak and revealed us the way we were twenty or thirty years before.

'I might have mentioned it to a couple of people in town. I also saw that lovely girl you used to date before you met the hussy Annie. Now what was her name?'

'Mad Mary by any chance?'

'No, I think it was Mary something, but not that.'

'You really are going doolally, woman, aren't you? What's for dinner, anything edible or are we phoning out for pizza? I know what you are like on Christmas Eve; the kitchen is now ready for the onslaught tomorrow so there is no chance of anything other than pie and mash tonight.'

'There's lasagne, smarty-pants. You will have to eat that and like it, there's no way you will get a pizza delivered tonight in this weather. Now why don't you come tell your old mother about your love life? I could do with a giggle.' She tapped the cushion beside her as if I was about to spring onto it like a cat.

'Tell you what, let's have nice quiet night in front of the TV and I will fill you in on the gory details tomorrow morning while we do the veg.' She looked at me as if I had simply sprouted a second head. 'Won't you be leaving me to it and taking your father to the pub to get him out of my hair?'

'I think we can leave that for the belligerent Beth to do, she needs the practice since I have done more than my fair share. Besides I am not stepping out in the village while the dating equivalent of Freddie Kruger is still prowling around. You know what she did to my back last time I saw her.'

'A mother should never have to see those things.'

After a few hours of typical Christmas Eve repeats and what turned out to be a surprisingly good lasagne, I figured I had time to get back to Sarah with a text.

TEXT: 'So is the head finally better? What are you up to tomorrow?'

I pressed send and wondered if she was out with Misty or even partying. I went into the kitchen to grab a beer, and before I got the opener from the drawer, my phone went ping. I really must change the ring tone so I can tell it's her or not (something suitable such as 'How Much Is That Doggy in the Window' or the theme from *Airwolf*).

TEXT: '80%, sorry again. Off to Mum's first thing, back late in the evening.'

Curious, I am not sure I could face my family without a drink, so the idea of going there for the day and driving back, assuming they lived a fair distance, was not one I would readily entertain. Now that got me thinking. Assuming they lived a distance, what was I saying. I had been chatting to this girl off and on for two weeks tonight and I barely knew anything about her. I am still not sure what it is she does, what her history is, or what her plans are. It is strange that she seems to deflect my passing questions like a bulletproof vest. Or maybe I am just a little self-obsessed. I have been so keen to tell her about the rules and prove that I am a nice guy that maybe I am simply showing her that I am everything I profess not to be. Oh bugger, I think I might be a little drunk and just a touch maudlin, but in our family that pretty much describes Christmas.

TEXT: 'I am back on Monday if Misty wants a walk. We could chat about you?'

So how often do you send a text and then think, oh damn, that could be taken more than one way. She has already made comments about me liking the dog more than her. She is going to start wondering what I might want to know. Or will she think I have been talking to someone about her.

TEXT: 'That would be nice. Misty says woof, I say sweet dreams.'

Well I think that was over and out. Maybe time I got to bed and prepared myself for the day ahead which would be the usual banter and probably painfully dull.

'Big brother, you finally got me something that I wanted for Christmas, are you starting to take advice from your colleagues, or do you have a new woman in tow?' As she unwrapped the fridge magnet with a goat on the front and a twenty pound note taped to the back, she actually smiled. I will not bore you with each separate ooh and ahh during the rest of the ceremony of the present opening but suffice to say, there were more positives than negatives. I rang Gerry to speak to the kids and Mum of course jumped in to thank both of them for their gifts. My Father was strangely absent from proceedings immediately after and I decided that I should investigate. Dad has a penchant for his garden shed in the way that naughty neighbours always did in 1970's sitcoms such as *Bless This House* (reruns okay, I am not that old). I have this image of my father laughing like Sid James while he blows up the shed in an ill-fated attempt at distillation (hence the moonshine comments). Before I walked into the shed, I had already worked out what was going on as the smell gave it away.

'Where the hell are you getting blow from, Dad? What am I saying, why are you using blow?'

'Adam dear boy'—sweet Jesus, he had turned in Richard Harris overnight—'how sweet of you to finally notice. Your sister has been getting it for me for a few months. You know it really helps with the arthritis. When she is not around, your lovely friend Mary can provide for me. She was not just hanging around for you in the pub, you egotistical little tosser, she was actually supplying me for the festive period. You, my dear lad, are just the icing on the cake to her.' With this he slumped back into the beaten-up old armchair that was nestling next to a paraffin heater keeping the place slightly warmer than freezing. I could feel the chill, but I suspected this was now beyond his cognition. He was quite high, so I am just wondering what it was he was being sold; it really did smell strong. 'Would you like to a little puff?'

'I think I will leave that to you, Dad, since it appears to be medicinal.' I should point out that I do not do drugs or go near people, girls or boys that do. I am no prude; I am basically all about live and let live, but I simply do not wish to imbibe or take part in something that is illegal, whatever the difficult moral argument that surrounds it. I wandered back in the house, whilst he mumbled something about it being my loss.

'Mum, are you aware your husband is in the garage getting stoned?'

'Yes, dear, it's because I won't let him do it in the house.' There was most definitely a witty comeback to this I could have used but you know I think the last one-liner had knocked the stuffing out of me.

The rest of the day was exactly how you would imagine it to be. Slow, tedious family life of people who had a reason to be together when we were all a lot younger but now we just met up to compare case notes from each of our own personal asylums once a year. I did however remember that in my bag was Sarah's present. A bottle of *Captain Morgan* rum (oh how droll) and a copy of *Women Are from Venus, Men Are from Mars*. Well believe it or not it made me laugh out loud, which is more than I could say for the Christmas TV. Before disappearing to bed, I dropped Sarah a quick line.

TEXT: 'Thank you, the presents are great, very witty. Hope folks were fine. Happy Christmas.'

I said my good nights and I was pretty much asleep before my head approached the horizontal. I don't think I dreamed, but just hung in the darkness, hoping for a better start to 2011. When the first light of dawn came around seven, it was more white than normal due to the snow, which had now stopped, but lay over twelve inches deep. On my phone I saw the indicator flashing.

TEXT: 'Misty loved her sausage. I love my warm hands. Thank you HC, GN.'

So I would say that was mission accomplished. Now I just had to concentrate on getting through the day and home again in the morning.

Chapter 14

Stuck in the Middle with You
26 December 2010

Boxing Day passed very uneventfully in the end. As unfair as I sound about my family sometimes, they are just a lot easier to get along with once the initial animosity dies away. It's a bit like a Grand Prix; a lot of jostling for pole position, but once the race settles down, we kind of rub along together. I also need to make allowances for my parents due to their advancing years, they really are rather amazing if you ignore Dad's recent tendency to self-medicate. In previous years this would have been through the homemade wine and beer. Now his distinct red nose has been replaced by slightly red-tinged eyes from the blow but he appears to be happy in himself and the move from booze to weed has certainly helped to reduce his girth. I am jealous of one thing and that is that he still has a full head of hair, although grey, whereas I am a proper carrot top but thinning badly with a definite widow's peak. There has always been a family joke about my parentage (rather like a certain royal) as I am the only ginger in the whole direct family line. Luckily there are no other gingers in the village, although occasionally the old milkman is mentioned. I can just hear it now, mother Marion Cooper, Father Ernie, the fastest milkman in the west.

Now where was I, oh yes, Boxing Day over with, I sloped off early on Monday morning in order to beat the traffic, but with the downside of having to brave the ice rink that was the local road system of country lanes. After about half an hour of *Drive by celebrity on ice*, I managed to make the motorway and got a good run home. When I got to the flat, the place was freezing having been away for a couple of days, so I whacked the heating up and decided on a little Christmas cheer in the local while the internal temperature rose. Oh, and time to catch up with Sarah.

TEXT: 'Busy today? How is the lady of the house, and how are you?'

What did I say about sending texts and then regretting the tone afterwards? Maybe that second pint was not such a good idea. However, it appears there was no harm done as ten minutes later she came back and suggested a pub we could meet in by the Thames that had a log fire and mulled wine. Right now, I would drink anti-freeze as long as it was warm inside (kind of reminds me of Austrian wine). I said I would meet her in an hour so I dropped back to the now warm flat and put on two extra layers before the trek across town. I may have overdone it as people on the tube were giving me strange sideways glances, and when I caught my reflection in the tube window, I saw that I looked like an extra from *The Day After Tomorrow*. Several days' growth on my face while at Mum's was not helping the picture. All I needed now was an ice axe and the image would be complete.

Getting out of the tube at Embankment, I regretted not getting better directions as five minutes outside meant my fingers and toes had now lost all feeling. Note to self, better boots and gloves in future. Fashion really is no substitute for function. Finally I rounded the corner and there it was (you will notice for once I am not mentioning the name as I don't want to broadcast the place, it is far too good of a secret for that). Sarah was already installed by the fire with a steaming mug of mulled wine in front of her and a definite absence of Misty.

'No mutt?'

'And hello to you too.'

'I am guessing she is all right, it is just I was expecting to see her.'

'I am getting worried about you and that dog. Don't make me get jealous. No seriously, we had a massive walk this morning and all she wants to do now is sleep. She gets grumpy when it'd too cold like this, so I left her home.'

'So how was Christmas? How warm are the hands? Nice scarf by the way.' She was of course wearing the scarf I had bought her for Christmas so I guessed that I had got that right too. I grabbed a drink from the bar and got her a top up while I was at it. When I returned, she slid across her seat nearer to the fire and made space for me. She patted the cushion in an inviting way and I had to admit I was half thinking psycho at that point. But I sat down and she snuggled in.

'So you wanna talk about me then. What brought about this change of heart, you have barely asked a question in the last two weeks.'

'Curious that; I just realised when I was at Mum's how little I knew about you. When we met, you were intrigued by the rules and we just seemed to spend a lot of time talking about them. But I would also say that you have ducked a few questions along the way. I was going to ask you some things the other night but you were not really in the right frame of mind for questions, more for looking at the inside of your eyelids. Let's start with that, you said agency party. I noticed the drawing board in your place are you some kind of technical draughtsman?'

'Did you also notice the pictures on the walls?'

'What the caricatures? Wow, are they yours? So what are you a cartoonist or something?'

'Freelance graphic artist. A pencil for hire. The caricatures are a hobby and I make money on the side doing corporate events. I have a big party on New Year's Eve that I am working at.'

'That is really rather cool, I am impressed. I am guessing it pays its way as that is a lovely place you have.'

'Actually, I inherited that from an aunt who died a few years ago. I could never afford to buy it on what I earn. Don't get me wrong, I make ends meet, but that place is something special. I actually own the whole building and I rent out the top flat. But it gives me a garden in central London for Misty which is important to me.'

'How long have you had her? I saw how she was watching you the other night when I put the throw over you. She is devoted, isn't she?'

'She was a rescue pup. Some idiot got her and after six months realised the fluffy ears and the oversized paws were not as cute when the animal is eating you out of house and home and needing two good walks a day. They tied her up at the canal bank and walked away. It's funny you should have mentioned Battersea the other day as that's where I got her from. She took a lot of nursing back to health but now she is my rock, my confidante, and the only thing on this earth that I truly trust.' Her face took on a rather hard look while she spoke, it obviously upset her a lot, but when she saw me looking, she forced a smile. 'I can't abide cruelty to animals.'

'Or humans?'

'Most humans.'

'So what did you do for Christmas day?'

'Mum lives in Suffolk, but I am afraid we don't get on that well, so I just went for the day. She lives like lady muck in her little village. Dad died ten years ago and she has been on her own ever since, but she has a massive circle of sycophants, sorry I mean friends. No, I was right the first time. They have a loathsome little community there; all sweet sherry, coffee mornings, and four balls in the week.' She looked at me expecting a reaction. When I did not respond, she carried on. 'Not a golfer then?'

'Rule 18. Long story, not worth you bothering with, but I am more into my football.'

'Playing or watching? Another armchair pundit?'

'Watching but actually on the terraces. Gerry and I have season tickets for Leyton Orient. We go to all the home fixtures if we can, although it is not often we travel, Gerry only gets every other weekend off, based on Charlie's rules.'

'Ah, I am guessing this is Gerry's better half? Sounds like my kind of woman, it's about time we started having rules of our own.' She got out a notebook and pencil from her bag and made as if to make a list.

'Where shall we start? No sniffing crotches; no drinking from the toilet, no muddy paws in the house.'

'For a moment there I thought you were talking about me.'

'I was.' She laughed and put the book away. 'So what else you wanna know. Me, I'm an open book.'

'Okay, why are you single? Are you single? Have you ever been, how can I put this, not single?'

'Do you have some issue with saying the word *married*? You still reeling from your ex-wife's so-called betrayal? You said she ran off with a Pilates instructor called Karen? Most blokes would end up finding it a turn on. You know, that two women thing.'

'Oh yes, two women sounds like fun, but not when there is no room for a man and one finds oneself supplanted. I simply don't say *married* because there are so many different forms of relationship these days. Married, Dinky's, Cuffs, civil partnership. Let's just assume any of those. So are you, or have you ever been?'

'I have been engaged.'

'Around our way when growing up, that was just an excuse for a party.'

'You cynical bastard. This was serious. Three years we were together. A guy called Andrew, lawyer, filthy rich. But in the end he was just filthy. Think of the most clichéd thing you think that could happen.'

'Oh I don't know. Turned out to be married already or maybe gay?'

'No, far worse, he ran off with my best friend, the chief bloody bridesmaid. That was seven years ago. For some reason I have had trust issues since. I have had a few flings in between, but to be perfectly honest, I prefer the company of Misty. She is housetrained and does not tend to let me down. Even if she does seem to have taken to you!'

'That girl has good taste.' I may have been preening myself at that point, puffing up my chest and feeling rather important. I should have known a put-down was on the way.

'Well everyone makes mistakes, even Misty doesn't get it right all the time.' I should have been hurt, but I was looking at the very distinct laughter lines around her eyes. She was smiling and so I left it at that.

'Any other dark secrets? Are you are serial axe murderer, etc.? By the way, what did you do on Boxing Day if you just stayed in Suffolk for the day?'

'I work for Shelter every Christmas, two days. I did Christmas Eve and Boxing Day this year. I can tell you, Christmas Eve was not fun with that hangover still lingering.'

'I am going to ask, what happened on Wednesday, you said a long lunch, but that appeared to be very long.'

'A few of the freelancers got together. As we work at home a lot, we don't get to meet up in the office like everybody else, so we went for lunch and then I stayed on for a lot longer than I intended. I felt awful when I woke up on the sofa and pretty guilty.'

'I would have left Paracetamol with the glass of water but I did not know where they were and I was not about to start rifling with Misty there.'

'You were very sweet to have left the water and the blanket. I was actually quite impressed.' With this she turned and planted a gentle kiss on my cheek. 'Thank you.' Then she raised her finger in a wagging manner. 'But don't get any ideas; just mates.'

'Okay, but I am right to assume there is no hulking great Mr Sarah somewhere that is going to get all testosterone territorial on me for being a mate?'

'Nobody you need to worry about, Captain.' With that she turned rested her head on my shoulder and stared into the fire. I guess the conversation was over.

Chapter 15

In the Ghetto
29 December 2010

I am one of those sad people that invariably works between Christmas and New Year, firstly because it is quiet, secondly because we need to maintain cover over the period as the markets are open, but most importantly, the singles tend to get the short straw. The Cuffs generally lodge their holiday requests very early or have very late whinging exercises to the boss because they have so and so coming for Christmas and they are 85 and it could be their last Christmas. I am guessing you have heard this sort of thing before. Frankly I don't really mind, because it's quiet, the days are shorter and I get to catch up on paperwork, get a decent lunch in, and maybe even use the gym. I don't want to overdo the gym bit yet, but since I have not used it at all in December and I really need to get ready for the January purge, it would seem like a good idea to reacquaint myself with the equipment and break myself back in gently.

There is that expression about the best-laid plans and unfortunately this was the case today. Some idiot had double booked a trade in the system which needed to be reversed out and there was a lot of noise for about three hours. When the dust started to settle, the lunch window had closed and I sat staring at a half full mailbox again. As I worked my way down the usual list of tedious requests, I found a message from the Sarah.

Rules for a Born Again Bachelor

From: *Misty.she.wolf@gmail.com*
Subject: Captain Hook

Captain, I find myself at a loose end and I wondered what you were up to later. I know you said you were working (hence sending to your work address). I must admit my request is also two-fold. Every time we have met so far you have come across town to me. With my normal level of suspicion (and from my little story you can see why) I am wondering if all this is lies and there is a little Miss Captain and some baby ship mates somewhere. Suddenly I have this image of Captain Von Trappe. I know you like to sing and quote lyrics. Is there any chance that the hills of East London are alive with the sound of music? Why not invite me over. I can leave Misty for an evening and you could entertain me. I await your missive.

Okay, she had a point. In my own way I just figured with Misty in tow she was not going to want to trek across London for a pint or a glass of wine, but apparently I was wrong. Well I had nothing on and with it being quiet here I had the chance to get back and make sure the place was in a good state. I have borderline OCD so it is unlikely to be a mess, but these things need to be checked out. I wondered if she wants a drink or to eat as well.

TEXT: 'Drink or food and drink?'
TEXT: 'Food would be great. Do you cook?'
TEXT: 'Is it still a Catholic Pope? Is there anything you don't eat?'
TEXT: 'Not keen on Offal, but other than that anything.'

With that I dropped her over my address and directions from the tube (no, I am not telling you) and got on with trying to clear my desk as soon as possible. Now I am not a gourmet cook, but the plethora of cooking shows on the TV over the last few years means I am capable of looking after myself and pulling together a fairly decent plate of food. I left the office bang on five and took myself off to the local supermarket on my way home. Only small issue was the number of people there. Why is it when we have any sort of disruption to normal service such as a bank holiday or Christmas, people act as if a zombie plague is coming and they strip the shelves as effectively as locusts in the Sahara? I struggled to find the bits I needed and had to modify on the fly what I was cooking, but that's what food is about these days (don't you dare mention fusion, it's a pet hate).

With the shopping done, I got back to the flat and did the basic food prep for a stuffed chicken breast and placed it in the oven. Now it was time to check the flat for acceptability. Luckily I was right about it being in a good state. How can I describe the flat? Let's start with the estate agent speak. Second-floor bijoux residence with easy access to the city and East London. Two double bedrooms (only just in the case of the second room), a functional kitchen and a lounge/dining space. What I should then add in terms of decoration is think minimalist. It is not all white or anything, nothing that stark, but I do not have a mass of ornaments lying around. My only real vice is bookshelves, which are unfortunately organised by size, genre, and alphabetic order by author's name (keep your thoughts to yourself, it's not like I am criticising your room right now). Yes, I admit it's all a bit organised. Even the PlayStation games are in a shelf in name order. It's just the way my brain works, and frankly it is one of the things that make me good at my job. I am a natural pattern matcher; in fact I think that is why the rules appeal to me so much. Deep inside my head somewhere I know there is the feeling that if I follow the rules I will eventually make the right choices and I will find the right person (or am I just deluded?). I have a phrase I have taken to using when it comes to the rules: having nothing is better than having the wrong thing. I think it is amazing but unfortunate that this sort of insight only came to me when I was nearly 40; but I suppose they do say that's when life begins.

I am drifting again, I will get on. The flat is acceptably tidy, I have showered and put on something less work like and the food is coming along fine. I have whipped up a quick salad and vinaigrette and put some music on. Here again is a difficult choice. You may not have it worked out by now, but music is massively important to me, in that I really love the lyrics and also quote them at apposite moments. I also happen to love to sing (don't worry, this is not an *X-Factor* moment when an ugly duckling turns into a swan). So for me music says a lot at all times. What I put on as background music is likely to be interpreted (well I would) and so I was being careful. Classical at this point would be too staid; country would make me sound like a hick and rap like I was trying to be trendy (mutton dressed as lamb). I went for the comfortable middle ground of Motown as in the worst case, people just mentally reference the advert they have seen. I was listening to 'Through the Grapevine' when the doorbell went.

'You found it then.'

'Why do people say things like that? If I had not, who the hell would you be speaking to?'

'Sorry, shall I try that again. Good evening, please come in and try to leave your shoes and sarcasm at the door. I don't like to leave marks on the carpet or my intellect.'

'Touché. Sorry from me too. It's still bloody cold and I am not sure whether I am coming down with something.' With this she handed me a bottle of wine and followed me into the room while I hung up her coat. She surveyed the room and took the glass of wine I offered her. Moving towards the bookshelves, Sarah began to scan across the titles. 'Um, this is nice wine. So the books, alphabetized? That shows a certain level or genius or insanity. You have a fair few.'

'Not as many as you on display. I have a load more in storage but I can't abide too much clutter so I try to keep a balance.'

'Oh yes, I forgot you had seen all mine. I am really sorry about that night, I know I said that the other day, but I do feel a bit guilty still and you did behave so well.'

''Nuff said. We all have our days. When I saw you there, I can honestly say I simply thought of all the times I had slept in a chair after a skin-full. Anyway moving on, I hope you like chicken, it's almost ready.'

'Yup, chicken is great. Interesting decision you made; cook rather than go out. You do eat out, I guess? Or do you have other conditions as well as your OCD? Yes, I have noticed how tidy this place is and then on top of that there are the little extra details. The coasters on the table; did you use a ruler? They look like they have been placed with mathematical precision.'

'It started when I was a kid. I used to tidy things up. Mum thought I was a freak. Dad would give me these tasks to do in the garage and garden that involved sorting. Do you play Pelmanism? It's also called pairs. I could not be beaten at it growing up. It's like I could see the cards in my mind.'

'You really are a freak, aren't you?' With this she smiled and I knew she meant it in a nice way and we sat down at the table to the food I produced from the oven. We ate in fits of silence and odd questions about the books and music. You know the usual sort of thing—favourite author, favourite genre. Do you think the movie is ever as good as the book? But eventually the question came back that I had failed to answer.

'You avoided telling me why we are eating in. So are you skint or embarrassed to be seen with me in your hood?'

'Please, ghetto if you don't mind. I am far more Elvis than I will ever be Eminem; on *a cold and grey Chicago morn*—thank ya very much. It's okay, Elvis has now left the building.' She looked at me smiled and clapped her hands. Then she looked at me and opened her hands in a gesture of well, come on, tell me. 'It is nothing about money or being embarrassed but I am not sure I want to drag you into the local here. I don't drink there very much these days. I had a couple of pubs I used to use locally which did okay food, but I stopped using them when in company due to rule 14.'

'Okay, I will bite. What is rule 14?'

'Avoiding territorial women, I had bad experiences.'

'Do you care to share?'

'Okay, but let me get the cheesecake and coffee and I will tell you the tale.'

Chapter 16

Hey, You, Get Off My Cloud
29 December 2010

I remember sailing down the Black River in Jamaica in the burning heat on a tourist boat. Funnily enough Annie and I were on honeymoon and the guide was waxing lyrically about the crocodiles in the river. Apparently, he says, you will see one every hundred metres, give or take. Now me being a typically cynical tourist, I thought, oh yeah, whatever, I bet we don't see any and this is all some kind of scam. But lo and behold, half a mile into the river from the basin we see the first one. Now I am not saying that there is an inner sprinter in me in terms of distance measurement, but approximately every hundred meters or so of river from then on we saw a very happy crocodile, bathing in the Jamaican sun (you could tell they were happy from the big toothy grin). They were not behaving in the way you would think they would. They were calm, placid, some might say maybe under the influence of some Marley magic medicine. I asked the guide if they ever got nasty. After the inevitable joke about not swimming and how he lost his arm (yes, he had just the one), he mentioned the only time you saw them get annoyed was when their territory was encroached upon. I was left wondering how you tell they are annoyed, I am guessing it was not a certain level of huffiness or not speaking over dinner. This our guide confirmed in his own special way, but I think his hand gestures were more repeatable than his patois.

Have I lost you yet, or can you see where I am going with this? Bear with me. The crocodile in the Black River is another fine example to be added to the rules. Did you ever realise that women, you know the slightly more bumpy type of adult, are way more territorial than us blokes? I can tell from that disbelieving sneer on your face that you don't agree with me; okay, try this for size. Why do you go to a pub? Is it for the company, the music, or the beer? Mostly, let's face it; unless you are a Sky sports fan and are too tight to pay for it at home, a pub is about the beer. So what happens when you break up from that girl that you were so dearly devoted to? Well, you go back to the pub and you enjoy the beer, in fact, a constant in a changing world. Ah, but now you see, there is the problem, your ex does not necessarily follow your masculine logic; I would say that's why they call it masculine logic, but I will get on to exceptions later. Oh no, your average female of the species is territorial in a big way.

What often happens is that your target audience, in Latin *humanus skirtius*, gets rather too attached to a certain watering hole, not for the beer, but in fact for the location. Location is incredibly important to the female psyche; this explains why they knock socks off men when it comes to reading maps. If you think about it, they are not in the pub for the beer in general, and although there are exceptions, girls tend to drink spirits or wine. You are not going to tell me they are enamoured with a broken pool table or a jukebox with a selection of eighties classic including 'The Final Countdown' and 'When Will I Be Famous'. No, sorry to break any misconceptions, but this is about territory and their mates of course (why else do females go off to the toilet in packs). Although both halves of an ex-couple may state a love of a certain local, in a fight to the death, I would always bet on the more aggressive female to come out on top. The more passive male simply finds a new source of beer!

What is supposed to happen when the relationship ends? Do you walk carefully away down the middle of the street like a gunfight in reverse? No, you go back to the same haunt and then she walks in. Now this can be dealt with gracefully, where the whole pub is on tenterhooks or the opposite. This is where there is a screaming match, although this

Rules for a Born Again Bachelor

often happens later in the evening; there are lines from helpful friends such as 'Leave him, Tracey, 'e's not worth it'. For Tracey, please substitute a name as applicable. Quite often these moments can subside over time and a gentle status quo can be established. You may pick different nights or even change pubs. However at some point you are going to fall foul of rule 14.

14. Never go into a pub your ex frequents with a new woman.

That is the rule, now comes the example. There was this girl called Tracey; damn, I knew there was a reason I mentioned her earlier (see appendix on Freud, no, I'm just joking about that). Well, we had been going out for about a month and I realised that Friday was a somewhat troubled night for her. She was a vet's receptionist and had access to what I can only describe as very-high-quality horse tranquillisers (please tell me you've seen *In Bruges*). She had a habit of mixing them with vodka and Red Bull to make what she called a Red Rum. This only happened on a Friday night as she had no work on the Saturday. The sex was great but the psychotic behaviour was not really worth what I was getting out of it, so we split. Well I spent the requisite one month alone (rule 12) and after that started chatting to a girl called Nathalie who happened to be an antique dealer, and no, don't start making jokes about my age. Anyway, where as I, oh yes, Nathalie. I had not really thought it through that on the second date with Nat, we went for an early dinner and then fancied a nightcap. We went off to the Crown as I knew they served a decent glass of wine and we grabbed a table close to the bar.

If I told you I heard the trouble coming before I saw it, you will get the general idea. There was a scream from across the bar rather like a crank shaft shearing. The high-pitched noise was followed by some of the bluest language it has been my displeasure to experience; when I say this, I am talking squaddies blushing, I think you get the picture. Well apparently my parentage was in question, not the first time that's been mentioned. The problem was, she then started on a very startled Nat. You don't get called she-whore and the like a lot in the antiques game, even in Lovejoy. The result of this was a very early exit from the bar, a verbal lashing from the lovely Nat, and me dropping her off early at her place instead of mine. To make matters worse, at two in the morning Tracey came pounding on my door demanding to have what was hers and asking where the tarnished lady was to be found (the language was in fact rather more colourful and colloquial). After a liberal application of the hotline to the local police station, I got a few more hours' sleep. Then of course came the next morning and the inevitable text from Nat as in reality I knew it was coming. Apparently she wanted to spend more time with people who do not have psychopathic exes, which meant a lot less time with me. I did say rule 14 was important.

Chapter 17

Happy New Year
31 December 10

When I had finished telling her about Tracey, Sarah was laughing so hard there were tears rolling down her face.

'And this is the reason we ate in tonight? How long ago did you stop seeing this psycho?'

'No, this is not the reason, but I don't see any reason to annoy anyone in the local, just in case. I stopped seeing her over two years ago, but I do see her in the pub occasionally. I made the decision I would not go in there on a Friday, just in case.'

'Right, anyway, thanks for a great dinner and as ever a fabulous insight into the mad, bad world of Adam. I really am starting to think of you as the Bionic Man, you know, a man barely alive but we can rebuild him. You are a little freaky but fun with it. What are you doing for New Year? I have this drawing job on so will not be back 'til the wee small hours.'

'Gerry and Charlie are having a little dinner party, but I won't be late. I hate having hangovers on New Year's Day. I do the month of January dry so it is horrible to start it feeling crap.'

'Excellent. I always try and take a dawn walk with Misty every year on that day. You fancy popping over and joining us? We can grab some breakfast afterwards?'

'Sounds like a plan.' With this I collected her coat and helped her put it on before showing her out with the promise she would text to let me know she found her way back safely. As she left, she turned and gave me a hug. Don't get excited, nothing too sexy, but gentle and warm.

<hr />

The next two days were spent in totally tedious tasks around the office. Honestly, when it's busy, it's like Liverpool Street Station in rush hour, but when it's quiet, it's like a morgue. I think the biggest issue is that we all end up becoming adrenalin junkies in the city. As painful as the tough times are, the quiet bits in between really do drag. Anyway, I had to focus on getting over to Gerry's for New Year's Eve. Charlie normally throws a pretty good dinner party, and this year with the Christmas present, I was hoping for a little bit of fresh pasta and a decent Italian sauce or two (she also makes a sensational Tiramisu). I was going to take my usual contribution—flowers, chocolates, a couple of cheeky cigars for midnight, and two bottles of bubbles. I am after all a creature of habit. In case you are wondering, no, I don't smoke cigarettes or have any kind of taste for my father's newfound drug of choice. I do however like the occasional cigar, on high days and holidays. Gerry and I have been indulging in this since we were 15 when he managed to smuggle a couple from his dad's stash.

After changing into something that I believed looked okay, without being too smart or too casual (why is everything so hard these days, everybody judges?) I set off for Gerry's. My evening had been planned so that I could get the night bus home in order not to be screwed for the usual extortionate cab fare. I swear the Mafia must have moved into the minicab business in the East End as everything after midnight becomes the equivalent of a small mortgage. I turned up at seven thirty in order to see the kids and help to put them to bed. Having been at Gerry's for the last few years, I knew this would not be a one-time thing and that we would have a series of visits through the evening for water, cuddles, or bad dreams (although now they are older, that is really only Ellie these days). They were very good kids, but even they got excited when people came to dinner. I had a small victory when it came to the bedtime story I had been reading Ellie. I'd read the current book of choice more than nine times and it was getting a little tedious. I had popped out earlier in the day and picked up the latest thing (according to the shop assistant) in children's literature for the age range. We first had the ceremony of the unwrapping where the old ones *helped* Ellie remove the paper. Then we got down to the serious business of reading. When we were about halfway through, I heard the doorbell go and figured that would be the first of other guests. Charlie and Gerry had invited a couple of other friends over but I had not asked who was coming.

'Adam, this is Susan; she's joining us for dinner. She comes into the school from time to time as a reading assistant.' I had just walked into the dining room to find the table set rather ominously for six. Bloody Charlie has done it again. This is the third time she has introduced me to an available female of her acquaintance. I am starting to think she does not like cooking for me after all and is trying to find someone else to take over. In all seriousness, I have known Charlie for so long that I know she does not have an evil bone in her body and all of this is well intentioned, but she knows the rules.

'Oh how delightful, will your husband be joining us?' I gave the dagger look to Charlie who looked more sheepish than normal.

'Not unless his name is Lazarus, he died five years ago.' She looked sad but at the same time somehow resigned to the idea as if this was a line she had been practising as a defence for some time. I now went as red as one of Nena's ninety-nine balloons and started to babble incoherently.

'When not working in the city, Adam spends his spare time doing odd jobs for the diplomatic corps.' Charlie clenched her fist and bared it in my direction. Susan walked over to Charlie, held her hand, and gave her a peck on the cheek.

'It's okay, Charlotte; I am in a good place with it now. He was ill and it was in the end a blessed relief for all involved. Anyway, Adam, you can call me Sue, I am not prissy about names but Susan does make me sound like an Enid Blyton character looking for lashings of ginger beer.' She approached me to shake my hand, but I thought I might try and recover some composure by giving her the three kisses on the cheek routine. 'Oh, very cosmopolitan, or is this your idea of working fast. Charlotte said I should keep an eye on you.' She winked at me while she said this.

'Not at all, it's just I work for a Swiss bank and have some spent time in Europe. I think they have a certain amount of style in greetings that we reserved English could learn a thing or two about.'

'How delightful, I have travelled a bit myself, where have you been? Did you pick up the language?'

'I had a couple of years in Munich but my German is now so rusty that you might end up with tetanus if I used it in polite company.'

'It might be nice to have a chat about it at some point over a drink. I've spent time in Austria, Germany, and Switzerland over the last few years. I have a marketing company that I used to run with my husband.'

'Yes, that would nice,' I said and gave her a card. I really had no intention of following up on this but I was being given nonverbal prompts from Charlie to behave. I needed to speak to Charlie as this woman broke so many rules that I was going to shout 'House' any moment now. 'Can I ask how long have you known Charlie?' I thought I would at least keep it light.

'As Charlie mentioned, I read at the school for the second-language students. I have been doing it for a few years and Charlie and I struck up a friendship over a couple of after school catch-ups.'

The other couple turned up just as the meal was ready to be served. They were Charlie's sister and her husband, Michelle and Michael. I think like Hart to Hart, Michael only married someone with the first initial as him so they did not have to change the monograms on the towels. I have met them as a couple many times over the years, though in Michelle's case for almost as long as I have known Charlie. Michelle was originally a lovely vivacious young girl, but I have to say life with Michael had really knocked the stuffing out of her and now they were just a fine example of Cuffs. They had all the glitter and the glitz on the surface but underneath you could not see a spark of passion or excitement about life. They reminded me of what I did not want to end up like. I suppose if I am honest, this is what my marriage to Annie must have looked like from the outside; no wonder she left. There I am all of a sudden back in the dock and the cross-examination is restarting. The next witness is Annie and there is cheering from someone in the public gallery but I can't make out the face. I snap out of it and try to get back into 'good company' mode.

Dinner was very nice and Charlie had indeed made good her threat and produced the most delicious homemade ravioli with the pasta maker. She finished off with the unsurprising but excellent as ever Tiramisu. The only disconcerting thing was that during dessert and into the coffee and petite fours, I became aware of something brushing my foot. We had been seated opposite our *partners* for the night and I finally realised that Sue was attempting to play footsie under the table. I pulled my feet back and ignored the gesture. About five minutes later it was no longer my foot that was being touched but she had managed to slip her shoe off and her foot was brushing my inner thigh. I looked across the table to her and her eyes were piercing into mine. She had a smirk on her face and all the while she was continuing to talk to Charlie and Michelle on the subject of children's education. I made my excuses to go to the bathroom. There I took my time washing my hands and wondering how to get out of the situation. I checked my watch and it was 11.15. There was no way I was getting away before midnight as Gerry would want to toast the New Year with the bubbles and smoke the cigars. I wondered if I could twist Gerry's arm and get outside for a breath of fresh air for the cigars early. His missus got me into this; he could bloody well help me get out of it.

'Gerry, I feel Cuba coming on,' I said and I walked back into the room. Gerry gave me a look and I knew yet again I was going to be in the wrong.

'Excellent', said Susan rather drunkenly, 'are we dancing?' She got up and flung herself in my direction. 'I would love a Cuba Libre.' I waltzed her back to her chair and plonked her down.

'No, I am afraid that we were referring to another tradition.' Gerry was now shaking his head at me and imploring me to stop. At this point, I must have installed my empathy head as I got a very ominous feeling. Suddenly I guessed how Susan's husband had died. I mouthed the sign of smoking to Gerry behind Susan's back and pointed to her while crossing my hands. Gerry smiled at me and nodded his head. Talk about a close call. 'I was only joking, Sue, of course we will all have a Cuba Libre to toast in the New Year.' I was now hoping our hosts had Bacardi in the cupboard.

'Let's stick to the champagne for the New Year toast since you brought it, Adam.' Charlie was now moving down the threat status on her face from def-con one to three. It seems the crisis was averted and also as a bonus I had pulled my chair out to a point that Susan could not reach me with her foot. I also think the booze was beginning to tell on her a bit as her eyes were looking a little red. The next thirty-five minutes went without incident. After the New Year toast and a quick look outside at the fireworks, I made my excuse to go. I had my bus to catch. Sue was getting a cab and I had no intention of chaperoning her, whatever the lovely Charlie had in mind for me. I arrived home by about one. As I got in, my phone showed a text from Sarah.

TEXT: 'Is seven too early? Hope you had a good evening.'

TEXT: 'Seven is fine. See you at yours. Woof to the mutt, HNY.'

TEXT: 'HNY to you too, mate.'

I lay awake for a while and thought there must be a better way spend New Year. The rules were meant to get me out of situations like that, not make it worse. Time for a New Year resolution me thinks.

                                                                                     ❧ ☙

Luckily the tubes ran early and I arrived at Sarah's place about quarter past seven to find her staring out the window. She waved and indicated she was coming out. About two minutes later the vision which approached me was dressed somewhat like the Michelin man. She was also snuffling into a handkerchief.

'I knew it, I am coming down with something. I just cannot get warm. Thing about having a dog, especially one as big as Misty, is that she doesn't care how bad I feel. She needs her walk.' Sarah almost flew down the stairs being dragged by a very excited Misty. I am guessing she had not got a walk last night when Sarah had returned late.

'Was it a good night for your art? How does it work? Do you get paid per piece?' We crossed the street and headed for the closest park which sits alongside the Thames. The pavements had now been cleared, and although it was still cold, the snow was beginning to disappear. We would be fine as long as no more fell.

'I get paid for the evening. Normally about three hundred quid, but last night being New Year I got five hundred. Some corporate bigwig putting on a function for his friends, being a bit flash. They certainly worked me for my money. I ended up doing seventeen caricatures. If you think about it, that's about thirty quid a pop, which is not bad for a personal portrait, although I must admit they were not all that flattering. What about you, how was the dinner party? Was it pasta as you suggested?'

'It was pasta which was very good, but the evening itself was a bit of a disaster as Charlie did one of her classics and provided me with a date for the night. She has done this before and it really pisses me off.'

'Is there a rule for that?' Although we were walking quite fast along the street and puffing against the cold, I could tell that Sarah was bit miffed about something.

'It broke a number of rules. I was very annoyed with Charlie and I shall have words with her at some point in the future when it's appropriate. There was no point in being unpleasant at the time, but I do not want or need my partners to be picked for me.' With this the annoyance on her face seemed to dissipate. We walked on in silence for a while and after a short time I plucked up the courage to speak. 'Penny for them?'

'Sorry I was miles away. Not feeling the best this morning. Not booze related as I barely drank last night. I was going to ask you if you fancied breakfast but do you mind if we keep it a short walk today as I feel like going back to bed.' Looking at her face, she had gone ashen.

'You do look really peaky. Of course let's get you back. Do you want me to take Misty for a run first?'

'No, she will be fine. She is not a fan of the cold either. What are you up to the rest of the weekend?'

'Actually very little. You know what it's like in reality living on your own. Clothes to wash, floors to clean. Gerry and I have the football on Monday. The mighty Orient is playing Colchester at home. Should be a good match. Then back in the office on Tuesday, but it's probably going to be a light week. We still have a change freeze on so hopefully not too busy. Happy to pop out for a drink midweek if you are up for it?'

'I like the idea, let's just see how I feel. I will text you.'

'Okay,' and with that I walked her back to her place, at an increasingly slow pace. She was looking pretty ropey by the time I dropped her off. I then shot off back across town to my flat. Time to get some breakfast in and see if there was any flak from last night.

Chapter 18

Back on the Chain Gang
3 January 2011

'Stand up for the Orient, stand up for the Orient.' It was a pleasure to hear the chant run around the ground. Our pulses were racing which was good as it was absolutely bloody freezing. Our seats in the North Stand should have been protected from the wind but the gale howling around the stadium seemed no slave to logic. Gerry and I were here for the first match of the New Year on Bank Holiday Monday. He had got a pass out for the afternoon but we had not had time for a pint before the off, so we planned a minor session in the Birkbeck after the match. The trouble with supporting the Os was that the tube station queue was a pain after the match and so Gerry and I always stopped in our favourite local hostelry just behind the station to let the crowd go down. The match? Pretty good actually, we were always the better team and scored just before halftime. We had reached three goals up just after eighty minutes, but with four goals going in between eighty and ninety, it all got a bit fraught. We ended up walking away winners four to two against the not-so-mighty Colchester and had by this time built up a thirst and the need for a warming chaser.

We did our usual shimmy through the crowds and got to the pub about quarter of an hour later. The Birkbeck is your typical East End boozer and I mean that in a good way. It is green-tiled on the outside, has a large inside, and for summer has an equally capacious beer garden. There is a great pool room and Gerry loves all the boxing memorabilia on the wall. They are not the fastest bar staff in the world and the management have a certain low level surliness, but I think for the all crap they put up with this is pretty good. I got the round in while Gerry found a couple of high stools to perch on. They would have been dangerously high after a few pints if people rocked on them, but fortunately the floor had so much spilt beer on it that they were stuck fast.

'Cheers, mate, what a great result.'

'The match? Or the beer?' I was confused for a second as we had just spent the last fifteen minutes dissecting every kick of the ball. Gerry then necked a third of his pint and looked at me. The bastard was actually smirking. 'Oh, I see. It's "have a go at Adam for drinking Coke" day, is it? You know I don't drink in January. My little annual detox. So now I guess you are going to make a meal of that.'

'Got any nuts?'

'Oh the man is a wit, my sides are splitting.' From my pocket I took a bag of dry roasted, knowing that this was not what he was referring to.

'Bless you, my man. But I was referring to what is supposed to hang between your legs. What was wrong with you on Friday?'

'I know exactly what you were referring to, you cheap bastard. You and Charlie are not in my good books right now. You know how many rules that woman broke. Did you know she was playing footsie with my thigh?' Gerry smiled, stuffed a handful of nuts into his mouth, and then started to cough as one went down the wrong way. 'Easy, mate, you're not supposed to pebble dash the pub on the inside.' Gerry took a slug of beer and the coughing ceased.

'Yes, I did know that she likes to play that game. She has tried it with me before. If you know about it beforehand, then you can watch her body to recognise when she is doing it. She sort of arches her shoulders to get leverage.'

'You two are complete shit bags.'

'Honestly, mate, I knew nothing about it before she turned up, it was all Charlie's doing. The poor thing was on her own for New Year and Charlie thought she would be just what you needed. Get your mind off this Sarah chick. She is obviously messing you about or you would have been out with her that night.'

'She was working, dipshit.'

'Oh, well, anyway, no harm done.'

'Can you please have a word with Charlie and ask her to keep her good intentions to herself from now on?'

'I can try, but you know Charlie. She's like a force of nature.'

'I think maybe the fifth horseman of the apocalypse is closer.'

'That's a bit strong, Ads.'

'Okay, what about Yentl the Matchmaker?'

'I know where this is going. There is no music licence here. Do not break into show tunes from *Fiddler on the Roof*.'

'Okay, well do something useful and get me another Coke. The pool table is free, I will go set up.'

Tuesday morning came as a shock to the system after the extended weekend. The weather had not improved and in fact blizzards were being predicted for the next two days. This was made worse by the fact that a month in the office without beer to compensate was always a long drag. I got into the office around the usual time. We were going to be light on staff for a couple of days as the Cuffs with kids still had childcare issues until the schools went back, so they were either off or 'working from home'. Mysterious that (I know I shouldn't whinge), but how is it working from home for me means more hours than when in the office but for some of my colleagues is an excuse to do everything from washing, shopping, and ironing to pruning the bloody roses.

Anyway it was not long after I arrived that Drew and Angie turned up. They were chatting conspiratorially as they walked into the office sharing a tray of coffees. When they saw me, they clammed up.

'Did you two find religion over the holiday period? You are early and together.'

'Adam dear boy, we simply bumped into each other at the coffee shop.' However Drew had turned a very pretty crimson shade which now matched his scarf.

'You have that "just pumped the neighbour's dog" expression on your face. You sure you didn't spend all weekend bumping into each other? Didn't you go to a party on New Year's Eve together?'

'Adam, behave or I shall come over there and twat you. I went along to watch Drew's band and they are a lot better than I expected. You should come along next time.' Angie took her coat off and slouched into her chair. She put her feet up on the desk, picked up the phone, and started listening to voicemails. It had not escaped my attention that Drew was hungrily looking at the length of leg that had now been exposed above the knee and she was making no attempt to hide it.

'Whatever. Rule 5, guys. Just bear this in mind when it all goes tits up.'

'You and your weird rules, no wonder you're single. Anyway, the next gig is on the eighteenth, you up for it? You could bring a friend? You got one that doesn't break any of the rules? Or your mate Gerry, he was a laugh last time we went out. In fact more of a laugh than you. Can we borrow your more interesting mate for the night?' Drew was now standing over me looking down. I lifted my elbow swiftly and caught him in the solar plexus. Not too hard, just enough to wind him.

'Sorry, sport, didn't see you there. I will go and get my own coffee then, as I see you have yours.' I walked out of the office singing, *'Happy loving couples, wearing matching white polar-necked sweaters, reading* Ideal Homes *magazine, Yeah!'* I do like a bit of Joe Jackson every now and then to make my point.

※ ※

Wednesday, midday, all quiet on the Western front. I am reminded of those World War I trench films as there is a blizzard outside and I cannot see across the street outside of the office. Pretty, yes; practical, no. We all have one of the weather channels up on our PCs looking for a break in the front so we can get home. While waiting I checked in on Sarah.

TEXT: 'You back in the pink now? All better?'

I'm not sure why, but I think it may be a function of the instant gratification lifestyles we all live, but when I don't get a response to a text for an hour, I get a little concerned. I sent a follow-up and no response. Now this was getting serious enough that I even tried to call. I am not a great one for picking up the phone normally when a text or email will suffice. Still nothing and I was thinking about calling out a dog sled team when the weather broke suddenly. As it did not look like it was going to last, the team all gave their excuses and made a break for home while they could.

I was literally thirty paces from my home when my phone started to ring. It was Sarah. I left it to ring until I could get in the flat and get out of my now cold and wet gear. I then called her back.

'Hello you, are you in one piece now? Sorry I missed your call just then but I was out battling with the snow. It's shocking out there.'

'Hi. I am rough as hell.' I could hear the huskiness in her voice. She sounded like Bonnie Tyler after the throat operation.

'God you sound awful. You need me to come over and cook some chicken soup? Or maybe as a handy pall-bearer?'

'Please don't make me laugh,' she rasped and started to cough.

'Seriously, do you need me to pop over and get some supplies in for you and walk the mutt?'

'I should say no, but that would be so helpful.'

'Okay, see you in about an hour or so, weather permitting.'

※ ※

To be honest, I did not really want to go out, but she sounded terrible. I got dressed up in my best polar gear and headed out over to her place. I stopped by the local 7-Eleven and picked up some bits and pieces mentioned in a text she had sent me. When I got there I am not sure who looked worse, her or Misty. The mutt had a, wait for it, hangdog expression on her face. I grabbed the lead and told Sarah I would be back to fix some food and warm up once I had taken Misty out. Saying that, for a dog that had barely been walked in three days, she was not keen to leave Sarah's side. But once the lead was on her collar, she seemed to perk up and we headed for the park.

Even on a cold night like tonight, the snow had stopped, the sky cleared, and the ground was now as hard as iron to quote the *Good King Wenceslas*, dog walking is a sociable business. Dog owners just seem to want to talk to each other. I am not sure if this is through some sort of shared joy or shared adversity. Same poor weather conditions and the need to pick up poo after the animal has completed their ablutions. I must had spoken to six dog owners that night, five of which were ladies. I was starting to think that dogs were almost as good as babies for meeting the opposite sex. But I could tell when Misty had had enough as she began to slow down. Sarah was obviously right in that Misty does not like the cold. I got her back to the flat and gave her a good rub with a towel (Misty, that is). Sarah was just lying there on the couch still looking like death. I made her some soup and got her to eat it while I warmed up with a coffee. Shame I was on the wagon; a brandy would have gone down well right now.

'So how goes the fitness regime?' Sarah croaked in between sips of hot chicken soup.

'God it is so boring during January. The gym is full of people that use it for a month and don't know what they are doing. The gym bunnies and the Nazis could barely get a look in. She looked at me quizzically.

'Is this another line from planet Adam? Or perhaps another rule?'

'Keep quiet and eat your soup, you're not well.'

'Come on, I am all ears now. Even Misty is interested.'

'Tell you what; you get better and I will treat you to some food out to celebrate. Then I will give you the full story. I have a bit of a trek back and I want to do it before it freezes hard out there. It will be like a skating rink in the morning.'

'Okay, let's see how I feel on Friday. I think Misty can make do with the garden until then. Thanks for being a mate tonight, it is really appreciated.' She reached up to give me a peck on the cheek.

'Get off me, you diseased woman, I don't want what you've got.'

'And that, my dear Adam, is why you are single.' I grabbed my coat, gave Misty a pat, and set off for Siberia.

Chapter 19

Physical
7 January 2011

Friday evening came and I had got a couple of texts from Sarah indicating she was a whole lot better than she had been two days ago. I tell you, that chicken soup is a bloody marvel.

'It's not a date,' I yelled down the phone. I am sitting in the office at seventy thirty in the evening as I have a call with New York due to a system failure. Why do these things have to happen on a Friday? It's one of those occasions whereby I have to explain to people who will not understand but who have a tether and stake and are simply looking for a goat to tie to it. There is a poster on the wall of the office showing a series of penguins moving in unison which is meant to be motivational but has been heavily covered in graffiti by the staff to make it slightly more ominous than Hannibal Lecter at a funeral home. While I was waiting to join the call and the office is empty, I had decided to give the delightful dog lady a call and see what she was up to later.

'Okay, what would you call it then?'

'We are simply two friends having a drink and some food. You mentioned you might want to do it on Wednesday.'

'Are you sure I was not delirious?'

'And you wanted to know about rule 11.'

'I am interested in all your weird rules. But I am not sure I want to know more than that.' So that's interesting; now she is being aloof or some might say playing hard to get.

'Okay, what would you like to do, if you are free? I'm done here in half an hour, or possibly we could catch up at the weekend?' I am trying not to sound desperate but I'm now starting to regret this interaction and I see my conference call is just about to begin.

'Same place as last time in ninety minutes?'

'No, the pub by the river with the fireplace was not dog friendly, what about somewhere else.' Well come on, that has got to win me brownie points. If I am willing to sit in a pub with the hound from hell, I deserve a medal (even though she is secretly growing on me).

'Wow, give that boy a prize, he's a quick study. You know that Misty is close to my heart. Okay, let me figure it out and I will mail you. Gotta go now, see you in a while.'

'Okay, catch you in a while,' the line went dead and I switched handsets. I jumped on my conference call and the predictable fun got under way. The uninvolved worked on raising their profile while the guilty let the Teflon on their shoulders get to work. While I was on the call, my email pinged with the suggestion 'The Orange Brewery – Pimlico, bring a bone'. I quickly looked it up on my phone, worked out my route, and sent a confirmation. Where the hell am I supposed to get a bone from at this time of night?

Now I am not stupid and I decided not to get caught out with the same trick twice. I dashed out of the office determined to be in the pub before she got there. When I walked in the door, I looked to see if Sarah or the mutt were present; no result. I got myself a Coke and scanned the room for other signs of danger. No exes, check. No heavily drunk people, check. No criminal-looking types fancying a fight, check. I know I am man of simple needs, but the rules thing can be a bit addictive.

After about fifteen minutes she walked in. The leather biking jacket, a pair of impossibly tight or spray-on jeans, and knee-high leather boots with a heavy hoodie on display against the cold. She didn't so much walk into the bar as make an entrance courtesy of being dragged in by Misty who was obviously on a mission; I was hoping that mission did not include eating or shagging my leg. She saw me, gave a huge tug on Misty's chain, and raised a hand in greeting.

'You look 100 per cent better than the other night. I was actually quite worried about you.'

'They make us tough where I come from.'

Misty seemed to realise that good behaviour was now required and wandered in my direction plonking herself down on the floor by my table, where I had surreptitiously placed a water bowl. I was also intelligent enough to get Sarah a glass of wine and Misty a chorizo sausage from the kitchen, which the latter took a great deal of interest in after slurping the water out of the bowl.

'Misty, you are such a tart. Don't get the wrong impression, Captain, she might do anything for sausage, don't imagine I am the same.'

'Bloody hell you're hard work. I do something nice for your mutt and you still try and twist it round. Is there any hope of redemption for me?'

'If you can't do the time, you shouldn't do the crime.'

'Oh you are so amusing. I just think that you have a little bit of a jaundiced view of me and maybe that is not accurate.'

'You have sodding rules for dating women and you hang about naked on Pimlico balconies, what am I supposed to think.'

'Fair play, but let me tell you some more and maybe you will see how I got to where I am. I am not a bad bloke.'

'Go on then, I'm all ears.'

'Rule 11 is related to gym bunnies. Now I am not the fittest guy in the world but I do try and get to the gym when I can. As you know this month is booze free and I am trying to get in there every day. I like to run, row, and possibly cross-train. There I am afraid I draw the line. I am never going to be found spotting weights, doing fifty reps on a multi gym or two-minute equipment rotations that are designed to burn. When I mentioned gym bunnies, I am not being sexist as I think the metaphor works for blokes and women alike. I am happy with my almost normal body shape and the fact that I can climb stairs without getting out of breath. I pretty much eat and drink what I want without over indulging. But then I go to the gym and I see the gym bunnies or worse still the gym Nazis. The bunnies are sad but acceptable. They keep fit; continuously. They eat right and they then don't seem to want to go out and have any fun. The body image of Madonna or maybe Lindsay Lohan does not appeal to me. Arms that are so thin that they seem like a strong wind would break them. Muscle definition on the abs that would make Mr Universe look like a slob. But then we get into the gym Nazis. The bunnies are passive, the Nazis as all fascists tend to be dominant and aggressive. They want you to become like them. They want you to change—I also have issues with people that want me to change, no rule, more a principle. They want to rebuild you in their image. Well that is where I draw the line.'

'Okay, these just sound like general principles, was there something specific? I am kind of sitting here waiting for the light bulb moment and currently you are definitely only hitting ten watts.'

'This is not a funny story, just a fact of life that I get bored being told what to be or being with people that are so serious about their health that they are a bore in the evenings. Life is about balance surely. Yes, there were a couple of girls, but if you hang around gyms long enough, you will see hundreds. Why would I want to spend my time with someone that when in a gym is looking continuously in the mirror as she flexes her muscles and shapes her butt.'

'So you just go for fat girls like me then?'

'Oh behave. If you wanna go fishing, then bring a rod!'

'I am just saying that you must like fatter chicks, so is that how you see me?'

'I like normal people who are healthy and not borderline anorexic. You know you have a nice body without me telling you. Shall we change the subject?'

'Go on then.'

'Okay, it's your round.'

'What do you want?'

'Diet Coke with ice and lemon I think.' With this she smiled and headed to the bar and Misty gave me a look. 'And another sausage for the mutt.'

Chapter 20

A New Flame
11 January 2011

Every day in the office I get an email with some of the potential spam emails in a separate file so I can see if any are genuine. I scan this most days but often I will look at the main site once a month or so, adjust any rules that are wrong, and release anything I really need. So it was with interest that I went into the antivirus portal mid-morning on Monday to find a string of mails from an unknown email address, S.Porter@Marketme.com. The subject lines of the emails made it obvious who they were from; it was Sue from New Year's Eve. I released them and then spent the next five minutes with increasing amusement mixed with a high degree of trepidation. I don't have a specific rule against stalkers, come on this is common sense, but I am not keen on people who are too eager. Passion I get, obsessive, I am not sure I have room in my life or indeed inside my brain for that. I will give you an example.

From: *S.Porter@Marketme.com*
Subject: Nice Bum

Okay, I can see that you are playing hard to get. Well I can handle a waiting game. I was rather impressed with your bum the other night, very pert. I am definitely one for a nice bum. I am not keen on budgie smugglers, but a decent fitted pair of

jeans would look good on you. I can admit to having spent a
fair amount of time imagining it. So, how about that drink?

The state of my bum aside (I have been told it is very nice by the way), I am not sure how all this unwanted attention was warranted. I get the feeling that her version of the night and mine were somewhat different. Either that or Charlie had been interfering again and winding her up. I read through the entire email chain and then wondered if I could get away without answering at all. The spam filter is one of the most obvious tricks in the book if you want to ignore an email, but I am not sure if she would know this. I decided the best idea was to play dumb for now. I really must have a word with Charlie about this on Thursday.

※

It's Thursday night and I am on my way over to Gerry and Charlie's for dinner. I am avoiding the pub beforehand as this is the weakest time of the month for me. Almost halfway through and the dry period and my defences are at their lowest ebb. I have failed once at this stage after a crap day in the office, so I try not to put temptation in my way anymore. Gerry of course is sulking about this as he fancies thrashing me at pool. I am a little earlier than normal as work is still light and I fancy playing a game with the kids if they are up. Peter has a PlayStation and I am starting to introduce him to some slightly more challenging games. Hopefully it won't be long before we can get him online.

Arriving I am greeted by the very gloomy face of Gerry at the door. I go to move inside and he comes out to meet me.

'Bit melodramatic for not getting to play pool, mate. If it is that serious, we can always go to the pub and I will have a Coke.'

'I am so sorry, mate. It's nothing to do with me.' Gerry was almost whispering, honestly I thought someone had died, just how bad could it be and what the hell was he talking about? 'I just turned up and she was here. Charlie and Sue are drinking already.'

'Sorry, who are we talking about?' And then the penny dropped. 'Please don't tell me Sue from New Year's Eve is here? I have been getting a load of emails from her, but they got stuck in my spam folder. That's it, I'm off.' With that I turned to leave but Gerry grabbed me by the collar.

'Oh no you don't, mate. You are not leaving me with those two.' He half dragged me back into the house. 'Now behave. Just grin and bear it, she isn't that bad and you can't afford to be that picky, you are not getting any younger.' I took my coat off and walked into the living room. There I saw Charlie and Sue lying back on the sofa both with a large glass of wine in their hands. Sue was wearing a short crimson skirt and her posture had provided it the opportunity to ride up to a point where I knew they were not tights she was wearing. Her top was black, silky, and cut so low that nothing was left to the imagination. Sue raised her glass to me and smiled.

'They seek him here, they seek him there; they seek that Adam everywhere.' I am not sure how long Charlie and she had been drinking but it was not an elegant manoeuver for her to lift herself out of the chair and I got to see that she was at least wearing matching underwear. 'Saucy boy, did you get an eyeful?' She came over, put her arm around me, and gave me a huge kiss on the cheek. 'Oh I almost forgot, you are Mr Cosmopolitan.' With that she kissed me on the other cheek and then went to kiss my first cheek again but stopped halfway and went straight for the lips.

'Easy, tiger.' I pulled back my head and detached myself from her. 'Evening, Charlie, glad to see you don't lose your touch. What's for dinner?'

'Oh I thought we would just dial out this evening. I was planning to cook, but Sue came into school today so I invited her over. We fed the kids and had a little glass or two for the chefs in that hot kitchen. What do you fancy, pizza, Chinese?'

'Why don't you show me what you have to drink in the kitchen?' I thought I could get Charlie on her own to get myself out of this, but she was not too keen on getting up.

'What I want to know is why you have not answered my emails, you naughty boy. Anyone would think you were looking for a spanking.' With this Sue slapped me hard on the arse. 'And that is why I said nice bum. It is so firm, not usual for a guy your age; I bet you work out hard. I like a man who can build up a sweat. Come and sit down with me.' She dragged me in the general direction of the sofa.

'Sorry, I have not seen any emails, I wonder if they got stuck in the spam filter.' I directed her down towards the sofa but managed to stay standing myself.

'Spam, spam, spam, spam,' Sue started to sing. 'Spam, spam, spam, spam,' Charlie joined in as harmony. It was like a Monty Python tribute act. Charlie got up from the sofa and walked towards the kitchen to get me a drink. Each step was taken in time with another spam being sung out loud. I followed her into the kitchen.

'Charlie'—I grabbed her by the shoulder and span her round—'what the hell are you playing at? You know I hate it when you start playing cupid.'

'Lighten up, Ads, she is lovely and loads of fun. She has the hots for you.' She touched me on the end of my nose with her finger in some sort of weird variation on a sobriety test. 'And she thinks you have lovely arse, which of course you do have.' She went to pick up a glass and pour me some wine. I took the glass out of her hand and put the bottle down.

'Charlie, she breaks at least three rules all rolled up into one. Let me go through them for your benefit. Rule 3: Blind dates.' She went to say something but I stopped her. 'Don't go there; I know she does not have a guide dog. Rule 13: No widows. Rule 15: No favours to mates. I won't even go down the line of I don't date psychos. I did see her emails in my spam. No, don't start to sing again. She is not right. She is a fruitcake.' I noticed she was now looking over my shoulder. 'Are you listening to me or are you having trouble focusing?'

'I think maybe you should shut up now.' I turned to see Sue standing in the doorway. To say she was not happy was somewhat of an understatement. The very flirty, happy drunk had been replaced by someone with thunder on her face.

'Oh, hello, Sue, didn't see you there. I was just saying to Charlie that I needed to go.'

'You bastard,' she started before flinging her glass of wine over me and then turning on the waterworks. There was, I have to say, nothing at all dignified about the way this lady was crying. I made a move to get past her and she slapped me on the face. As I entered the dining room, Gerry moved towards the door with me. He knows when the house is an unsafe place and frankly he was getting out with me while the going was good. Grabbing my coat and shooting out the door, we moved off in the direction of the pub.

'I'm guessing you are getting that game of pool after all,' I said to Gerry as we sauntered down the street. Looks like my spam filter was set just about right. I really must learn to trust it in future. The worst of it was, in the middle of January, I was covered in alcohol, I smelt like a brewery, and yet I still not had a drop to drink.

Chapter 21

Band on the Run
15 January 2011

It is Saturday morning I am looking forward to walking Misty through the park in order to catch up and vary my exercise routine (careful this could become a habit). I have been busy with work and we have not really spoken much in the week, whereas Sarah seems to have plenty of time on her hands. I am not sure which is worse.

'Did you fancy coming to see Drew's band? They are playing in some dodgy watering hole in Fulham on Tuesday night at eight. I know it's a school night, but hang on, I never asked, do you like live music? If so, any particular type? Drew's band plays a mild-mannered fusion of grunge, punk, and rock. You know, covers and a few things they have written themselves. Bit of Greenday here, bit of Marillion there.' As we chat we are walking past the most beautiful trees which line the bridle path that the household cavalry are currently training on. Sarah gets Misty back on the lead to let them pass before she tries to chew on a horse chin bone, while still attached to the horse.

'I do like live music as it happens. In fact I love the passion of live music, the genre isn't that important as long as it's not thrash metal, rap, or extremely avant-garde jazz.'

'I know what you mean, when they go off on a long solo that loses the melody completely, it's like manic musical masturbation.'

'Adam, you do have a rare turn of phrase. Even I am picking up on your alliteration these days. What is it some kind of game?'

'It's Mum really. She used to do it to me all the time when I was growing up. Sort of game we would play. She was always into her crosswords and Scrabble. She still is a demon for that. Whereas me, I can do it, but I prefer numbers. Give me a Sudoku any day over a crossword. So the band, you up for it?' The horses had now passed and I use the ball thrower to send Misty off on a long run. My God those things are more effective than a Scud missile.

'Are they any good? What are they called?'

'Three and a Half Horsemen. Stop it, stop smirking. You know what it's like trying to think up something original. They all went to university at Imperial and they thought that the big time beckoned. I'm pretty sure they only finished their degrees and got jobs to pass the time until fame came knocking. I'm told they are good, but then it was Angie who said that and I suspected that her motives may have been less than pure.'

'Oh Captain, my captain. Please try not to take the moral high ground when you are around me. It is so unbecoming and frankly a little rich. Or are you jealous?'

'She is almost young enough to be my daughter, and no, I have no interest.'

'Do I detect a little ageism here or are you now going to try and disguise this as a rule?' Sarah is now mocking me, using her finger to wag at me like a disapproving parent.

'It is a rule, number 17, but one created from a distance not through any personal experience. It's the fifteen-year rule. I will not date anyone fifteen years' difference in age from me.'

'Older or younger,' she says with a big smile on her face. 'As if I don't know the answer?'

'Both of course and for exactly the same reason.' Misty has now come bounding back and I send the ball flying again and then realise I have sent her in the direction of another dog. I keep an eye on them to make sure there is no fighting. Misty grabs the ball and goes to say hello but Sarah raps her thigh twice with her hand and the mutt is suddenly inbound again like a well-behaved boomerang. 'I am not interested in that sort of thing because although on the surface it would seem incredibly flattering for one party, what the hell do you have in common?'

'Isn't that just a cliché?' I think Misty has now had enough of the ball as she has flopped down at Sarah's feet.

'Not at all. Look if we talk about music or TV or films, we have a common set of language, icons, and heroes. There is what, three or four years between us? However, in general if you mention something culturally, I know what you are talking about, unless particularly obscure. But how would it be if one of us was continually having to educate the other? It would get really painful playing teacher all the time.'

'I thought that was every bloke's fantasy? You know, a little gymslip and warm custard action.'

'Oh behave. You know what I am saying.' I reach down and scratch Misty behind the ears and in response she rolls over so I can tickle her tummy.

'Misty, can you stop giving him ideas, he is bad enough already.'

'So is that a yes or a no to the band?'

'Yeah, why not. Let's see you on the back foot when I meet your friends.'

'These are work colleagues, not really friends. I think I can handle it.'

'And how will you explain who I am and how we met? The fact I saw your bollocks before I saw your face?' Sarah reached down and put the lead back onto Misty and started to head towards the park entrance, leaving me to talk to her back.

'I am pretty sure you could pass for a friend and that you do not have to mention the whole balcony thing at this point. Just come out and have a laugh.' I was now jogging to catch up with her.

'I see laying off the booze is working, you seem to be getting a little fitter.'

'I am doing okay, but it's a shame the gig is in a pub. One more night of temptation. Shall I pick you up on the way?'

'Yup, get to mine about seven thirty and we can catch a cab over there.'

※

I got changed into jeans, a band tee shirt, and a leather jacket in the office so I would not have to go back to the flat on the way to Sarah's place. As I emerged from the tube at Pimlico, I got an alert on my phone.

TEXT: 'Sorry. Still coming, but running late. Will explain.'

Now I am as curious as the next, but cryptic messages make me nervous at the best of times. Let alone when I'm just about to pick a girl up and take her to an event where my workmates are going to be. I was thinking hair cut or colour gone wrong? Wardrobe drama? Running late due to work? I got there and as I went to knock on the door it was opened by an elegant lady who was probably late sixties but dressed and appeared a lot younger. She obviously looked after herself.

'And you are?' she said with the air of someone who thought she was better than me and wished to prove the point.

'Late for an important appointment. So if could buttle off and get her ladyship for me, and I do mean Sarah and not Misty, that would be appreciated.' With this Misty stuck her head through the lady's legs and came to say her own special hello to me in the time-honoured crotch-sniffing tradition. 'Saved by the belle. Watcha, Misty, how are you, me old china.' For some reason I went all Dick van Dyke at this point; I think potentially just to annoy the old girl.

'Mother, if that's Adam, tell him I'll be there in one minute.' Sarah's voice appeared disembodied from somewhere deep in the flat.

'Oh, darling, I think the street urchins are rubbing off on you. Prince Charming heard every beautifully enunciated syllable you screamed.' I had guessed right, it was the mother and now Christmas made an awful lot more sense.

'Pleased to meet you, Sarah's mother.' I held out my hand and she looked at it initially with disdain. Finally she took it lightly and shook it, but it was like holding wet lettuce. 'I can see where Sarah gets both her looks and her quick wit,' I said in an attempt to be charming.

'Yes, nice try, but unfortunately she got her judgement from her father.' At this Sarah appeared, reached down, and patted Misty. She squeezed past her mother in the doorway.

'Try not to speak ill of the dead, Mother, I know it's hard but one of us misses him.' She gave me a peck on the cheek and turned back. 'Now you be good. No getting into trouble.'

'Misty is always good when I come to stay,' her mother crowed in response.

'I was talking to you, Mother, I am leaving Misty in charge. Come on, Adam, take me away from all this.' With this she put her hand to her forehead in a heyday of Hollywood Lillian Gish–type pose and swanned down the stairs.

'Be home before midnight or you know what happens, you turn back into an ugly duckling.'

'And that, Adam, is one of the reasons why I am still single.'

We arrived at the pub with about three minutes to spare but I was not surprised to find that the band was still only half set up. I waved to Drew and went to the bar to buy some wine (maybe a bottle and a straw) for Sarah as she was still in shock and a Coke for me. I saw Rick and said hello.

'This is Sarah; she's a mate of mine. Who else is here, I haven't seen Angie, isn't she the number one groupie.' Rick reached across and shook Sarah's hand.

'Shut it, Adam, don't bring that up, for God's sake.'

'Don't tell me they have had a bust up?'

'Last night after you left the office, she came in from an afternoon drink with a real cob on. Apparently she caught him at the weekend with another woman. A proper groupie she reckons.'

'Lucky guess? Coincidence?'

'Yeah right. You know Angie is a bit of an IT whizz, Miss Geek girl? Well apparently she turned on "find my phone" on his iPhone and then tracked him to a bar.' For some bizarre reason I subconsciously reached down and looked at my phone.

'Feeling guilty, Adam?' Sarah grabbed my hand as it rested on my phone.

'Just Freudian, mate,' I said to her to emphasise the fact that she was a friend not a date. We moved towards the stage and got a decent place at a table to watch the band and rest our drinks in with a small crowd. Rick was there with a girl called Diana whom I had never met before but apparently he had been seeing for over a year. She lived away down in Southampton where she worked but was up for a few days to spend time with him. I had the funny feeling that she was way too good for our Rick until she started to laugh and I got flashbacks. I looked at Sarah and she stared directly into my eyes and tried to keep a straight face. 'Remind me to tell you a story later.'

The band struck up and they were not bad. They went through a fairly passable set list with 'American Idiot' and 'Give Me Novocaine' with a few of their own numbers thrown in. Drew was trying to look uber-cool on the bass doing a passable impression of Mark King, bass-slap and all (which did not really suit the music). He spent a lot of the evening looking at a girl staring at him from the front row of tables and going through my mind was the thought, is she the one that Angie caught him with? At the interval I asked Sarah if she wanted to stay for the second half or shoot off for some food on the way home. She didn't want to be too late so we made our excuses and walked down Fulham High Street to a local burger joint which was an oasis of peace and quiet by comparison.

'So that was your mother then? She's . . . well, interesting.' I slipped a chip into my mouth which was so hot it burned.

'I'm not sure I want to talk about her. Even now after I have had my anaesthetic. She just turned up you know. She has some event in the city tomorrow with the ladies so she rang me from a cab as she got into Liverpool Street. Mother never takes tubes don't you know.' Sarah was lacerating the burger in front of her with a knife in the way a surgeon would not (I must admit her with a knife after a bottle of wine was a little scary, especially when this wound up). 'Misty doesn't like her either. I mean come on, Misty even likes you more than my mother.'

'Oh the compliments just keep coming. You're spoiling me.' I took the knife out of her hand and put it on the table. 'I think the patient isn't going to make it.' She looked at me with rage in her eyes but then she saw I was smiling and the moment of frustration subsided.

'I'm sorry, Adam, this is not your fault and once again you are proving to be a good mate when I am having a bad day. It's just she gets under my skin. And she winds me up about Dad.' She took a mouthful of dissected meat, grabbed my hand, and gave it a squeeze. 'So you said to remind you of a story when we were in the pub.'

'Oh yes, rule 69.'

'Oh come on, that's bit of a cheap one, isn't it?'

'It's not what you think at all.'

Chapter 22

Tears of a Clown
18 January 2011

Now, I like to laugh as much, or in fact probably more than the next man. I am not talking Bernard Manning or Jim Davidson, but either something puny or intelligent. You know the sort of thing, plays on words and the like. The trick to humour is simply to enjoy yourself whilst not annoying or hurting others. That is where the unfortunate laugh comes in. I called it rule 69 not for the sexual connotation but rather in celebration of Frankie Howard of *Up Pompeii* fame, i.e., titter ye not. Now there was a man who knew the true meaning of a double entendre. It has happened to me twice now, because the trouble with an unfortunate laugh is that is it not always obvious when you first meet the owner. Whatever you say, funny or not, if a girl is laughing like a maniac within two minutes of meeting me, there is probably something else very wrong in that particular belfry or I have spinach in my teeth.

The first time a strange laugh had an impact on me was with Claire. My god she was pretty. She had some job in magazine publishing related to marketing that I never really got to the bottom of. Boxes were being ticked though. She was young, but not too young. She was pretty but not up herself. Degree educated at somewhere red brick and quite importantly to me these days, she was solvent (I have been a bit of an easy touch in the past). Do you ever get that ominous feeling that something is wrong? When too many things are in place, you start to think there has to be a catch. But we had a couple of dates and things seemed to click quite nicely; even a little kiss and a cuddle on the doorstep after the second night out. This was beginning to look promising.

I am a fan of theatre when I can run to tickets. So I booked to see a humorous play in the West End that was getting great reviews but had already been running for a while so as not to break the bank. We met up for a drink beforehand, couple of glasses of fizz each to take the edge off and to wipe the dust from our shoes of another day working in the city. She seemed okay and was in high spirits without being intoxicated. We took our leave and headed to the theatre, where I ordered an interval drink and then we took our seats.

As the first few moments of comedy seeped away and the audience got the flow, I started to notice the most awful noise. Now I have seen *A Midsummer Night's Dream* and so I have heard a theatrical donkey bray. Well let me tell you now, this was more impressive, but with the added bonus of being slightly behind the action. She was just getting started when the audience began to die down from each comic line.

Even in the dark, people have a sixth sense if you are staring at them and I was most definitely staring at Claire. As the show went on, the braying got worse. I leaned over the next time I saw a punch line coming and kissed her on the neck. She looked at me lovingly and luckily the bray was averted as she focused on my apparent amorous attentions. I checked my watch and calculated how long until the interval. As I did this, I missed the next witty retort and Eor was unfortunately let back out of the corral. This of course had not gone unnoticed by my fellow theatre goers, who were showing signs of annoyance as they were rather in danger of missing the next one-liner while the farmyard cantered through the stalls.

Three more pecks on the neck at opportune moments (the reviews had been kind, it was not the funniest show ever), and the lights came up for the interval. Lights in this context equal visibility to a slightly hostile or at best bewildered audience. They were not sure if this was an avant-garde theatre with a member of the cast in the audience or whether Care in the Community had been extended for the evening to Shaftesbury

Avenue. Claire seemed oblivious and was really rather enthusiastic about the second half of the show.

'Let's get our drinks in the bar,' I suggested in an effort to distract her.

'That was so good. I really enjoyed it. I can't wait for the second half.'

'You like it that much? I'm not really impressed myself.' I thought maybe if I could convince her it was not brilliant, we could get away with slipping out for a drink and dinner rather than staying for the rest of the show. I led her up the passage between the seats and into the bar where we found our pre-booked glasses of champagne. It then occurred to me that maybe it was the booze that was making her worse. I wondered, seriously, how I could get her out of there without fuelling her laugh even further. I know I have rules about honesty, but I was just not able to directly address the issue at this point. I am aware cowardice is not admirable in a man, but what would you have done?

Well actually, I will tell you what you wouldn't do. You wouldn't fake tripping over the carpet and throwing a very expensive glass of champagne down the front of her dress. Wet T-shirts are not that faltering but a dripping wet cocktail dress is probably ten times worse. What was worse is that I swear everyone in the bar knew exactly what I had done and why.

'You idiot', she screamed, 'my dress is soaked and I smell like a wino.'

'I am so sorry, it was the carpet. Can I get you a towel or something?'

'I can't sit through the second half like this.'

'Do you want to go and get changed or just go home?'

'Let's just get out of here,' was her sullen reply.

The trip home on the tube was almost without incident, apart from a wino trying to inhale the fumes from her dress as we waited on the central line. Also the looks on the tube from the other passenger just screamed *Look at the drunk*. After walking her from her tube stop, I made my way back to my place and decided to give her a day or two to get over it. Well even in this I appeared to have made a good call as she left me a voicemail the next day suggesting she did not want to spend her time with careless people. She also made some comment about me being inappropriately amorous in the theatre. I think I dodged a bullet.

I don't even know the name of the other girl as it was one of those close escapes. I am not really one for nightclubs, but occasionally when there is a work to do or a mate's birthday, I can have my arm twisted. I do like a dance and it does not take much persuasion to get me on the floor. Well one night I was in Mackenzie's and the crowd from the office was drifting off. This nice-looking girl started getting closer on the dance floor; there was just the odd bit of eye contact. Within a couple of tracks we were next to each other and she was shouting something in my ear about a drink. I pointed to the loo and said I would be back. I thought if nothing else I could freshen up a bit. She went back to the bar and entered a gaggle of girls who were looking on. I guessed it was another office party as I wandered over to the cloakrooms. Splashing water on my face and washing my hands, I walked back out and started to approach the bar.

The girls were so loud that I could hear them above the music but in particular I could hear one shrill scream above the rest. Now I am no ornithologist but I was convinced this was the mating call of some eagle or hawk that you would normally hear stalking sheep over a moor, not in a nightclub in central London. I walked to the bar to grab a beer and the crowd parted in the way that you see the heavens open up in those great religious epics. In the middle of the girls was to be found the cute young lady in question. I then realised from the lip-synching that the noise was emanating from her mouth. I will not be able to tell you her name, as I decided then and there that I was once bitten twice shy with embarrassing laughs and so I slunk off back towards my colleagues, made my excuses, and left.

I'm thinking that maybe I need a very funny opening line in the future to test the water, but that is still a work in progress.

Chapter 23

Crushed by the Wheels of Industry
19 January 2011

I wouldn't say that the office was quiet the next day, but it was clear that a ceasefire had broken out in the reported war between Angie and Drew. Not that I wish to bang on about being right (but I get so few opportunities normally so I shall) but I did mention rule 5 at the time. I have seen this so many times before (and lived through it once, but not this close to home). There is an expression about not *Dumping on your own doorstep* and for the hard of thinking this means do not do things too close to home that might come back and haunt you. A fling with a colleague is one of the dangers of working long hours in proximity to like-minded people. The issue comes when it is over and invariably the relationship will end (not many successful marriages start this way), but you are still sharing the same work space with someone who is now no longer the centre of your world, but rather the centre of your enmity. So it was for poor Angie, who when all is said and done, is not a bad girl, just a bit idealistic and naive. She knew that her outburst coming back into the office after beer could have repercussions as this was against the rules of drinking at work. You can normally get away with it if you are subtle, but arriving back into the office and going ballistic at your ex is rather like dressing up in fancy dress, putting a sign around your neck, and calling HR. Angie was now being quiet and the model of office good behaviour, but the atmosphere surrounding her was so cold when Drew approached that there had been three calls today already to Corporate Services to adjust the air conditioning.

As things calmed down, the day followed a familiar pattern of business, but then around midday came an invitation to a meeting at one o'clock in the main auditorium. The thing about group emails that go to the whole team is that they arrive at pretty much the same time. Everyone does not have the same new mail indicator set and some even have the sound turned off, but with mobiles tied to the email system as well what happens is a slow ripple of alerts through the office. How big the ripple defines how important the email is. When this alert ripple continued through the entire floor, some four hundred people, we started to look at each other in a confused manner. Something was most definitely 'up'.

'Don't tell me we've been fined again, there goes my bonus.' Ralph immediately flicked on the internet search engine on the usual news sites to see if any information had been leaked to the press. Who would have thought the BBC News would know about the cuts before the staff, but invariably they found out pretty much the same time or just after. It got so bad in the industry that one day a mail was sent to all staff asking them not to pass on emails to external media companies as this was a breach of company policy. Within one hour this email appeared on a certain city gossip site (social media for bankers). 'Nothing on here so far.' Ralph continued in his role of official office internet translator. There appears to be at least one in every office who has their eye on the internet, because it simply won't surf itself.

We knew how big the problem was before we knew the problem itself simply by the fact they were webcasting the announcement due to the fact that the auditorium only seated three hundred. When we got there, it was already standing room only and they had started to turn people away due to overcrowding. The noise quietened down as the bank's CEO started to speak. I won't bore you with the intricacies of the speech as management terminology is both very standard and designed to hide a multitude of sins. In fact the image you should have in your head is the teacher from the Charlie Brown cartoon. All you effectively heard for the first ten minutes was 'Wah, Wah, Wah'. At the end of this time we got down to the serious brass tacks. Poor trading performance, a need to cut overheads, and finally staff cuts mostly in IT and the back office. Notices of risk of redundancy would be going out before the end of the day and a ninety-day process would be kicked off to allow people to find other roles. For those of you out of the loop on this, think of a ninety-day notice as the sort of thing a cancer doctor gives you. If you start to show signs of recovery in the first thirty days, i.e., find yourself another role internally, then you have a chance of survival. However, if you go past thirty days, the medication is then turned off and you go to spend a lot of time working on your garden until they pay you off; by the way, I live in a flat, so this will never do for me.

We all traipsed back to the office and everyone was mumbling. Little groups of twos and threes were gathering and dispersing. Each looking for a way to make themselves feel better about their own chances. Angie and Drew still kept their distance and I think secretly were both hoping the other one was going to get chopped to save their discomfort. It was with this mood that we started getting called into the boss's office, one at a time. It was one of two conversations, you are definitely staying or likely to be going, but with each person, the same standard crap had to be said. I could go through each conversation in detail, but I won't, suffice to say by the end of the afternoon we were two Party Animals and a Cuff down. Angie and Ralph had both been put at risk on the Party Animals' side and from the Cuffs we were likely to lose Bernard (although I think his booze issues were more likely a cause of his selection than his work abilities). Even if we are an unruly bunch, nothing pulls together a team like shared adversary and the mail went around very quickly that we were going to the pub for a session at four. This was one thing the management expect in circumstances like this and so a blind eye was turned.

It was about three thirty and I got a text from Sarah.

TEXT: 'Mother is staying and wants to go for dinner. Can you come?'

TEXT: 'Sorry, we have an office drink in All Bar One at four; job cuts.'

TEXT: 'Adam, my mother is asking for you to come and I need support.'

TEXT: 'Sorry, but so do my colleagues. Call you later?'

TEXT: 'Don't bother. I won't ask you for help again.'

Well that had not gone as well as it might, but what did she expect? Her overbearing mother clicks her fingers and I am supposed to attend? I have things to do with my own people. I think she is a great mate, but sometimes she has no idea about what goes on over here. I would try her later, or maybe that was a bad idea after beer. Oh and bang goes my booze-free January, but needs must when the devil is your bartender.

It's easy to drink a pint or two. At that point there is always the opportunity to stop. When you have consumed four or five and some idiot decides that ouzo is a great idea, then your judgement can waiver. Flaming Sambucas sound like such a good idea until you burn your mouth on the glass, but suddenly a Jaeger bomb numbs the pain. Finally, six hours later and the bar is looking at a very healthy till while we are sitting on the benches outside. I am wearing a beer jacket with a Jack and Ginger in one hand and a Havana in the other. My arm is around Angie as she needs a fair amount of consoling, but before you get any idea, although I may be drunk, I'm not stupid. However I do decide to look at my phone and see seven missed texts from Sarah which I had not noticed during the evening. I'm still wise enough not to open them now as I will make a real mess of things. I slip my phone back into my jacket, slip my arm back around Angie, and look up straight into the face of Sarah. I would have said something, but before I had time to speak, she had slapped me so hard on the face that she spilt my drink. Angie chose this moment to walk to the railing and throw up in the river. Sarah turned on her heel and walked away. All I could think was thank God she did not bring Misty with her. January was obviously my month for getting slapped.

Suitably shocked and without a drink, I got up to leave, there was no point in following Sarah as that ship had sailed for the evening. As I walked toward the door, Drew grabbed me and explained that we were all going on to a club. Angie had gone and washed her face and looked a lot brighter and so eight of us got cabs and headed for the city. I know I danced, I know I drank; I know I got home at three twenty-five in the morning, but the rest is a mystery unless somebody from the office lets me know in the morning. For now, I fell asleep on the couch in my clothes.

I am not sure but I may have gone blind. All I can see is blackness. Suddenly I realise I am on the couch and I must have pulled my jacket off in the night and put it over my head to stop the light. The problem with this is that I have not set an alarm and the light has failed to wake me. My mouth feels like the bottom of a parrot cage (don't ask me how I know) and my head is about to explode with the pressure of a small hammer smashing my skull from the inside. I always remember on the day after why I don't go on benders anymore. I check my watch and see it is eight forty-five. I can still make it into the office by half nine if I am quick but moving is hard. Then the paranoia begins. My hands go instinctively to my wallet, check; my phone, check; and my work bag, nope. Then I remember I left it in the office and feel the weight come off my shoulders. Checking my phone for missed calls and messages, I see the seven messages from Sarah (now opened, although I have no memory of reading their content) but then no other calls from her. Then I check my phone log and see I have made four calls to her at various stages of the night after she left. Will I never learn? None of the calls appear to have been answered, so I guess she is ignoring me. I jump in the shower (after undressing) and make myself as presentable as possible before heading in.

On the tube I read Sarah's texts. Let me summarise, they go from *Are you ignoring me* to *I thought you were a friend* and end up with *I am coming over there to talk to you as I am worried*. Shame I didn't read that last one, it could have saved me from a painful face and probably stopped the need for this hangover (okay, not really, but maybe reduce it a bit). I wouldn't mind so much, but I remember this has also put an end to my booze-free month. Anyway, I thought I would leave her to it today and let her cool off. I would contact her in a couple of days and try and explain. For God's sake, it's not like we are going out or anything, we are just mates.

Arriving at the office, I was not the first one in as usual, but I came a close second. Drew had arrived and Malcolm followed me up in the lift. Angie did not make it in all day; we got a message about a broken toe and a late-night dash to Casualty (apparently some big guy stepped on it in the club last night). Ralph called from the pub at eleven thirty and said he was having a Bloody Mary for breakfast and did anyone want a coffee brought in on the way? Bernard arrived at around twelve which for him for par for the course. He looked his normal self with the spider veins on this face doing a fair impression of the London Underground Tube map. I guess the reason being was that last night was simply business as usual for him.

Chapter 24

Who's That Girl?
24 January 2011

It's now five days and there has been nothing from Sarah. I have of course tried to text to no avail. I have no illusions to my suitability for friendship or more, but I did think that maybe this was an overreaction. Yes, I was drunk. Yes, I was outside a pub with my arm around another woman, but come on, there was nothing going on. Then earlier today the penny dropped. Drew came sniffing around for any gossip about the night out and to find out about Sarah.

'So are you seeing that girl or what? She seemed a bit pissed with you the other night.' He was staring at my screen trying to read my email while we talked. I minimised the window and turned to face him in my chair.

'I didn't realise you had seen Sarah, I thought you were getting a round in.'

'She came in the pub first looking for you. She spotted me and I told her you were outside with Angie.' With this he laughed. 'Did I drop you in it, Ad-man?'

'You shitbag. You deliberately set me up. Why the hell would you do that?'

'Well she is just a friend, that's what you told Rick the other night. I thought I would test the waters myself but she stormed off to find you after I spoke to her. I followed her out with the drinks just when she let fly with the slap. She has a hell of a right hand on her.' I felt my face and rubbed it. 'Anyway, does this mean she is single?'

'Get out of my sight, you odious little troll. I have some repair work to do because of you now.' With this I walked off to get a coffee, not forgetting to lock my workstation. The trouble with work is that they are all a nosey bunch, no point giving them ammunition.

I left it to the end of the day having tried Sarah a couple of times more on text with no response. The easiest thing was to go over there and talk to her directly. Between you and me, I may not have any idea of romantic inclinations towards her, but she has been good mate over the last few weeks and I would not like to lose that. As I just fancied a chat, I went straight from work saving me the round trip home first, but I didn't bother to change out of my work suit and tie.

The walk from Pimlico tube is now becoming quite familiar and I have been sorting out shortcuts as I have become familiar with the streets lined with smart terraced houses. A very different vibe to the area around my flat in Mile End. Sometimes this involved coming at the house from different directions and one time I did get lost. I arrived from a wholly new angle tonight and as I approached I saw the door open and Sarah appeared. I thought she must be off to walk Misty and I was going to call out when I noticed a man walk out with her and the distinct absence of a mutt. It is a truth universally acknowledged that inside every man is a small boy who wants to be a spy. I immediately snuck behind a car and watched where they were going. Once I saw they were walking away from me, I started to plot my route down the street to follow them. I know it's pathetic, but be fair, what would you have done? I'd gone all way to Pimlico to see her, so there was no point in skulking back now.

Obviously I had no trouble following Sarah, but I also wanted to know more about him, so if they split up I knew who I was going to stick to (in hindsight, this sounds weird). I would have put him at about six foot two as he was taller than Sarah and older by about ten years. Greying hair, although a full head of it and well cut (it started to annoy me how many men older than me have a lot more hair on their heads than I do). I could not tell what he had on apart from what looked like a very nice great coat and smart jeans with patent leather shoes that caught the streetlights every now and then. How am I doing so far on the spy school skills? They headed off towards the river and I followed at a discrete distance. Although Sarah had only seen me the once in a suit (five nights earlier), I did not want to get caught as this would be hard to explain.

After about ten minutes, I saw them enter a Chinese restaurant and by the time I walked past the window they were sitting at a table in the front and he was holding her hand. She looked up as I walked past but I am pretty sure she did not notice me. With this I made my way back to the tube station and set off for home. Well as Drew had said, it's not like we were going out, she is free to see whoever she wants, so why was I so disappointed? Maybe I did want to be more than mates, or maybe she was right and I just wanted access to Misty!

─────

I am well aware that I had failed to keep *dry* during January, but now the seal had been broken, I must admit that I'm happy to accept my failure and not keep turning down people for drinks. There is still a heavy mood of defeat in the office due to the lay-offs. So far none of the three have managed to find themselves alternative roles, and the longer it goes on, the more maudlin they become. In this context maudlin equates to a propensity to go and out and drink more. This also has the effect that a lot of work gets passed on to us survivors. I swear my day feels like it is an hour longer already and they are still working here. The gym regime has already gone by the wayside and the chance of a lunch has once again become a dim and distant memory. I don't want you to get the idea I am after sympathy or bankers, but what with the survivor guilt and the uptick in work, it felt like the pressure was really on. I have been avoiding any more evenings out after the last one, but once in a while one should participate for appearances if nothing else.

'You coming for a few sherbets tonight, Adam?' It was not like Ralph to include me in his plans, but he has been looking for drinking partners most nights recently and I wondered if he was slowly tiring the office out. Ralph is actually not a bad guy, but his world centres on heavy drinking and casual encounters so he is most definitely chalk to my cheese. Don't get the wrong impression, everybody in the city is not out every night or we would be dead. 'We are going to The Slug for a couple and then over to Shoreditch to one of my favourite little haunts.'

'Will I be needing to bring pound coins for the jar?' I started to fish in my drawer for spare change (lap dancing bars must have a real big bag of change for the bank in the mornings).

'Ah, I see you are an aficionado of the ancient art form.' It was odd, when he said this he rubbed his hands together and the effect was somewhere between a proud father and a pimp; think Fagin but without the Jewish connotations. 'I can get us into one of the bars for free as I am a special guest. This is one of the ones not run by the Russians. It's mostly Polish girls, but be fair, you are not there for the sparkling conversation, more the sparkling G-strings.'

'I swear you worry me sometimes, Ralph. Tell me again why you are single?' I was hoping the inflection at the end of the sentence would imply that this was a rhetorical question and not a request for Ralph to answer.

'We should have a chat later, Adam, you are only six or seven years younger than me. You too could enjoy life the way I do instead of being a slave to this place. You know why I am not bothered about leaving?' I went to answer, but before I could, he responded himself. 'Anyone with a brain has seen the writing on the wall for a long time. I've had twelve years here and I will get a nice package with money that will last eight to ten months. Why rock the boat? I've been trying to get a package for a couple of years now. That's why I don't bend over backwards like I used to. Having said that, I know a couple of girls tonight who can and will if you are interested.' I looked at him and tried not to be too contemptuous. He was not a bad person in reality but his views were everything that I did not want to be. A different woman every time you talked to him, with a tendency to misogyny. Simply surviving at work but not putting himself out in reality. His body was a mess from far too much real ale and I don't think he had ever seen the inside of a gym, unless he was staring at the scantily clad and panting women through steamy windows. He reminded me of Toad of Toad Hall. But in the same way Toad was a bumbling fool, Ralph did not have a nasty bone in his body and that is how I felt about him. Well, when I say that, I discount the bad bone in his trousers (if the rumours are be believed), as I can't believe it is very nice by now.

There were ten of us in The Slug to start with, just beers and no stupid drinks for a change. We stayed for two rounds and then Ralph stated he was leaving for Shoreditch and the crowd split like the Red Sea. Apparently there had been a visit on Friday night and the others were not keen to return so it looked like I was to be Ralph's wingman for the night. This is very *Top Gun*-esque except that he does not look like Val Kilmer and I don't look like Tom Cruise (Laurel and Hardy or the Chuckle Brothers might have been a more accurate metaphor). We grabbed a cab over to Commercial Road and approached what was an old London boozer that has since had most of its windows blacked out for the sake of the girls' modesty and the neighbours' sanity. The doorman nodded to Ralph in acknowledgment (obviously due his regular patronage) and indicated that we could go in without paying the entrance fee.

The next two hours, and they were expensive, were spent in conversation with a set of scantily clad woman who circulated the room before each record to collect pounds coins in a pint jar. Once they had collected what they thought was sufficient, they got up on stage and performed a wardrobe change from something to nothing in approximately four minutes. While they were dancing, other girls who were not performing would pass by the table and ask if a private dance was required (ten pounds in this bar, twenty in others I hear). Ralph was literally like a celebrity walking in there. I swear I could almost hear walk-on music akin to the World Wrestling Federation or Rocky. They fawned over him and used him as a way to introduce themselves to me. They shared their latest gossip with him as long as it took to convince him to have a dance with them in a booth. After we had spent a lot of money on pots, overpriced drinks, and Ralph having three private dances, it was time for me to drag him to a normal bar.

'Come on, Ralph, there is only so much anatomy I can study in one night and the girls are now starting on their third rotation.' It does go from shocking to arousing to boring very quickly.

'But of course, Adam, the best is yet to come.' With this he did a round of cheek kisses with the girls that got a lot of dirty looks from the punters who wondered why he was not getting pummelled by the bouncers for touching them. 'Come on then, let's go, if we stay any longer they will start to ask for massages and that will be awkward at this time of night. In the middle of the afternoon, management turns a blind eye, but at this time of night I will get lynched.' We moved towards the door and although it would be wrong to say a room full of heartstrings snapped, I am not so convinced that at least ten G-strings didn't. So now I know what Ralph spends all his wages on.

After about ten minutes walking through Shoreditch towards Hoxton we had only been accosted by three girls offering certain services for a consideration (apart from dinner and a show, I have never paid for it, I do have some scruples). We arrived at what looked like another downmarket bar, but this time the windows were not blacked out.

'What's this place? Not more strippers I guess looking at the decor?'

'It's a kind of singles bar.'

'Not one involving payment I hope?'

'Adam, what do you take me for? No, this is the sort of place where you meet ladies who want to have a good time, no questions asked. If you look at their hands, you might notice tan marks on their wedding finger. It is my preferred pub of choice after watching the girls for an hour or two. There is likely to be someone here who wants sex with no comeback, if you will excuse the pun.' We walked inside and the place was heaving. I saw a couple leaving from a table in the corner and sent Ralph to the bar while I grabbed it. I am not a spy or a gunslinger, but I do feel safer in busy bars when my back is to the wall. I can sit down and I can see the door, just in case of trouble.

'Here's your drink, Adam.' Ralph passed me my pint and settled down to look around the bar. 'See anything you like? We have a rare Smorgasbord tonight.' I think he was talking generically and not in reference to Scandinavians customers, apart from what looked like an ABBA tribute act on a hen night in the corner.

'Is this what you do, Ralph? Don't you have any interest in something more meaningful?' He looked at me with a mixture of humour and disdain.

'Oh dear Adam, you really are a PC, new-man, bleeding-heart Liberal, aren't you. Well I'm sorry to disappoint you, but welcome to the Tao of Ralph. My life is not the search to be the latest greatest advert for masculinity to be found in the pages of GQ magazine. I don't cry, I don't cook, and I don't have any intentions of a serious relationship in the near future. I don't want any ties right now. Work is about to dump me and it's just what I both want and need. I will be a free agent and I can do some travelling, see the world. Why would I want to drag someone else along for the ride, probably on my ticket at that?' I wasn't saying anything, partly through the fact I had heard bits of this before and partly realising that he was serious and this is what passed as a life plan for Ralph. He was late forties and planning to go on living his life like a twenty-something. You know there are times I realise that my rules are exactly what I need. Ralph the Toad may be mostly harmless, but he is not how I want to turn out to be. 'Have you seen the blond girls in the corner, Adam, they are giving us the eye.'

'Ralph, I don't do double dates. Wingman in name only.'

'Why are you thinking you will get the ugly one?' He smiled at them and raised his hand in greeting.

'Don't call them over, for God's sake. No, I'm not worried about getting the ugly one, I'm not worried about getting either of them. If you are going to chat them up, I am going to disappear.' I started to gulp my pint.

'Don't be a wuss. Let me at least chat to one of them and you occupy the other so I can suss out the lay of the land.'

'Ten minutes, no more. I need to get home at a reasonable time for a change and most definitely on my own.' Ralph started to chat to them, they were in fact work colleagues and not Swedish at all as I had suspected. They too had cuts going on and wanted a bit of fun. I think I must give off pretty obvious vibes when I am disinterested as they flocked around Ralph while he waxed lyrical about their looks and the night being young. He made a couple of wise cracks about a threesome and that seemed to be my cue to make my excuses to go. I am not saying I was invisible at this point, but I think the threesome thing may have been closer to the truth than even Ralph had expected. Heading for the door I just got this overall sense of what in the midst of all this laughter and drinking was the most depressing place I had been to in a long time.

I walked for twenty minutes avoiding the tubes to get my head together and catch some fresh air. The Tao of Ralph just made me want to redouble my efforts to find the right person. There is nothing bleaker than the thought of the future having me as the oldest swinger in town. I thought back to my life with Annie and how it was supposed to be forever. How did I manage to find myself back in this position at my age? In many ways I should thank Ralph for an insight into a way of life I simply did not want. I checked my phone and realised I had been doing this a lot over the last few days. Not a sign of any messages. Oh well, with that thought I got on the DLR and headed out of the city to home.

Chapter 25

Who Were You with in the Moonlight?
29 January 2011

It's Saturday morning and I'm having a lazy start to the day. After the night out with Ralph, I decided to a have a nice, quiet week to get myself back on track, despite failing to sustain a dry and fit January. I have been in every night and I didn't even go over to see Gerry as I think I am still not in Charlie's good books. On the positive side, I have not received any more emails from Susan the Psycho so I am guessing that little issue can now be considered dead and buried. Gerry and I are chatting (football this afternoon in fact), but there really is no point kicking a hornet's nest until you really have to. Charlie will most definitely forgive me next time she needs a babysitter. As I have been in so much, the flat is spotless, the ironing done, and I am catching up on a bit of PlayStation action when the door goes. As I open the door, Misty shoots past me and starts to sniff around the flat. There staring at me is Sarah. As I was not expecting this, I stand dumb for a few seconds.

'Are you going to invite me in, or are you planning on dognapping Misty?' I stepped out of the way and invited her to enter with a bow.

'Sorry, I was speechless there for a second. I thought you were not talking to me anymore. Please come in, as much as I love your dog, I am not sure I want her moving in.' I closed the door behind her as Misty came bounding through the hall and skidded on the laminate flooring. 'Drink? Tea, coffee, hemlock?'

'If you are going to be funny, then I will go again.' She turned her body as if to head for the door.

'No, no, I will behave; I am just a bit taken aback. Sorry, let's start again. It's really nice to see you. I didn't know that Drew had managed to wind you up that night until a few days after. He thought if he got you angry at me, he could chat you up himself.'

'Let's review. You went out in your *dry* January, got drunk, and ignored me, and then when I turned up as I was worried about you, I find you draped around some slapper. What would you have thought?'

'There are a few points I would make in my defence. Firstly, I did say that we had job cuts announced that day. Angie, the aforementioned "slapper", was the girl that Drew had just dumped and she was on the list to lose her job. I was not doing anything other than supporting a colleague. My rules would be broken in about twenty ways if I went near her.' The kettle had just boiled and I made a couple of coffees. I looked in the cupboard and found an appropriate bowl for Misty and gave her some water. 'Secondly, we are not actually going out. Thirdly, last time you were drunk, I was the perfect understanding gentleman.'

'Okay, points two and three I agree with. I didn't know about her being cut and you are right Drew did wind me up. I thought I was coming over to support a drunk mate and I found you in a fairly compromising position. Is that it?'

'Well, the final point is aren't you currently seeing someone anyway?'

'What do you mean?' She looked a bit confused at me.

'Well a couple of days after the *incident*, I came over to apologise.'

'And? I never saw you, did you get cold feet?'

'I think you were too busy staring into the eyes of the guy in the Chinese restaurant while he was holding your hand Boyfriend? You said there was no one, was that a lie?' She stood up and glared at me.

'Have you been spying on me? Is that in your bloody rules?'

'Hold on. I came over and saw you leaving your flat with some old guy. You know, six two, six three, great coat, trendy jeans, and patent leather shoes? Sorry, I followed out of curiosity. Since you were not talking to me I thought I would try and work out why. So who is he?' Sarah sat back down and sighed.

'Okay, fair shout. I was going to get angry at you then, but the funny thing is I was doing something because of you. The *old guy* as you call him is Gary. He works at the agency I work for. Occasionally over the last few years he has been what is euphemistically call a *friend with benefits*.'

'You mean a fuck buddy?' I laughed out loud.

'Adam, don't be crude, there's no need for that. I have known Gary through the agency for about ten years. There was a time a while back when we were both single and after a long lunch one thing led to another. Since then there have been moments when it has happened again. He only really phones when he has had a few.'

'So what has this got to do with me?'

'It's your damned rules. The day you met me drunk, I had said no to him. He asked me out last week to try it on again and over dinner I told him I was not going to continue with this way anymore. You made me realise that there are some things I don't want to put up with anymore.'

'How did he take it?'

'Well to use a quaint Americanism, the only thing he stiffed me for was the bill. He was angry that things had changed and could not understand why. He was convinced I was seeing someone and he kind of lost the plot at that point.'

'Well, good riddance to bad rubbish as they say.' I stopped pacing and sat down beside her. Misty came over and put her head in Sarah's lap.

'It's not that easy, all things come at a price.'

'Sorry, but surely he will take a hint, right? He isn't going to keep bothering you, is he?'

'It's not that, it's more of a financial thing. I said that Gary works at the agency, what I didn't say is what he does. He is the coordinator who hands out the assignments. Business is not good at the moment and none of us are getting enough work. But I don't know if he will give me my share of the assignments now he is hacked off with me.'

'He wouldn't be that petty, would he?'

'I am sorry to say, yes, he would.'

'Sorry to hear that. So what about us? Are we going back to being mates?'

'Well I'm here, aren't I? But we need a no-jealousy ground rule. I think we both overreacted a bit. Me as the madwoman and you as the stalker. Let's have no more of that.'

'Agreed. You fancy a quick bite to eat before I shoot off to the football?'

'Why not. Is there a greasy spoon nearby? I could murder a fry up and Misty loves bacon.'

'Yup, let me get my jacket.' With this we set off for the local Weatherspoon's as they are dog friendly and do a mean (cheap and good) fry up.

I met Gerry just before two in the Birkbeck for a sharpener ahead of the game. We hadn't actually seen each other since the night of the falling out with Susan. He was as perky as ever.

'All right, mate. How's your life?' He was halfway through a pint and my Coke was standing there with condensation dribbling down the side of the glass looking particularly unappealing. I hadn't mentioned to him about falling off the wagon. 'I got them in, didn't know how long you would be. You getting any?'

'Hold that thought, mate, had a small incident with the January wagon.' I went to the bar and got a pint of lager and returned.

'Now, where was I, oh that's it. There are times, Gerry, when your front might get you slapped, you know. Are you like this at work?'

'Course I am, as I am coarse. They just love my sense of bluntness on the site.'

'You can say that as often as you like but it still doesn't make it a palindrome.'

'Oh, dictionary boy, you would so get punched if you came to work with me! So anyway when you coming round to dinner again? The other night really was like dinner and a show as they say on the telly.' I wouldn't say I had his full attention as the early match had kicked off and was being shown on the screen on the wall. It was the local London Derby of Spurs versus the Gunners and he was keeping one eye on the match.

'When Charlie has forgiven me and will not try to use my bollocks for a doorstop when I turn up.'

'You're all right, when she found out how much Susan had been mailing you, she kind of understood. It's just she thought Susan would be good for you as you have not had much luck lately. If you want her to stop, just get a girlfriend and let her vet her. Try saying that when you're pissed.'

'So is it safe for me to come round?'

'You are starting to sound like Marathon Man. Yes, it's safe, Dr Mengler. She needs your help.'

'With what, the kids?'

'Yup, we've got a dinner out booked and she needs a sitter next Saturday. Why don't you come over on Thursday night and sort out the details? We can get pizza for the kids so we won't have to cook. Yes, get in!' Gerry punched the air as Arsenal scored and went two-one up, with ten minutes to go. 'Get 'em in, Adam, it's your round.'

Chapter 26

Family Affair
3 February 2011

The Thursday night dinner at Gerry's turned into a bit of an anti-climax in the end as I was expecting the battle royal and Charlie just wanted to smooth things over. It was obvious from her comments that she was not impressed with Susan and her email deluge. They got on really well when they saw each other at the school. As I mentioned earlier, Charlie worked there part-time and Susan came in to read to the kids. It's a big thing in the city to give back to those less well-off than oneself and literacy is a very common way that people help out. Charlie was even more annoyed when I told her about Susan playing footsie at New Year and Gerry had never told her before that she had tried it on after a few drinks with him in the past. I would just love to be a fly on the wall next time they meet in the staff room.

Anyway, the meal went well and we were back to the good old banter so I knew the request was coming (it did help that Gerry had primed me at the football on Saturday).

'You doing anything on Saturday, Ads?' She took on that little girl lost look in an effort to wrap me round her finger.

'Oh for Christ's sake, stop squirming, woman. Gerry already told me you want me to babysit.' The reaction here was two-fold. Gerry gave me a filthy look and she did pretty much the same to him.

'Adam, you tosser, don't drop me in it!'

'Charlie, don't blame him. Your psychopathic friends aside, they are my godchildren; you know you only have to ask. Where are you two off to, somewhere nice?'

'One of the guys on the site is retiring and they are having a meal and then dancing afterwards in some new swanky hotel in Stratford; they seem to be multiplying since we got the Olympics. Not often we get a chance to get dressed up. And as for the dancing, I get to bust a few moves.' Gerry had got up, dragged Charlie to her feet, and started to waltz around the room while whistling the 'Blue Danube' or something not too far from it. After about thirty seconds of this, Charlie pushed him off and started to booty-shake.

'Stay away from me, you pasty white boy.' That girl could still move. She got up and put some music on quietly as the kids were in bed and then sat back down. 'So are you coming on your own or bringing a friend?'

'You know this isn't school or even some American teen movie? I'm not about to turn up here with some bird and end up getting off on the couch while the children sleep upstairs. What do you take me for?' Although the idea probably wasn't quite as abhorrent as my indignation suggested.

'What about this Sarah girl? Gerry said you seemed to be getting on okay with her these days? Isn't it about time you brought her round for her vetting?' With this she mimes putting on a mask and donning long surgical gloves.

'I am surprised your children are not mentally scarred with your sense of humour, woman. Gerry can't you keep her under control or discipline her?'

'Don't go down that road, Ads, she likes it too much.'

'Yuck. You two are my oldest friends and frankly there are some things I don't need to know. What time on Saturday? There's no game this week so I am not up to much.'

'Don't change the subject, are you bringing her with you?' Charlie had the bit between her teeth now.

'No, I am not. Sarah and I are just mates, we are not going out and you are not going to meet her anytime soon.'

'Adam, you are going to end up like some little old woman with cats if you are not careful.'

'Charlie, with blokes it's a dog. I will end up with a dog on a string if I am not careful.'

'Well at least you agree with me. Shall we say six on Saturday, that way we can say good night to the little ones and you can play games with Pete. He likes having fresh cannon-fodder.'

I turned up to bedlam. When Gerry let me in, Ellie was in the middle of bath time and Gerry was on the phone to the local pizza place to deliver.

'The usual, Adam?' Gerry quizzed me while he held his hand over the receiver of the phone.

'Yup, that's great. Charlie, aren't we doing things in the wrong order? Bath before pizza? I remember last time.'

'Yes, Mr *Know It All* super parent, and just like last time we are running late again. It's either this or you bath her afterwards.'

'Fair deuce. I will keep quiet. How can I help?'

'Stick a kid's movie on and sit them down in front of the box will you. I am just finishing off Ellie and then I need to get ready.' This was easier said than done. Peter and Carly were engaging in what appeared to be a military skirmish in which they were both crawling around the carpet while firing incredibly realistic guns at each other complete with ear-splitting sound effects.

'Guys, *Cars* or *Shrek*?' Of course they disagreed so in the end I decided, *Shrek* it was. I got the DVD player set up and sat down in front of the screen. I had found in the past that if I ignore them and start watching the movie, within five minutes they will be on the couch curled up beside me. Of course we would not be alone, but rather would have a host of Ellie's and Carly's fluffy pets with us making it almost impossible to move.

The pizza arrived and the relative calm was lost. Ellie was now in her pyjamas but Charlie had successfully negotiated a tea towel around her neck for the pizza feast. I spent the next twenty minutes juggling a godparent police action while swapping the occasional comment with Gerry and Charlie. Honestly it was like they had forgotten how to dress like proper grown-ups. When the time came for them to go, the kids had eaten enough for me to claim victory and to allow them to get down and wash their hands and faces before going near their pristine parents.

'You scrub up well, Charlie. Who's this stranger you are going out with?' I said in Gerry's general direction.

'That's Daddy, you silly,' interjected a very serious Ellie who was not quite ready for the world of banter.

'Have a great time, I have your number, don't panic. I've managed this before.' Charlie kissed her little troops who were lined up for inspection like something from the *Sound of Music* (Sarah would have loved that after the Von Trappe comment). Gerry made a big deal of giving them all bear hugs before he left.

'Half hour, one hour, two hours, okay?' I knew the drill but Charlie always thinks if she says it to me in front of the kids that they will listen (they never do by the way).

Ninety minutes later, fed, watered, and put to bed, it was just Peter and I left and the TV had switched from DVD to PlayStation. He was a great kid and liked to play platform games; this evening we were off to Little Big Planet. His hand-eye coordination amazed me and I wondered just how much practice he was getting.

'Uncle Adam, can I ask you a question?' This conversation would take the usual format. However serious or trivial, his eyes would remain 'glued' to the screen. Who said boys don't multi-task?

'Yes, mate, go for it.'

'Do you have brothers and sisters? If you do, do they live nearby or with your mum and dad?'

'That's two questions strictly speaking, but I will let you have two for the price of one. Yes, I have a sister called Beth who is 33 and a brother called Paul who is 37. And no, they don't live near me. Beth lives out of London in a place called Northampton and Paul lives upside down in Australia. We call him Kangaroo Jack.' It's not often that Peter will pause a game, but he pressed the button and turned to me with a big grin on his face. I am not sure if it was my brother's potential orientation (upside down) or his nickname that had won the smile.

'How come we've never met them? Are they like you?'

'They are both very bright but they don't work in the city in a bank like I do. Paul is a lawyer in Perth. He went there when he was a student and he ended up staying. Every now and then the government there lets people admit they should not be there and allows them to stay. It's called an amnesty. Well Paul wanted to stay as he found a lady he fell in love with called Stevie and he has a daughter about Carly's age.'

'Don't you miss seeing him?' His smile now morphed into something far more serious. 'I know I would miss Carly and Ellie if they lived a long way away.'

'A little, but it's different when you grow up.'

'What about your sister Beth, do you see her?'

'I saw her at Christmas when I went to see my parents. Did you like your presents from them?'

'Yup, I got a new gun for the PlayStation.' He got up and came back having collected a very well-used plastic weapon. 'So what does Beth do? Is she a lawyer too?'

'No, she works for a charity. She helps people that can't help themselves.'

'She sounds nice,' and with that the play button was pressed and my interview was over. We played on for another hour or so and as usual I let him stay up watching the box with me until he fell asleep. I woke him and walked him up to his room. After he climbed in to bed, I covered him up before going back to sit on the couch. So my question is this. Do kids really have a way of cutting through all the rubbish we tell ourselves every day, or do we just listen to them in a way we don't listen to ourselves or others? This 11-year-old boy had just made me think about my own siblings in a way I had not for a long time. As I sat there and put the telly back on, I got my mobile out and texted Beth.

TEXT: 'You free for a chat tomorrow sometime?'

TEXT: 'Are you drunk?'

TEXT: 'No, just thinking I should make more effort.'

TEXT: 'Okay. Phone tomorrow after ten.'

And with that I put my phone away and waited until midnight for the wanderers to return. It was not a pretty sight. God help them in the morning when the kids wake up.

※

Sunday morning was not an early start as by the time the terrible twosome got in half-cut and wanting to chat, it was nearly one when I got home, stone-cold sober. I had literally just gone straight to bed and after a busy evening with three exhausting godchildren didn't see anything but the inside of my eyelids until just gone nine. I should have set an alarm as I hate wasting the day but I did admittedly still feel tired. I made myself a cafetiere of decent coffee, a bit of a rare treat reserved for weekends, and then sat down to call my sister. At this point I was not even sure what I was going to say. Her phone rang for about thirty seconds and then went to voicemail. I looked at the clock and realised it was still only nine-thirty. Our Beth was never an early riser. She, like my dad I have recently discovered, is a great exponent of the Saturday night spliff and so I can imagine she meant ten when she said ten. I drank my coffee, walked down to the paper shop, and tried again about ten fifteen. This time she answered.

'I guess that was you earlier. You always were bloody early for everything, Adam. I wonder if that was the problem with Annie.' She still sounded half asleep and I guess was hacked off that I woke her up early on a Sunday.

'Good morning, sis, any chance we could be friendly and try to keep off my failed marriage for five minutes?'

'Okay, fair enough, bro, but come on, it's not like you to call, what's up?'

'I am not sure you would believe me if I told you.'

'Oh please don't tell me the midlife crisis has finally started. Have you bought a Porsche yet like your banker mates? Or have you gone for a good old tattoo? Knowing you it would just be henna. Nothing too permanent in your life. Sorry, I said I wouldn't mention your marriage. By the way, do you ever hear from her?'

'No, why on earth would she contact me? Once she had got what she wanted from the divorce, that would swapping me out for an improved model, she just disappeared. Her mum calls occasionally to see how I am but even that has dropped off luckily. It was all a bit painful. All I got left with from the marriage is a much bigger mortgage than all my colleagues.'

'So why have you called?'

'I was babysitting last night with Gerry's kids and Peter and I started talking.'

'What is he, 10 now?'

'Eleven. I can't believe where the time has gone. Anyway, the subject got round to brother and sisters and he asked me why we don't see each other. When I thought about it afterwards, I am not sure I know myself. It made me think I should try a bit harder with you and Kangaroo Jack.'

'Well you could start by using his proper name. Calling him that really winds Mum up. You know she is proud of him and her only grandchild is on the other side of the world.'

'Okay, you have a point. Do you fancy coming down to stay one weekend, or even going down to Mum and Dad's together?'

'We could do that, you could even come up here.'

'North of Watford? You serious?'

'Honestly, Adam, you are such a Kentish man. And I am not making a pun at that. We even have running water and electric light here now.'

'All right, let's sort something out. Can you let me have Paul's Skype address if you have it?'

'Okay, I will stick it on an email.' That was it, a bit more chit-chat and she rung off. Did I feel better? Maybe or maybe I just felt a bit weird. Deep inside me there was this nagging doubt that if I couldn't get on with my own family, how was I supposed to share my life with a stranger? I wonder if the problem was me all along.

I am back in the courtroom and they are calling for character witnesses. Sitting in the public gallery are Mum, Dad, Paul, and Beth. When another call goes out for witnesses, they all look the other way. They all hear the call, but none of them appear to want to stand up for me. I get that sinking feeling. Suddenly I see Annie there and she starts to walk towards the witness box. This isn't going to end well.

Chapter 27

Kissin' in the Back Row
12 February 2011

After the snow comes the rain. I am not saying that the flooding has got bad locally but I have noticed a carpenter turn up with a bunch of animals in pairs. The worst of it is that Leyton's ground has flooded so Gerry and I are now at a loss for Saturday afternoon. Charlie has not missed a trick and made it clear that no football means Gerry has DIY to do and I am left to my own devices. After my chat with Beth recently, I even thought about asking her down this weekend, but I don't want to make it look all last minute. Instead I have agreed to drive her down to Mum and Dad's in a few weekends' time. Strength in numbers always seems like a good idea when seeing the old folks and more importantly when I might bump into Mad Mary. I am still wary after Christmas and my father's newfound interest in her for purely pharmaceutical reasons is not helping.

I thought I might go and check on progress at the Olympic Park to see how things were going. It is amazing what they have done with a really crappy area of the city and it is pretty cool how much my flat has gone up in value in the meantime. I bought just around the time the Olympics were announced. I remember the euphoria of the day; everybody was in Trafalgar Square, all trying to avoid the prevalent cynicism. You know what people were like back then. We won't get, if we do the city will never cope and the buildings won't be ready. I also know the hell that was the next day at work as the bombs went off around the city, we all knew someone who had been there or witnessed the events.

It's funny that it is four years on now and we are almost done with the main building work and the Olympic site is starting to look pretty cool. The best bit is the rumour that Leyton Orient might end up sharing the stadium with West Ham from 2015 onwards. I bet we won't miss any more matches due to flooding then.

I was on my way back from the park when Sarah texted to see if I was busy. She too was a bit bored and Misty was not keen on long walks when it was so wet. I am pretty sure she is the most picky bitch I have ever met (I am talking about Misty still). It is like trying to walk Goldie Locks, honestly, too cold, too wet, pretty soon we should find a season she likes. When I said I was free, Sarah suggested going to the cinema. Oh this was going to be fun, agreeing what to see, let's find out just how good at being friends we can be. The problem with cinemas in the centre of London is that they are a wee bit expensive so I would rather go to somewhere on the outskirts. I convinced her to meet me in Canary Wharf where there is a decent cinema on West India Quay. We agreed to meet at three and either have a drink before or after depending on what was on and when.

'So what do you want to see?' Sarah asked as she walked up to me outside the cinema. She was dressed in a very cute-looking top that was a lot more flattering than the average clothes I saw her in. Maybe it was getting warmer or possibly she was not dressing to walk a huge German shepherd.

'You look nice. I'm really easy. I can do action, comedy, sci-fi?' I stared up at the board to check what was starting soon.

'No chick-flicks then?' She was smiling when she said this and I hoped she was simply joking. Don't take this the wrong way; I have seen some really good films of this category such as *The Devil Wears Prada* but I am not sure I was in the mood for some of the more depressing or predictable elements of this genre.

'Do you like Mike Leigh? You know the guy behind *Secrets and Lies* and *Topsy Turvy*?'

'Don't treat me like an idiot, of course I know Mike Leigh. Yeah, I like his work, what's on?'

'*Another Year* has just come out and it is getting a lot of good reviews.' Looking up at the board, it was going to start in twenty minutes so we could grab a coffee and go in.

'Done. Let's get popcorn. I know it sounds childish, but it's not really going to the cinema without popcorn.' She was almost squealing with delight. It is always nice to see people get genuinely excited, as I often find the muted responses of people quite depressing.

'Cinderella, you shall go to the ball and you shall have popcorn.' With that we headed to the door and sold one kidney to pay for the popcorn and coffee. We found our seats and settled in for the thirty minutes of adverts and trailers.

<hr>

Almost three hours had passed by the time the film was over and it was already dark. The temperature had dropped and it looked like more rain was on the way with the wind whipping up the waters around the docks.

'Drink or food and drink?' I asked Sarah as we walked across the Wharf in the direction of the tube station.

'Food would be nice, but nothing too pricey, I am watching the pennies.'

'I'm sure I can stand you a meal if you can keep your pride under control. What about Thai? There is a brilliant one at the bottom of the island with views over Greenwich.'

'I'm not after charity, but I admit that does sound nice. I am a huge fan of Thai food.'

'Okay, then we need to head for the DLR, not the tube.' We jumped on to the train at Heron Quays and headed down to Island Gardens.

When we arrived at the Elephant Royale, we managed to get a table by the window as it was very quiet still. I'm not sure many people were going to brave the evening as the sky now looked heavy with rain. In the fifteen minutes it took to get here, the trees had gone from moving gently to being bent double by gusts of wind.

'I love being inside watching storms, especially with a real fire or hot food.'

'So one out of two isn't bad then. This is a great menu.' We took the next ten minutes to order and then settled back in our chairs with a large glass of wine each and watched the storm break.

'I loved the film, it reminded me of the complexities of your life when you talk about your past issues. You seem to have a fair bit of baggage,' Sarah said and smiled.

'Don't we all at our age.'

'Speak for yourself, you cheeky sod. I am younger than you.'

'You are not without any issues; you haven't said that much but you did mention your engagement and Gary so it is not like you have lived in a glass case.'

'Okay, you have point, but you need your own baggage handler.' This was a bit of a low blow but I will concede the idea of the rules makes me sound like a bit of a basket case especially when I tell stories about what has happened to me along the way.

'Getting back to the film, I loved all the interaction with Tom and Jerry, and yes, it was very realistic when it came to more mature relationships. You know the way that friends of friends keep turning up at social occasions. It's a bit like that David Nobbs series, *A Bit of a Do*? The only part of the story that was wrong in the film was the handling of kids.' I thought a subtle change of tack would be a good idea.

'In what way?' She was drinking a lot faster than me and started to top up her glass from the bottle in the wine bucket.

'Well kids in those situations, you know multiple partners over the years, and finding new partners with kids. That's where it all gets tricky.'

'I didn't think you were a kid hater. I know you are not keen on women who are looking for a baby father, but what's wrong with those with kids?' Things appeared to have taken on an edge or it could just have been that the sky was lit up by an enormous shard of lightning which made all the waiters stop and look out.

'No, I love kids, remember Gerry and Charlie's. No, my issue is that women I have met and dated who already had kids are really hard work and most of the time unless you meet them and become a couple when the kid is really young, you are destined to always be on the outside looking in.' The Tom Yum soup had arrived in a big steaming tureen for us to share and we ladled out bowls full of the tempting and very strong-smelling liquid. It tasted delicious and I could tell she was enjoying it as I got a moment off from the interrogation. After the bowl was emptied (and I mean scrapping the pattern off), she came up for air.

'Were you hungry? You eat like you haven't for a week.'

'Sorry, but I think I could inhale Thai food and especially the soups. That is amazing; great choice of restaurant. So this issue with mothers, you implied personal experience of this. Wanna share? I think we have time while I hoover up the mains.' I am not sure if it was the food or the wine, but she definitely relaxed at that point. She sat back in her chair as the bowls were cleared, refilled her glass again, and waited for me to start.

Chapter 28

Kids Say the Darndest Things
12 February 2011

In many ways Sarah is right about baggage. In this modern day and age of multiple marriages and living together, it is common to go through a number of relationships in your life unlike our parents. Sometimes I feel like a failure because of this, but then at other times I think of all those marriages where people stayed together for appearance's sake while living through personal hells, and I wonder if we do not have a better way to live now. If you meet someone in their thirties, forties, fifties, or older, they are most likely to have a history of failed relationships and family ties that will shape the way they behave. Did you know the highest growth sector in divorce stats are the empty nesters? After twenty or so years of bringing up Tarquin and Esmeralda, husband and wife look at each other one morning over the cornflakes and realise they don't know who the other one is. He is probably seeing his secretary on Thursdays and she has fantasies about her tennis coach. After a somewhat less than amicable divorce, once their friends take sides, they will spend the next twenty years blaming the other while they talk through their woes with a series of equally bitter substitutes (or do you suspect I am being a little harsh?).

On top of this statistic are an increasing number of single parents who have split with their other halves through a variety of reasons, but a common one is the husband failed to wait the agreed twenty years before going to work on his secretary (if you will excuse the pun). There are three ladies that I have been out with (I think when they have kids you can't call them girls anymore, however old they are) who had children in tow (CIT). Don't start to judge me here, only two of these relationships broke up because of the kids. The failure of the third relationship was due to a completely different rule that came into play. Nancy, the lady in question, was a paragon of virtue when in charge of her little darling and was a hard worker the rest of the time, but on the odd evening she had off with me, she could do red wine at a rate of a bottle an hour. After two bottles (on three separate occasions), she became what is affectionately known as a booze monster. She could not talk apart from at high volume. She would slur her speech and eventually would both fall over and throw up. After the third time this happened, I realised I didn't see myself with a partner who needed to attend AA meetings (and she didn't share the driving, if you know what I mean).

When I talk about issues with mothers who I have dated which relate directly to the aspects of parenthood, I must cite the cases of Michelle and Romy (names not changed, and neither have the names of the kids, but purely for comic effect). I met Michelle at a charity do one evening after work in the city. A bunch of people from various banks had run or wobbled five miles, paid their dues, got the tee shirt to prove it, and were mingling socially to wallow in it. Michelle worked for a rival bank, Swiss not German, but it meant we could practice our poor language skills on each other (please no jokes about cunning linguists). I thought the evening was going to go on for a while as I was between disastrous relationships at the time and things were looking promising. She was erudite, obviously fit, and pretty good looking if I am honest. I was just about to go all deep and sensitive about her fabulous blue eyes when she looked at her watch and got up to leave in a hurry.

'Something I said? I thought we were getting on well there?'

'We were, too well, I forgot the time and I have a sitter, sorry.' She pulled out her phone and sent a quick text to say she was on her way. 'Look, have you got a card or something? I would like to do this again.'

'What, you want to stand about with a cold beer in your hand while the sweat from running dries on your body surrounded by a bunch of bankers?'

'Not exactly, but certain parts of that equation appeal. I'll call you.' And with this she was gone.

Wonders will never cease; a girl takes my card and actually calls. It was in fact about three hours later and I may not have been in my best state. I thought I was being suave and sophisticated but in reality I was more likely to have sounded brutish and drunk. However I came across it seemed to do the trick and we arranged to meet on the following Saturday. She picked a pub, but after we met up, I noticed she spent quite lot of the afternoon looking at her watch while we were talking.

'Do you have somewhere to be?' I asked her after a while. 'Hot date?'

'No, I only have two hours as my ex has Mitchell for the afternoon.' I nearly spat my drink out (who names their kids after themselves when they are opposite sexes?). 'It's a shame you couldn't have met him.'

'Your ex-husband?'

'No, Mitchell. He is such a little star but his father is a waste of space. Mitchell is four but he is already showing a lot of skill with a ball. He will be the next Wayne Rooney.' Many things were going through my mind at that point, the first of which was, what a footballer who needs a hair transplant? Once I got my head into a slightly less sarcastic place, I thought hang on, I have just met you and you want me to meet your 4-year-old. Isn't this a little freaky? If I had a kid and I was looking for a new partner, I would make sure about things before introducing the poor little thing to a new person. 'I wanted him to go to the David Beckham football camp over the summer but they closed it last year much to my disgust.' Oh, I thought, that explains Wayne Rooney, not a fan of Becks anymore.

'Well maybe next time we meet up,' I said as if to quell any fears for her and to move on to the subject of anything else, but I could see it was not going to be that easy.

'Maybe I could cook for you one night? We love having guests. Mitchell helps me set the table and he has impeccable table manners. You would be very proud of him.' Oh sweet Jesus, where was this going? I now had this image in my mind of a proud mother manacling a new surrogate father to the child in place of the now defunct one. Maybe what I needed was a pint with her ex to find out what the score was.

'So what is he doing with his dad this afternoon, something exciting?' Maybe she could talk about him for a bit and I could find out some history. It was at this point I think fear had taken over as I was drinking my pint a little too quickly. She already signalled for another drink from the waiter so there was no escaping at this point.

'Oh, that waste of space. The sooner I can get him out of Mitchell's life, the better. He is not the sort of role model I want for my son. He used to have ambition but then he lost his way and now reckons he wants to be an author. I just call it laziness, it's not like it's a proper job.' I had a growing feeling of discomfort that the lovely lady in front of me with the fantastic eyes was looking for a Tetris block boyfriend to replace the husband of the same shape that had since lost a few edges through the trials of life. I actually felt sorry for him and in many ways a little worried for me.

We finished the afternoon and she went off to get *der Wunderkind* and I exited the pub pretty sharpish in case she had any intentions of returning in the near future, child in tow. I made myself scarce for a few days, but she persisted in sending invitations for evenings which would of course involve meeting the aforementioned child. On the fourth night she phoned.

'You seem to be avoiding me. Did you want to come over for dinner tonight?'

'Just the two of us?' I thought I would be subtle, but I am sure it was as subtle as brick on the other end of the line.

'Oh, is that the problem, that I have child?' You could hear the steam venting from her even down the phone. 'I've met men like you before, never wanting to meet anyone with a past life.'

'Honestly, no. I love the fact that you are a mother; I just can't believe you want me to meet your child just one week after meeting me. It is way too soon. What if it doesn't work out? What if we don't get on, what does Mitchell say then? Is there to be a long list of "Uncles" in his life akin to some seventies sitcom?' The line went silent and I think I may have overstepped the mark, but hell it's true.

'Goodbye, Adam.' Well that showed a fair degree of restraint. I was hoping there would be no reprisals and then I remembered, she didn't know where I lived. Not a rule, but just plain sensible; don't share your address too early.

Now Romy was a very different kettle of fish. She ended up being one of the longest-serving girlfriends after splitting with Annie. The reasons for this were two-fold. Firstly she was always so busy and secondly she kept cutting dates with me that it took ages to get to know her. At least once a week we would book something and half an hour before we were due to meet she would cancel. After a couple of months, this got a wee bit frustrating. Unlike Michelle, I knew Romy had a little girl of around 8 called Juliette (see I told you the names were funny, Romy and Juliette, is that weird or what?) but I was never invited to meet her. I thought this was positive in that Romy was concerned that we should be an item with a future before I got introduced to her daughter; wow, for once a mother I could agree with. But she still kept ducking dates. I would have thought she might have had another man, but I could not imagine how she was fitting this in with a job and a child.

Eventually I had it out with her as the excuses were getting more and more bizarre when she let me down.

'Romy, this is the eighth time in two months you've cancelled me at the last minute, what is going on? I am sorry but you have had more punctures than a balloon factory with a porcupine problem.' She was on the phone once more explaining that my evening was being ruined because another tyre had exploded on her car.

'I'm really sorry, Adam. If you really want to know, it's Juliette; she is feeling poorly and I need to spend time with her.'

'Why didn't you say, well that's okay then, I'm not a monster. Go look after your daughter; I hope she is better soon.' I put the phone down and thought what a wonderful mum to give up so much for her daughter.

It took another two months of broken dates to meet the aforementioned offspring and then suddenly the penny dropped. We met out at a funfair so it looked like we were just friends and Juliette would not get the wrong idea about me. It was not as if I was going to their house or anything. Anyway, we met and immediately I got the feeling of oh my God what a princess (the fact she was dressed as a Disney princess may have given this away), but what I mean is the way she acted.

'Mummy, I want this. Mummy, I want that.' The problem was that Mummy almost fell over her own feet to provide. Everything from money for rides to food was 'I want, I want, I want' and she simply got it. I had the funny feeling that all those missed dates were actually the little madam stamping her foot and demanding Mummy to act like a cross between a servant and a drone. At one point I thought I would test the water.

'Juliette, surely you mean please?' I said this as she demanded more money for another ride. Well, I think either the heavens opened or there was a metaphorical split of the tectonic plates because the whole scene froze. Tears began to well in the eyes of the little princess and rage began to show on the face of the lovely Romy.

'May I remind you whose child she is? What right do you have to tell her off?'

'I merely suggested she say please. My mother would have beaten me as a child if I acted like that in public.' It was one of those lines which should always be followed with *"I'll get my coat, shall I?"* but I think since I was already wearing mine, the best thing to do was to walk away before Krakatoa had a chance to repeat its famous explosion. It is safe to say I heard no more from the repressed Romy, which in many ways is a real shame. She was intelligent, good looking, and the sex was amazing, if only every now and then!

Chapter 29

My Hometown
19 February 2011

Beth arrived at my place just after seven on Friday evening which gave me time to get in from work, get changed, and throw a few things in a bag. It is harder than it used to be to go away for the weekend. Phones need chargers, so do cameras, toothbrushes, etc., so it's always a mad dash to make sure you are not going to get caught *run down* as it were. I offered her a coffee, but she just used the loo and we headed off. I should bear in mind that she had spent nearly three hours travelling already. As the rush-hour traffic had died down, we set off in the direction of the Blackwall Tunnel and the road to Mum and Dad's. It was quiet in the car and I was not sure if Beth was just tired or thinking. I was worried that an argument was brewing. Tuning the radio to Magic FM, I hoped that the music might lessen the awkward atmosphere.

'Do you remember this? I think they are playing an '80s night,' I said as 'Blue Monday' started to emanate from the radio. I turned it up as I love the sound of the syn-drum.

'I know you think I am over the hill, dear brother, but please try to remember there are seven years between us. I was always more "Happy Mondays" than "Blue Monday".' I'm relieved to say when I peeked across at her (no, this is not an American movie where they sit there looking straight at the person next to them while driving) she was smiling not frowning. Maybe the ice was melting. When the song was finished, she turned down the music. 'Do you want to talk about it before we get back to the homestead?'

'Talk about what?'

'This urge you have to get back in touch with your roots. Visiting the folks when it's not a holiday and talking to Paul and myself? I can't see one conversation with an 11-year-old boy is the whole reason behind this sudden change in direction.'

'I'm not sure entirely. That is part of it, but also there is this girl I have been seeing.'

'I knew there was a woman behind it. What is she, born-again?'

'It's not like that. I'm only seeing her as a mate. No physical stuff.'

'Too much information, Adam. Anyway, what's wrong with her, why just friends, or can she simply see through you?'

'Oh please stop, my sides are splitting.'

'What's her name for a start?'

'She's called Sarah. She's a freelance graphic designer and she lives in Pimlico with a German shepherd called Misty. I can get you a CV if you want?'

'Behave. I only asked her name. Anyway, what happened to the "no girls with dogs" rule?'

'Who told you about the rules?'

'Mum did at Christmas after you flipped your lid over Mad Mary. I don't think any of us knew at the time you guys were going out, quite how weird she was around you. All the exhibitionist stuff sounds so strange. She is still a little whacky but she has calmed down a lot.'

'She slapped and groped my arse in the pub. How much calmer is she, please remind me?'

'Okay, fair deuce, maybe it's just you that brings it out in her. She still has the hots for you twenty years on. Now, back to the subject in hand. Why would talking to Sarah make you reach for your family like Linus reaches for a comfort blanket?'

'Love and Pride' by King started to play and I wanted to turn it up, but as if to anticipate my intentions, she reached across and turned the radio off. 'No, you cannot have your other safety blanket of loud music either. I swear when we were growing up you used to live through your song lyrics. I'm sure that's why you can be so bloody weird now. It's not normal you know. You honestly used to fixate on a song. Mum would get so cross when you played them over and over again. Tell me then, with this Sarah, what's the score? Is she the real deal?'

'Okay, Jesus, sis, I don't think I can get the car seat to recline into a couch *while* we are driving. Sarah has a terrible relationship with her mother and doesn't really see any other family. Her father is dead and she misses him. Peter asked me about my brother and sisters and frankly it scared me a bit that we have grown so far apart. I don't think there was a single incident, but over time I suppose I got "fixated", as you so kindly put it, with work. I know I avoided people after Annie left. I was embarrassed, wouldn't you be? Paul has his marvellous marriage, Mum and Dad are blissfully happy in that way dotty pensioners can be, and you are content to be single. You seem to thrive on it. Maybe I just thought it was time to get back on the horse. We used to have a laugh, right?'

'We did and I had the greatest two brothers in the world when I was growing up. Paul and I have managed to remain close despite the distance between here and Australia. Did you know I am going later this year?'

'No. Wow, I thought you were always broke with your charity work?'

'We can all save, Adam, even if we don't work for banks. I also ought to tell you that you are wrong about one other thing.'

'What's that?'

'I'm not content with being single. I am content with being in a relationship.'

'Is this where you tell me *you* have found religion?'

'No, this is where I tell you I have found Janice.' I think I may have lost concentration for a moment as the car did a little swerve on the carriage way. 'Watch the road, you looney.' With this she turned the radio back on, when she recognised the song and she turned it up very loud. After a minute of listening, over the top of the music she started singing along *I'm coming out, I want the world to know.* I am left thinking, is God a DJ?

⁂

Once she had recovered from her little revelation, Beth turned the music back down and reclined her seat for the rest of the journey. After ten minutes I realised she was snoring. I wondered just how long she had been bottling up that news. No wonder she seemed on edge. I woke her just as we started to drive through the village.

'Sorry to talk practicalities, but do Mum and Dad know?'

'Know what? That I am no longer single or that I am gay?'

'Either.'

'Neither. But it's okay, I will go gentle on them.'

When we arrived at the house, I grabbed the bags from the car and Beth went to knock. It seemed to take a while for Mum to open the door. As I got near I saw she looked tired. On her feet she had those zip-up booties, not the usual *Mother Mules* that we had called them as kids. It was only two months since Christmas but she seemed to have shrunk in that time. I gave her a big hug but she was in some way less substantial than I was expecting, as though my arms should have found more of her there than there really was. Beth bundled into the house to find Dad and I just hung on to Mum for a bit.

'You okay, Mum, you look a bit tired?'

'I'm feeling old, Adam. Your father is becoming a handful to look after and I am no spring chicken myself. This cold weather then non-stop rain gets into your bones. Anyway, come in, let's get you a drink. Tea, coffee, or something stronger?' We walked into the kitchen where Beth was sitting next to Dad with a glass of wine already in her hand.

'You don't waste much time, sis.'

'Don't be a prude, Adam, grab a glass and dive in. And get one for Mum while you're there, I have news to share.' I looked at her and thought, so this is treating them gently. Once we were all seated around the big kitchen table, in the room made inferno hot by the real fire that was burning in the grate, Beth began.

'Mum, Dad, I have someone new in my life and I wanted you to know.'

'That's nice, dear. You could have used the phone though. It's always good to see you but this is a bit dramatic.' Mum was sipping from her glass of wine. She was looking at Dad and then she winked. When she saw me watching, she smiled.

'Well I came down to tell you as I did not want to shock or upset you. Her name is Janice.' Beth then took a rather exaggerated swig of wine from her glass.

'Well I am glad we have finally cleared that up then.' Mum was now looking at me. 'You two need to remember I am not made of glass, I won't break that easily. Beth, your father and I have talked about it over the years. You have never been comfortable around any man we have seen you with. If you have finally found someone to be happy with, it's a weight off our minds.' My father, the man of few words, simply nodded his head sagely and patted Beth's hand.

'Oh. But what about grandchildren?' Beth interjected, seemingly slightly put out.

'I have one already, and you never know with Adam.'

'Thanks for the vote of confidence, Mum.' With this I went to the garage to get another bottle.

***

Saturday lunchtime was going to be a bit of a treat for Mum and Dad as we were going out to eat. They were not poor but didn't really have the cash to splash out on a regular basis. There was also a little bit of the *have you seen the prices in here* syndrome going on when we walk into the sort of restaurant I preferred to eat in. I am no food snob, but an extra tenner a head makes a hell of a lot of difference to the result. I had done some searching on the internet for reviews of local places and found a new gastro pub just the other side of Ashford, so I said I would drive. In the car on the way over, Mum was chatting away about Paul and her wonderful granddaughter Daisy. Apparently Paul managed to Skype with them once every couple of weeks, so Granny had a lot of news about what was going on in their lives. When we arrived at the restaurant, fifteen minutes later, Dad had fallen asleep in the back of the car and Mum was struggling to swing her legs out of the door.

'You need a hand there, Mum?' I asked her as she struggled.

'What do you think, you daft bugger. Come here and help your old mum.' With the commotion, Dad woke up and Beth helped him out the other side. I am guessing she was more aware of what was going on than I was. She got down to see them once a month and phoned twice a week. I had got lazy over the years and needed to get back involved for both my peace of mind and their health. Paul was not going to be able to support them from Australia as they got older and frailer.

The meal was a quieter one than I had planned. The food was too foodie for Mum and both her and Dad seemed to struggle with the portions. We didn't even look at desserts as they were full. I could see the disappointment written all over Beth's face. When I paid the bill and we headed for the door, Mum again struggled to get up from the table. I walked round and helped her.

'I just get a bit stiff now when I've been sitting down for a long while.'

'I know the feeling, Mum,' I commented and giggled.

'Trust you,' she said and gave me a warm hug. 'It's nice to see you for no reason. Not Christmas or birthdays. It's been too long and you have been a bit of a stranger.'

'I will try and make it down a bit more often, Mum. This was nice.' I took her arm and walked her to the car. When I got her installed in the front seat, I watched as Beth walked Dad over to the car. She stopped at one point and rubbed his knee vigorously.

'How bad is Dad's arthritis?' I asked Mum before Dad got near enough to hear.

'Bad enough that he can't sleep at night and I have to help him move sometimes, which is a struggle.'

'Can you get any help? You know, social services or whoever you need to call?'

'I tried to call them but I didn't get anywhere.' Dad was now being manipulated limb by limb into the car.

'I will take the details off you and give them a call on Monday, Mum. Leave it to me.'

In the evening Mum just wanted to crash in front of the TV and Dad suitably drug-fuelled from a trip to the shed was keen on getting a pint with his kids while we were both around, so we went off to the local pub. When we walked in, I stopped dead as Mad Mary was rocking on a bar stool talking to a couple of her friends, one male and one female. I'm pretty sure I knew the bloke from school, but it is difficult to tell sometimes. I took Dad to a table and went to get the drinks. Beth had gone off to talk to Mary who by now had seen we were all in the pub and was smiling at me and trying to catch my eye. I got the round in, nodded in her direction as I took our drinks back to the table. Beth came over and sat down.

'What were you saying to Mary?' I asked her.

'I was just saying hello. She asked after you by the way.'

'Please don't tell me you wound her up again?'

'Actually, Adam, I told her you had a girlfriend called Sarah and you were very happy with her.'

'She's not my girlfriend.'

'Oh okay, I will let Mary know, shall I? Or would you prefer to simply have a quiet pint without being hassled?'

'Sorry, sis, I owe you one.'

'Call it quits for driving me down. How you doing, Dad?'

'Bloody knee is agony. Even the pot is failing to make a dent in it tonight.'

'Dad, I have to ask. Is there not a proper drug you can use to relieve the pain? Pot seems a little, well, illegal for a start. It's also unproven in terms of any pain-relief properties or side effects. What do the doctors say?'

'Doctor Lakeham, you know the man we have trusted for forty years and who delivered Beth and Paul, recommended it. He says it is just as good as anything he can give me legally if used in conjunction with other prescribed painkillers. It means he can keep the prescription doses down at this stage.'

'What do you mean at this stage?'

'What do you think he means, Adam,' interjected my sister. 'Dad is worn out and getting more exhausted by the week. This is impacting most of his joints, but being that he was on his feet his entire working life in the factory, his knees are bearing the brunt.'

'Sorry, Dad, I didn't know it was this bad.' I went back to drinking my pint in silence. When I had finished, I said, 'Another, anyone? One for the road?'

'If you don't mind, Adam, I would rather go back, I'm shattered and I don't like to leave your mum on her own for too long as she worries. We go to bed earlier these days as she is getting more tired helping me. She thinks I don't know, but I do.'

As we walked into the house, the TV was still on, but Mum was softly dozing on the sofa, a blanket over her legs. Dad turned the sound down and woke her up to take her to bed. They said good night and left the two of us together. I flicked through the channels and found some rubbish on. I went out to the garage, opened a bottle of red, and brought it into the front room with a couple of glasses. When I walked in, Beth was wiping tears from her cheeks.

'Sorry', she said, 'I shouldn't get so upset but they are just getting so old.'

'I know, I can't believe they are so much worse than at Christmas.'

'Mum let slip they had been putting on a brave face for us, but yes, the deterioration is accelerating if I am honest.'

'I have a number for social services from Mum which I'll call on Monday.'

'Thanks, Adam.' I handed her the red wine and we clinked glasses. 'Welcome back to the fold, brother, I think you returned just in time.'

Chapter 30

Misty
20 February 2011

Beth and I arrived back into London on Sunday afternoon at around five. We had cooked lunch for Mum to give her a break and then left after the doing the washing up. I think the most relieved person in the room was Mum not Beth as she had thought beforehand. Mum now knew she didn't have to keep up the pretence of coping. First thing tomorrow I would get on to social services and see what could be done. Rather than going to the flat, I dropped Beth off at Kings Cross to make her journey back home a little easier.

'Come up and meet Janice, Adam. I know you will get on with her; she has your musical geekiness in common with you. And she loves movie trivia too.'

'I'm really pleased that you're happy at last. Just me to go then!'

'You'll get there, if you can work out what you are looking for that is. I mean, look at me. It took me years to get my head around what my heart was saying. What about this Sarah girl, why are you so adamant about her just being a friend?'

'She breaks my rules.'

'Who are the rules for, Adam, to protect you from them, or them from you?'

'I don't know what you mean.'

'Come on, since Annie, you have just tried to avoid any real commitments. The rules are just a shorthand way of you cutting ties when things get difficult.'

'Bit harsh, sis. On that subject, you know I have to ask?'

'No, Adam, I never had any idea. I was way too young and whatever you hear about Gaydar that's not the way it works. Annie may not have known herself until she met Karen. You don't get to pick who you fall in love with.' She opened the car door and took her bag out. She leaned back into the car and gave me a peck on the cheek. 'If this Sarah is the real thing, then take your time and don't screw it up.' With this she disappeared into the station concourse.

I made tracks back to the flat. When I was driving I noticed the message indicator on my phone, but I avoided picking it up until I was parked. There were three missed voicemails from Sarah. I could barely hear what she was saying as she was obviously crying her eyes out, but it was something about Misty and an accident. I tried to return the call, but got no answer. I texted her and immediately got a response.

TEXT: 'Elizabeth Street veterinary clinic, Belgravia. Please come.'

I was not sure where it was, but the quickest way to get there was to stay in the car and use the Satnav to find Elizabeth Street. I got an ETA of thirty-five minutes and texted back to Sarah to let her know I was on the way. When I got there it was the typical pig to park London on a Sunday evening. I found somewhere on a meter, rammed in some change, and looked for the clinic, which I eventually located at number 55. I walked in and immediately saw Sarah in the waiting room. She looked like she has just come from a war zone. There was dried blood on her jeans and jumper. Her hair was bedraggled and her face showed the evidence of a lot of crying. She had obviously managed to stop previously, but as soon as she saw me, the waterworks went back on and she erupted into sheets as she launched herself around my neck.

'Are you all right, you are covered in blood. What happened?'

'It's not mine, its Misty's,' she said though the sobs. I let her cry while I held her, very aware of the look I was getting from the receptionist behind the counter. When she had managed to regain composure a little, I gave her my handkerchief to wipe her eyes with and sat her down. I pulled up another chair and looked into her face.

'Tell me what happened.' I was holding her hand, it still had dried blood on it and it cracked like an old painting.

'I was taking Misty for a walk as usual this afternoon. I got outside the house and locked up. When I turned round, she had seen a squirrel across the road. She made a dash for it and then I saw the car. Oh, Adam, it was just like they say, I felt everything go into slow motion. The car was speeding and Misty didn't have a chance, she was flung over the bonnet and hit another car as she fell. The driver slowed down, saw me, and then sped off. He didn't even stop, the bastard. Who would do that?' Not wanting to get drawn into issues around the driver, I tried to steer the conversation back to Misty.

'What happened next, how badly hurt is Misty? How on earth did you get here?'

'Misty is pretty bad. They say she has a broken leg, but also some internal bleeding. That's what the vet is working on now. Adam, what am I going to do if anything happens to her? It's all my fault, she should have been on the lead.' Again I needed to get her to think about something else as this was not a healthy frame of mind.

'Sarah, look, the driver was going too fast. There is no way this is down to you. Misty is young and strong. She will pull through. Sorry to be curious, but I still wondered how you got here, did you carry her?'

'No, I got her out of the road, but I have insurance. This is her vet anyway and they have an ambulance service. That young lady costs me an arm and a leg to keep; I don't think you have any idea how expensive dogs are if you look after them properly.'

'Wow, I had no idea. On the positive side they know her here and can give her the best care. Have they given you any idea how long they will be?'

'The vet was just finishing up when you came in. They want to make her comfortable before I see her.'

'What, she won't come home tonight?'

'No, she will need to stay here for the next 2–3 days to make sure they have stopped the bleeding according to the nurse. She is still in danger and so she needs to have constant care.'

About five minutes later the vet came in and gave Sarah an update. He then led us both through to where Misty was in a 'doggie cot' for want of a better expression. She was still knocked out by the anaesthetic for her own good and she had a saline drip going into her side. Her paws were just limp on the cloth. Sarah started to cry again, but then pulled herself together and gently rubbed Misty's head. She thanked the vet and we left together. I took Sarah back to her place and walked her in to make sure she would be okay.

'Will you be all right here? And no, I am not trying to be forward, just offering to help.'

'Thanks, Adam, you have been a real mate, but Mum has offered to come over. She can be a real cow but she knows how to come through in a crisis. She will stay with me until Misty comes home'—with this she started to cry again—'or not.'

'Can I get you a drink before I go or would you like me to wait until she gets here?' Out of the darkness of the kitchen I heard a familiar voice.

'You can go now, young man, the situation is under control. I don't want you taking advantage of my daughter in her moment of distress.'

'Mum, stop it, Adam has been a brick.' She gave me a kiss on the cheek and a hug. 'Thank you. I will call you tomorrow with an update.'

We spoke through text quite a bit over the next few days. There was a tricky moment on the first night where they found Misty was still bleeding, but once that was sorted out, she made a very good recovery. By Thursday evening it was time to go and get her and I offered to drive as my car was big enough to lay Misty flat in the back. Sarah agreed and after work I picked Sarah up on the way. Her face was pale and drawn. I don't think she had had much sleep in the last few days.

'You look tired. I know you are worried about Misty, but at least she is now on the mend.'

'It's not just Misty. Remember, I have had three days with my mother. God that woman is wearing.' She managed the briefest of smiles.

'Glad to have you back.'

After we picked up Misty and got her back to the flat, the enormity of the recovery became plain. She was sporting a plaster cast on her leg, still had a bandage around her middle, and finally was wearing what the vet affectionately called *the cone of shame* which is that protective head gear they make recovering animals wear to stop them scratching. Misty really did looked ashamed and sorry for herself. Sarah made Misty as comfortable as possible in her bed which appeared to have a new lining in it for added comfort (now I think I understood the true cost of this dog). Her mother had since departed and Sarah offered me a glass of wine, but I declined due to the car. I settled for a coffee and a chat to keep her company.

'You got much on at work? You don't seem to have a lot of papers on your board. Or have you been unable to do much with your mother here?' I scanned around the room, and although she did not seem an untidy person the last time I was here, this was pristine. I had the feeling her mother had been working her hard.

'To be honest, with the vet's bill that is coming, work would be very nice. Even with the insurance, I still have to pay an excess and for the drugs. You remember Gary of course?' I nodded my head but did not comment. 'Well it's just as I feared. My commissions are almost non-existent since I said no to his advances. I am not a pauper because of the income from the tenants upstairs, but my finances are pretty low. What I earn, I burn on Misty if the truth be known.' She sat cross-legged on the sofa holding her wine glass and staring at Misty. Misty just lay on her side with eyes fixed on Sarah.

'What about exploring other avenues for your talent to make money? That caricature work you do, any thoughts on that?'

'It's really only Christmas and summer party work. The corporates are cutting back as well. You must hear the same things as me? I suppose that's why they are laying people off in your place. Any more word on your guys, have they found new roles?'

'Angie has managed to get something more junior elsewhere in the bank. But both Ralph and Bernard are going. I think it was something they had been expecting or in Ralph's case hoping for over a period of time. I just hope they don't get stuck looking for too long. Some of my friends have been out of work for over a year. Anyway, back to you, what about gallery work? Your pictures are great.'

'Adam, you're very sweet, but realism is not what they are looking for in galleries. You need shock and wow factors. They need to be a metaphor or make a statement. You need to be either weird, cross-dressing, or put your lover's names on camping equipment. That's not really me.'

'Okay, another agency then, there must be more than one?'

'There are loads, but like most industries, the communities are tight knit. There would be a lot of gossip as to why I would be changing and Gary may already be blackening my name.'

'Can you manage with all the expense of Misty?'

'Just. But I don't need anything else to go wrong right now.' Sarah was looking at Misty when she said this, but I think she was just avoiding me. I was sure that she was hiding something. I wondered just how close to sinking the ship her finances were. But it was not my place to pry.

'Well, yell if I can help in any way.'

'Adam, you keep helping and it is appreciated. Misty appreciates it too.'

'Okay, well I'd better make a move and let the patient get some sleep.'

My drive back to the flat took a while as traffic was heavy in the city and I had plenty of time to think. Sarah was someone I actually worried about, it was nice having a mate, but was it more? Beth had got inside my head and now she was busily rearranging the furniture. Maybe it was time to go and see her and Janice.

Chapter 31

Lady Madonna
26 February 2011

Sarah kept me fully up to date with the progress of Misty, and over the next few days, I went over to Pimlico to help her with walking the poor thing. She was okay to hobble along, but much happier when the vet allowed her to take the cone off. On the Wednesday at work I got a text from Sarah:

TEXT: 'I need a favour. Mother wants to have dinner.'
TEXT: 'It didn't end well last time you suggested this.'
TEXT: 'Pretty please. I am not sure I can face it on my own again.'
TEXT: 'Okay, when?'
TEXT: 'Tomorrow?'
TEXT: 'Okay, let me know where and when.'

As it was a Thursday night, I had to break it to Charlie and Gerry not to expect me for my regular weekly dinner. I knew I needed to make a bit of an effort with dressing up as Sarah's mother would be judging me from the moment I walked in the door. Things had not gone brilliantly on the couple of occasions I had met her so far. She certainly had an acerbic wit on her (or more accurately an acid and vitriolic tongue).

On Thursday morning I got a call from Sarah saying we were going to be eating at a restaurant in Marylebone called the Potting Shed. Her mother loved to eat at new places in London and she was planning to shop in Selfridges in the afternoon so the place was ideal. Due to this it was easier if I met them there according to Sarah, but as the agreed time approached I was regretting my choice of transport. I was now stuck on the Jubilee Line due to a failed tube in front of us. There is no coverage in the tunnels so I could not communicate with them to say I was going to be late. Anyone who travels in London regularly will be familiar with this. The tubes are at their best a marvellous way to move the masses around the city. However the system is so close to capacity at all times that it takes just one simple issue to really screw your journey up. Eventually we got moving, but now I was fifteen minutes' late, and even in February, it was pretty hot with the sheer volume of people in the carriage. Whatever time of year, the tunnels trap heat and the only real ventilation is the movement of the trains; if they are stopped in the tunnels, it is like being in an oven.

I had warned Sarah this was not my idea of fun. We are mates but in the past meals with partner's parents have been fraught with disaster. The biggest issue is that people seem to get ratty with those that work in banks. One particular guy, the father of my then girlfriend, was very vociferous in his indignation with my chosen industry. I tried to explain, but as this guy was already at retirement age (Katherine the lady in question was a few years older than me), apparently I was the antichrist by the way he went on. I, personally, and all my mates were responsible for his income dropping, his pension being worth nothing and all the ills of the modern consumer world. Honestly I was like the Dire Straits track 'Industrial Disease'; I was surprised I didn't get blamed for the paedophilia scandal in the Catholic Church and the state of childhood obesity. As you can tell that meal did not go well and it was one of the things that caused the lovely Katherine and myself to separate. She seemed to think that I stood up for myself a little too aggressively with respect to her elderly father. God knows how this was going to go tonight but I was already late and looking hot and sweaty.

Luckily, by the time I walked from the tube to the restaurant, the night air had cooled me down, so now I was just late (but that was bad enough). As I walked into the restaurant, I could see Sarah in the corner in what looked like a heated debate with her mother. I looked around the place and it was a marvel of space creation. It was located downstairs in the basement of the Dorset Square hotel and extended out in the vaults under the pavement. On the walls were cricketing memorabilia (we were only half a mile from Lords). I signalled to the waiter (or should that be umpire) that I knew where I was going and approached the table.

'So sorry about being late. Tube broke down in front of me. Couldn't text.'

'And that, my dear Sarah, is why I will not get on those infernal machines.'

'Mother, I swear you have come over all nineteenth century. Hi, Adam, no worries about being late, that sounds like a bitch of a journey.'

'Sarah, language.' I was now precisely aware of how this evening was going to go. Watching my Ps and Qs was going to be essential.

'Mother, may I introduce you to Adam. I know you've seen him at the flat before, but I think formal introductions are probably wise at this point. Adam, this is my mother Isobel.' Both ladies stood, I kissed Sarah on both cheeks and went to do the same to her mother but thought better of it and shook her hand.

'I'm glad,' I said. 'It was going to be embarrassing calling you Sarah's mum all night.'

'I have never been Sarah's mum, I am her mother. You can always use Mrs McKenzie if you want?' She withdrew her hand almost immediately; it was cold as ice. We all sat down and the waiter came over to see what I wanted to drink. By now the haughtiness of the old goat was starting to annoy me a little bit so rather than joining them in the wine (which looked delicious), I asked the waiter for a beer. There was a most definite look of disgust on Isobel's face, but Sarah was smiling at me. For a moment I was side-tracked by the decor. On the wall was a set of flowerpots that kept being randomly lit up. I finally realised they were spelling out quotes related to cricket. I became aware I was not saying anything and must have looked like an idiot staring at the wall on the other side of the restaurant.

'First things first, how is my favourite bitch.' I looked at Sarah to see if she reacted. I heard a slight gasp from Isobel.

'Misty is much better, thanks. The vet says the bandage can come off now. She has about five weeks to go with the plaster cast though so she will not be chasing squirrels in the near future.'

'Did they get the guy?'

'Strangely enough, the police have managed to catch him. He jumped a traffic camera just afterwards and they saw the dent on the car. They have charged him with driving away from an accident. It doesn't help Misty, but it might make him think twice next time.' Isobel was obviously bored with this conversation and after examining in the menu while we talked, she called over the waiter. We placed our orders and once the waiter had walked away, Isobel turned to me.

'So, Adam'—you would think the words were sticking in her mouth—'what is it you do when you are not chasing my daughter?'

'Mother, I asked you to behave.' As she said this, Sarah took a sip of wine and stared at her mother in annoyance.

'It's okay, Sarah, I am a big boy. When I am not being chased by your daughter, I am employed by a bank.'

'What you work behind a counter?' Honestly I swear that this woman could sneer to a level of professionalism I have rarely seen.

'No, global investment bank type. You know traders shouting buy, buy, buy. Not that I do that myself, but I work for a large Swiss bank in the city.' The sneer most definitely dropped away.

'Oh, well, that is very different. One has to be protective of one's children you know. Poor Sarah was treated terribly by the last buffoon.' Poor Sarah was of course going redder as each moment passed. 'Jilted her at the altar, well almost.' Isobel looked like she was getting into her flow now and turned her chair slightly to allow herself to face me. 'She was a broken woman you know. I feel I have to keep an eye out for her now.'

'Oh I don't know about that, Isobel'—I don't think she liked being called that—'I think she is rather capable of looking after herself. She has obviously managed to keep me at bay so far.'

'Eh, hello. I am here and not mute. I can speak for myself.' Sarah was a little indignant that she was being spoken about like property. 'Mother, Adam and I have a very nice friendship. He has been really good in supporting me when I was ill and over Misty's accident as well you know. Adam, will you stop playing up for my mother and try and be your normal self? It only encourages her.' With her piece said, Sarah took another drink and went off to powder her nose (or do whatever it is that takes ages to do in the bathroom).

'She can be rather headstrong when she wants to be.' Isobel looked annoyed at the outburst.

'Come on, Isobel, she has a point. We are just mates, I'm not chasing her and we shouldn't argue over her like a pair of carrion crows. How about we agree to behave for the rest of the meal to let her relax a little? It has been really stressful for her lately what with Misty and not having much work on.'

'I think I can agree that; a truce it is. I know I can upset her sometimes, but a mother worries you know. Another thing, before she comes back, why are you not interested in her?'

'Honestly, my sister asked me the same thing a little while ago and I really can't say. I actually like her and get on with her. She is great company and it's fun to have someone to do things with. Maybe that is enough or maybe if we take it any further I am worried it will all go wrong.'

'If you are not careful, someone else might beat you to the treasure.'

'Since she is coming back I guess we had better change the subject.' Sarah approached the table with a renewed glow on her face. She had put on some more lipstick and brushed her hair. Sometimes I forget that she is such a good-looking lady. 'Hey you, just in time for the mains. I'm happy to say peace has broken out so we can have a bit of lighter conversation from now on.' The waiter deposited the plates and played around with condiments and water for a few moments. We ate in silence for about a minute before Isobel broke in.

'So, Adam, Sarah tells me you have a place in the East End. Is it anywhere near the stadium?'

'Yes, about three miles away, I get a great view of the construction works. It is starting to look like we might put on a good games. The only sticking point is the transport system and after tonight's little debacle it is still a concern.'

'There is not a lot that can be done about that though, is there?'

'We are being asked to make plans to work from home or from our disaster recovery sites. For me it's not too bad, I could use a bike if I wanted, I just choose not to. The last thing I want to do is be that vulnerable on London streets, especially when you have nutters driving around like the one who hit Misty. Is anything happening with your agency, Sarah?'

'We are pretty much all home workers unless we go to pick up a piece so no change really. With the lack of work recently, I am not sure how much it will impact me.'

'You didn't say you were short of work, Sarah darling. Is there a problem?' Sarah looked sheepishly at me and made it clear with her eyes that this was not up for discussion.

'I'm afraid it's the same all over, Isobel. We are laying people off at the moment. In fact I would go as far as to say I can't remember any time in the last ten years, since the Millennium boom, that we have not been cutting numbers. We either give the work to other companies for less or shift it offshore to somewhere cheaper.'

'I do so dislike these telephone call centres. One cannot understand a word they are saying. It is so frustrating. But I thought according to the news they were bringing some back to England?'

'What they do bring back will just be phone support for language. We are offshoring technical roles and they will never come back. The knock on effect of all this downturn hits other industries like Sarah's I guess.' Sarah reached across and squeezed my hand, while her mother looked on suspiciously.

'Thanks, Adam, I don't think you could explain it any better.' With that the subject seemed closed but I am not sure if Isobel was suspicious or not. The rest of the meal passed off without a hitch and the conversation remained light. Once the prickly armour was off, Isobel could be quite funny and charming and Sarah got more and more relaxed as the evening progressed (that's relaxed not sloshed by the way).

When the time came for us to leave, the ladies' coats were collected from the cloak room and I walked outside to hail them a cab. As I flagged one down and it stopped, I kissed Sarah's cheek and went to shake Isobel's hand. At this point she presented her cheek to me and I did the double kiss routine having now won acceptance, if not yet approval. As they drove off, I started to walk to the tube station. By the time I came above ground again, some thirty-five minutes later there was a text waiting for me.

TEXT: 'She likes you. Thank you.'

Chapter 32

Here Comes the Sun
05 March 2011

March began well with a two nil victory at home against Notts County although it was not really what you would call a good match, more gruelling and ground out. There was a bit of warmth in the air but the pitch was still cutting up badly from all the flooding of February and it seemed to be the main topic of conversation in the Birkbeck after the match. The talk of the Olympic stadium being used as our home ground was on the increase. Every divot in the pitch appeared to be reaffirming the issue. It was good to feel the sun on our backs despite the cold wind. It had been a tough winter and the signs of spring were just beginning to show. As we were in a good mood post victory, we slipped into a third pint, more than we usually consumed post-match.

'You not in a hurry to go dog walking? By this point in the afternoon you're normally looking at your watch.' Gerry was playing the usual game of multi-tasking, talking to me while scanning the results page on the TV in the pub. It was getting to that point in the season where the threat of promotion or demotion was looming.

'She seems to be busy at the moment. I have texted a couple of times, but she's simply not available. Would be good if she had some work on, she seemed to be skint all the time.' Gerry turned to me and stopped looking at the screen.

'Working on a Saturday afternoon? Are you innocent or simply naive? She's got someone new, mate, and your services are no longer required. You've been replaced.' And with that he had pointed out the obvious that I had not even considered. We are not an item; she is free to go out with anyone. I am just surprised she had not said something. Maybe it was early days and she was just seeing how things panned out.

'You could be right, but since we are only mates, then it's not really any of my business, is it.' But then why all of a sudden did I feel sick in my stomach. I was pretty sure it was not the beer.

'If you're just mates, how come you look like you have just found a penny and lost a pound? You stupid sod. Charlie and I were chatting about it. You have been going out with her in all but name for weeks now. You do loads of things together, often around that dog. Then you politely peck her on the cheek and say good night. Then you act all surprised and wonder why she has gone off with someone else? That boat, my friend, has sailed.'

'You don't know that, you are just guessing.' But unfortunately Gerry's comments had hit home. It made sense. Vague comments on texts, no emails, not being available for a walk with Misty. I was just so dumb. Bloody Gerry was right as well, which also didn't help. I had spent a lot of time focused on Sarah. It was easy and simple. I had not had a date since I met her and wasn't bothered. I had not actually put two and two together, just bundled along without giving it enough thought. 'I'll text her and ask to meet later. Then I will ask her outright.'

'Go on then, I bet she blows you out, and not in the way that you hoped.'

'That is not helping, Gerry.'

TEXT: 'Fancy dinner this evening, or walk tomorrow?'

'There, it's done. She will come back sometime later and I will end up going over tomorrow and walking Misty. Then I'll have a chat with her about this.'

'She will be busy, stop kidding yourself.' The phone vibrated with a new text. Gerry made a grab for my phone but I managed to keep hold of it and I looked at the screen.

TEXT: 'Sorry, busy all weekend.'

TEXT: 'Work or bloke?'

TEXT: 'I said I am busy, Adam. Sorry.'

And there it was, Gerry was right and I felt like someone had kicked me in the teeth. I am not sure why I had not seen this coming. I quickly finished my pint and made my excuses to Gerry. He for once decided not to take the Michael as he could see I was in a mood. I set off for the tube, but while I was walking there, I thought I would at least make use of the rest of my weekend. I sent a text to Beth asking if she fancied lunch tomorrow. I could meet Janice, get my head away from London and Sarah. About twenty minutes later I got a response from Beth agreeing and suggesting a pub for me to find near them. When I got to the flat, I looked it up in the Satnav. It would take me about an hour and a half. I sent an acknowledgement and agreed to meet them at one o'clock.

❦

It would be fair to say I did not sleep well. I wrote a number of stroppy texts to Sarah, which of course I did not send and deleted immediately. I had stopped drinking after the third pint with Gerry as I knew that getting maudlin was a bad idea. I got up early on Sunday morning and collected the paper to read with my coffee and toast. No point overdoing it as I knew the sort of pub we were going to would be good old-fashioned Sunday roast with all the trimmings. I had a brief text exchange with both Charlie and Beth. Charlie was making sure I was all right (I did mention they were my best friends) as I guess she and Gerry had talked the previous night. She had offered me lunch but I mentioned I was going to see Beth. Beth on the other hand was new to this entire *brother being interested in talking to her* stuff and simply texted to confirm we were still on for lunch. I let her know my ETA and left it at that.

The drive was pretty uneventful (as the North Circular and the M1 goes, that could mean anything less than a full-on road-rage incident) and I arrived pretty much bang on time, although I do suspect Satnav manufacturers employ a few comedians in their ranks. There always seems to be one road which you can't enter due to it becoming one-way or being closed for some building work. I knew that Beth was very green but I suspected she would at least have a car, but had no way of knowing if they had arrived. I walked in and looked around; I saw Beth sitting at a nice corner table over the back of the room with a very pretty and extremely petite blond girl. It brought to mind the image of a pixie. I was about to start looking for mushrooms when Beth saw me and beckoned me over.

'Brother dear, this is Janice. Janice, this is Adam, my prodigal brother.' I kissed both on the cheeks in greeting. Whatever was going on between the two of them, it must be really good and as they both literally appeared to shine. They were completely relaxed and looked incredibly comfortable with each other. I can't remember ever having seen Beth look like this.

'A pleasure to meet you. I would like to say I have heard all about you, but my wonderful sister has not mentioned a thing.' I took my seat and glanced at the menu.

'Well let the interrogations begin,' Janice said in a lilting way that was not at all in line with my idea of interrogation. It turned out that she worked in a library, although she did not look like the librarians you probably remember from the films of our youth. She did a lot of work as an archivist and performed some research for the local university. At 31 she was just a little younger than Beth. When I had got as much as I could out of direct questions that I could without being rude, I asked how long they had been together.

'We've known each other for about six months. We met through a mutual friend at a party. We had both been single for a while and hit it off as soon as we met. We did a couple of movies together and then just after Christmas we sat down and had a proper talk. We had missed each other a lot while Beth was at your parents' and we realised we had fallen for each other. Well that's the simple version, but you get the picture.'

'That sounds nice. It might also explain why Beth was a bit uppity at Christmas, she was obviously missing you too. And was that the gift you brought but didn't open? Mum mentioned that to me.' With this Beth scowled at me but also squeezed Janice's hand. 'Are you going to move in together at some point?'

'Ever the practical, Adam. Brother dear, Janice moved into my place a month ago. We are really happy and didn't see the point in waiting any longer.'

'Wow.' I'm not sure, but I think I felt a pang of jealousy. I was really pleased for Beth but I was also thinking about my own situation. 'I am really pleased for you both.' The food had now arrived and we were tucking into three plates of roast beef and Yorkshire pudding. Janice had a second glass of wine, but Beth and I were making our Cokes last (there is nothing worse than driving to a pub, is there?). I know there is alcohol-free beer option, but frankly it tastes disgusting.

'So, Adam, what's your news? Lunch today was all very last minute, not that I am complaining at seeing you though. Anything to tell us? I was looking to see if you had brought anyone with you. How is the Sarah thing going?'

'It's not. We appear to have hit a bump in the road. She is busy all weekend and not able to see me. The texts over the last week have been very vague. Gerry thinks she has another bloke.'

'You mean "a" bloke, Adam. Unless you have talked to her and made it clear what you want, you are just a friend.' She held up her hand to quell me. 'Your words, Adam, not mine. "*We're just mates*", that's what you said. Maybe she wanted more, did you ask her?'

'We had a great friendship, maybe I didn't want to spoil it. I told you her dog Misty got knocked down, right? Well I was a mate and helped out with the walks and the vet visits.'

'And did you tell her what you said to me at the station? You said you actually cared about her. Please don't tell me there is one of your bloody rules that stop you being able to say how you feel?'

'Beth, you are being a rough on the poor lad. He looks in shock.' Janice was staring at Beth and pleading with her eyes to turn it down a bit.

'Sorry, Adam, but you are you own worst enemy. You know you felt it was more than friends and now it looks like you may have screwed up the opportunity.'

'Let's be clear, I don't know if she has a bloke. We are making assumptions here.'

'Well then I suggest you find out and soon. If she has not, then tell her how you feel.' We finished off the meal if not exactly in silence, but with little more than pleasantries. I was thinking about how to find out the score with Sarah, as I got up to leave after paying the bill and thanked them both.

'It was really nice to meet you, Janice. It's fabulous to see Beth looking happier than I can remember. Whatever you are doing, I suggest you keep doing it.' I went to kiss them goodbye and they both gave me huge hugs. I wondered that if one door closes in my life, another one truly does open. Seeing them there together made me think momentarily of Annie and I wondered if she was happy. Yes, my pride was dented when she ran off with another woman, but as Beth said, you can't pick who you fall in love with.

<hr>

Never drive if you have something weighty on your mind. I spent the journey home going over the whole situation and frankly it did nothing for my concentration. I missed one turning altogether and ended up stuck in a back double around Wembley; I suggest you don't do this yourself. When I got back to my flat, I resolved to find out one way or another. I would send one more text and see if she would respond.

TEXT: 'Sarah, I need to know the score, why are you avoiding me?'

I got the ironing board out (oh, the practicalities of single life) to sort out my shirts for the week. I was halfway through Wednesday when my phone beeped. I finished the shirt (as I am not a complete heathen) and picked up the phone.

TEXT: 'I am now seeing Gary. He does not want me to see you anymore.'

And there it was. In as close to black-and-white as a mobile will allow. Sarah and I were apparently through as mates.

Chapter 33

Secret Lives
10 April 2011

I would be the first to say that March dragged. The initial signs of an early spring were dashed by a return of the rain and even a cold snap that threatened snow (and the football was correspondingly poor). I said before that God must be a DJ, but I now suspect he (or she) is a weatherman. The weather matched my mood. I was not really willing to admit quite how much I missed hanging around with Sarah. I needed to use the aforementioned phrase as Beth was right, we were not going out. Charlie and Gerry were great as ever but there was a certain amount of walking on eggshells going on. You know things are bad when your mate's wife doesn't try and set you up on a blind date for a change.

I did see someone a couple of times for a drink and movie, a really nice chartered accountant called Zoe. I met her through a wine and cheese social night at one of the local wine bars. I'm not convinced if I would have found her more appealing prior to having met Sarah, but I know that I kept comparing them in my head. She was quite funny, quite good looking, and quite intelligent, but there was no acerbic wit or sarcasm. I am now mimicking the action of a widow (see rule 13) in that anyone new is likely to be compared with Sarah. The reason I won't date widows is that on the two occasions I have met them, they spent the evening wistfully remembering their now dead partner to a point at which no living human could compete. On the second occasion, I felt like we could have set the table for three at dinner it was so bad (I was tempted to ask him to pass the salt at one point). I swear if I ever do this again, I will take a bell, book, and candle with me. Anyway (I have let the level of embellishment distract me, apologies), getting back to Sarah. I don't think Zoe stood a chance against the image I was now holding for my friend who was not so much dead as Missing in Action (what a quaint military euphemism that is). On the third date, or rather on the attempt for Zoe to set up a third date, I cried off and simply said it was not working. She was upset but frankly not that surprised. Apparently, I had no fizz in me (she made me sound like a defective Alka-Seltzer).

I had also been hitting the booze a bit, I had the final parting drinks with Angie (off to pastures new internally, but still a good excuse for a leaving drink), Ralph, and Bernard. Amazingly the recalcitrant pair had both landed contract jobs, one at each of our Swiss competitors, so the drinks were more of a celebration than a wake. It is something to get a package and then walk straight into a new role, it helps reduce the mortgage or buy a new car (or so I am told).

I had seen Drew's band play again and he was on a high as they had actually made a single and video which was up on YouTube. It was okay, but frankly never going to be more than a bit of fun. This evening, as it is Sunday, I find myself unwinding before the week at work begins again. I had a very healthy lunch with Gerry and the family and then I may have imbibed a few more cheeky pints on the way home over a game of pool or two in the local boozer. I'm slightly woozy and wobbly and the worst thing in the world is going to happen in about four sentences. I should create myself a rule for not using the phone when drunk. I did think about inventing an app for a mobile phone that would breathalyse you before you could use it, but apparently it would never sell according to my friends. Here we go then; I scroll through the call log on my phone and find a number that has no name against it (I deleted Sarah's contact). I know the date of the last text, so I know it's her.

TEXT: 'So how is the world of Sarah and Gary? Woof to the pup.'

I did not expect to get a response, and after I had sent it, I sat there and stared at the phone thinking *You complete and utter berk, why did you do that?* But the thing about cats and pigeons is that they are rarely easy to separate once entangled. If, dear reader, you are now expecting her to respond immediately, then all I can say is behave! Life does not work like that. I turned off the lights and went to bed with a pint of water and two Paracetamol (pre-emptive strike against my hangover in the making).

⁂

Monday morning was bright, so it's lucky that one of us was. I'm not saying the pills and water had not helped, but I looked and felt like crap. The last month had seen me let a few things slip and so I decided to get back to the gym and try a bit of detoxing this week. Mind you, who doesn't say that when they have a hangover and a *head like a robber's dog* as my old man would say?

I was still first into the office and immediately got to work on the mundane and the minutiae of the modern world of banking. I wonder sometimes if we really do hire clowns or if the unfortunate humour is just a secondary consequence of the way things happen in the real world. Sometimes when I read the missives from my colleagues in other time zones (non-English-speaking, but don't accuse me of xenophobia), I think they have been randomly put through Google translate and back just for fun. I now see how wars might begin.

The rest of the motley crew emerged; we should have now been a team of six rather than nine, but somehow we had collected a new contractor (so more money, but easier to dump). I never failed to be amused by the way these things happen. By mid-morning there was a good buzz about the office and work was busy but not overloaded. Having done a round of extremely high-priced coffees from the canteen (sorry, staff restaurant, they get so precious), I returned to my desk to see an email from *misty.she-wolf@gmail.com*; now this I was not expecting.

Rules for a Born Again Bachelor

From: *misty.she-wolf@gmail.com*
Subject: Blast from the past

Did your phone malfunction in some way last night? I got a cryptic text. Misty says woof back. Gary however does not say hi. In fact Gary does not say anything as he is not part of my life any more. I am sorry for the way I acted, I shouldn't ask, but if you fancy a chat sometime, just yell.

Well I am no fool and I was not simply going to reply and make it look like I was desperate. I needed to show her exactly who she was dealing with. I must have taken at least twenty or thirty seconds before I started to write a response.

To: *misty.she-wolf@gmail.com*
Subject: New Rule Alert

My phone is working fine, I just happened to come across your number in an alcoholic state. Maybe fate simply smiled for once. I have a new rule to tell you about if you fancy a laugh. One of my colleagues tried speed dating; it's a cracker as they say. Let me know, I could do Wednesday (or are you having the same feeling of déjà vu I am having right now?).

The fairly rapid response stated that Sarah was planning to cook and I should be over there about seven thirty. Now, you have been privy to all this, what should I do? What would you do? I opted for playing it cool, but to be honest that didn't work so well last time. All I knew was that I was sitting in the office with a stupid smile on my face and I realised my heart was beating just a touch faster.

I turned up pretty much on time with a bottle of wine, flowers, and a dog chew (I still needed to keep Misty on my side). It was great to see her run to the door (Misty, focus!) as the plaster cast was off her leg and she looked like she was back to her old self (apart from a sizeable nick out of her ear). I gave Sarah a kiss on the cheek, but she stopped and gave me a big hug.

'You look well,' I said, thinking, *Oh my, what a charmer, please try harder.* She looked pretty amazing if I am honest, but she was also a little sheepish.

'Come in and have a drink, we have some catching up to do.' We walked through to the kitchen where she had something bubbling on the stove (it looked like pasta and a meat sauce, beyond that I am not an expert at that distance). She handed me a glass of red and turned the cooker down.

'Let's grab a seat; this won't be ready for at least twenty minutes.' We moved through to the lounge and sat together on the sofa facing each other. She drew her feet up to her chest and wrapped her arms around them. 'I suppose we should talk about Gary before you start talking about your dating activities?'

'Tell me if you want to, I'm not going to push. The only thing I would say is that I was disappointed by the way you told me, or in fact didn't until I pushed. You just sort of avoided me.'

'I am so sorry.' She reached forward and squeezed my arm. 'Gary turned up one day sober with flowers and said he missed me. He wanted to make a go of it. When I told him what I was doing with my time and how much you had helped, he got more and more annoyed about you. He basically said if we were going to make a go of it, I had to stop seeing you. After a few days of him saying this, I agreed. It was really good for a couple of weeks. I got a bit more work suddenly and then he became distant again. I found out from another girl at the agency, he was still seeing other women. Two weeks ago I confronted him and we had a really bitter row. I threw him out. I then made steps to move to another agency who already have given me more work than I have had in the past four months. That's not the worst bit though.'

'Which is?'

'I felt really bad about the way I have acted with you as you had been a really good mate, but I could not contact you as you might still be mad with me. When you texted the other night, drunk or not, I was so happy. I left it until the next day to make sure you didn't send any retraction when sober and then emailed you at work. I am so pleased to see my mate back. Anyway what's this about a new rule, what went wrong this time?' And there it was, the story was out there and she seemed to relax. I could tell it had been eating away at her, but I was not yet ready to share the impact it had on me. Once bitten and all that.

'Just to correct you, it's not about me dating but a mate. I did have a couple of drinks with a lady a couple of weeks ago, but no other dating. I have however been drinking out with the boys a bit and there was some sharing of stories.'

'Oh I bet you have had a field day over this heartless bitch.' She pulled her legs in tighter to her chest once more.

'Charlie, Gerry, and my sister are the only ones that know. All they were worried about was me. You came out smelling of roses, don't worry.' With this she looked more curious than anything, but I was not about to elaborate. 'So anyway, I was in the pub with Ralph one day and he had one of his drinking buddies with him, a guy called Nigel. Well this Nigel had done some speed dating.'

'A couple of my girlfriends have tried it, they were not impressed.'

'He said it was like a cattle market. Like the worst singles club you have ever been to, but without the music and with people trying too sickeningly hard to impress you.'

'The ones my girlfriends went to had the added bonus of being packages including drinks. This meant that at least half of the people there simply got drunk and one girl was almost speechless by the time she spoke to the fifteenth person. The blokes were mostly losers and the girls were desperate. Why on earth would you date someone after five minutes of talking?'

'Yeah, you're right. We must have spoken for at least ten in Pimlico that night.' I glanced across to see here expression to see her smiling while her hand slapped me playfully on the leg.

'We are not dating.' She stopped mid-sentence and looked down at her feet. After a few seconds (and no, I was not going to help her dig out of the hole this time), she looked up. 'So does this rule have a number?'

'I am going with number 25.'

'Christ, how many are there, you never said?'

'Twenty-six at the moment.'

'So what other odd forms of dating have you tried? What about online dating?'

'Rule 8, that's old school.'

'Okay, I have my opinions on it, but what are your objections?'

'When did you ever meet someone from the internet that was legal, decent, and truthful? I cannot remember meeting someone either online or in person after hooking up with them who actually looked like their picture. Their interests don't match what they say. Mostly it appears to be people looking for uncomplicated sex with people they only meet in the ether. Also, I met a lot of psychos and damaged people. I deleted my profile and vowed never to go near those things again.' Sarah walked out to the kitchen and turned the food off. She walked back in with the bottle.

'The food is ready. I have to admit I could not agree with you more on this. I ended up over a one-year period with a series of guys who just wanted one thing and it was not deep and meaningful unless you mean getting deep into my knickers.' We walked through to the kitchen and I pulled up a chair to the table. Sarah had laid it with candles and she turned off the kitchen light once she had served out the food. She raised her glass and chinked mine.

'To new beginnings.'

'To new beginnings,' I echoed.

Chapter 34

Do You Know (Where You're Going To)?
15 April 2011

The level of text messaging and emails have returned to a pre-Gary level, which is nice. I appeared to have my mate back. Oh you fool, I can hear you saying, have you learned nothing from this? Well you have a point (you as the reader either exists, or I have mild schizophrenia). Getting back to the plot then, I'm aware that my laissez-faire attitude previously did not work well. I needed to see where this was going and what her thoughts were. The way she stopped mid-sentence the last time we talked made me think she too was considering things on a more long-term scale.

Sitting in the office on Friday, its mid-morning and I'm thinking of the weekend ahead. Leyton had a poor nil-nil score draw on Tuesday night and we are away to Exeter at the weekend so I'm free. I feel I should try and get some time with Sarah to talk properly. I text her to see if she is available tonight or for *walkies* in the morning (oh how we miss the irrepressible Barbara Woodhouse). Within ten minutes we have agreed to meet for a drink later in the Marquis and plan some weekend activities. I got talked into a rather impromptu Friday lunchtime pint with Drew down on the Wharf, which turns into two. It's quite unusual but he wants to fill me in on the band and where it is going (he can't really talk about it in the office). When we return, I'm suitably emboldened for the evening ahead and I rush through the rest of the paperwork to clear things down before the weekend.

I arrive at the Marquis on time and see Sarah walking up towards me. She has Misty with her and I look to see if there is any outside seating free as this pub is not one for dogs.

'Sorry, Misty needed a walk; we can always find somewhere else if this place won't let her in?' She reached me and gave me a kiss on the cheek, and as usual I bent down to make a fuss of Misty who was noticeably more pup like since she had fully recovered and got her leg back to normal.

'Let's walk and talk and see what we can find.' With this we headed off towards the river as it is the best place around this part of London to walk and it has wide-enough pavements for the pup. When we had been walking for a few minutes and talking about her day (she really had hit a rich stream of work with the new agency, hence why she has not had time to walk Misty), I decided it was time for something a bit more intense. 'Can I ask you a serious question?'

'You always ask me serious questions. You know, wine or beer? Meat or Fish? Are you free for a walk?' She was avoiding and she damned well knew it.

'Where are we going?' We stopped, looked out over the river which was flowing fast. There was a serious spring tide, so the level was high.

'East towards Westminster?' She chuckled at her own joke just a little too vociferously.

'Do you want to talk or simply avoid the question?' I turned to her and looked straight into her eyes. Misty was pulling at the lead to walk on, but Sarah pulled her back and got her to sit.

'Oh, that question. Is it important?'

'Answering a question with a question is just another way of avoiding. Okay, let me be frank.' I held my hand up to stop her. 'This is not a comedy routine.' She bowed and swung her hand across her body to show deference. 'Are we mates or more?'

'Don't you like being mates? I thought you were happy with that? When we first met, you just wanted a drinking partner.'

'And in the time I knew you up until you disappeared off with Gary, I had not dated anyone.'

'Well neither had I.'

'Exactly. When you went off with Gary, I was hurt.'

'You mean jealous or possessive?'

'Don't play games, I am being serious. Charlie, Gerry, Beth, they all know I care about you and they also know that we need to work out where we are heading.' She stifled a laugh as she looked back down the river.

'You know you are actually quite attractive with the combination of serious and pomp. I missed you too, but I went out with Gary as you were continually making it clear you wanted to be just mates.'

'Well what if I am saying different now? What if I am saying I want a relationship with you? That I care about you and I think you care about me.' Misty was now looking bored and a trifle confused with whether we were walking or not walking. Sarah moved towards me and gave me a kiss, but for once not on the cheek. I was about to respond when she was dragged away by a now-agitated German shepherd. 'We could do with continuing this conversation without the matchmaking skills of that mutt.'

'We come as a package and don't you forget it.' I could not help but notice there was a definite bounce in her walk.

'I wouldn't have it any other way. So tomorrow, what about a proper date. Early evening drink and dinner?'

'Okay, but bearing in mind the last time few times that we've eaten out, I was skint, so I'm paying. I am now back to being a woman of means. Any ideas where?' I looked down the river and the site that met me gave me all I needed. Almost straight across from us was the MI6 building and that got me thinking of James Bond and surveillance. So where was the best view point in the city that was easily accessible to the public—genius.

'Yes, leave it to me. I'll book it all and tell you where to meet me tomorrow afternoon.'

'Oh, a mystery man. How exciting; will you be wearing a mask like Zorro?' I let that go as we walked off down the river.

❦

My quite brilliant idea (well I thought it was brilliant) was that a great way to start a date would be a ride on the London Eye to see the city we both lived in and loved, followed by a meal in the Archduke at Waterloo, a fabulous restaurant built into the arches at Waterloo station. They often had live jazz on a Saturday night and so during the day I booked a table for two and the tickets for the Eye. I asked Sarah to meet me at Westminster Tube station at six o'clock so we could have a walk and she would not guess where we were going.

When she arrived, I could see she had made even more of an effort than normal as she looked stunning (or maybe the scales were falling from my eyes). She was wearing a tight-fitting red dress and a long coat with knee-length leather boots (another pair, this was getting interesting, note to self to check her wardrobe out). I guess she was going for sexy but practical, I love the way this girl thinks. However, she was now taller than me, but that is not one of those things that bother me. I waved to her when she came out of the tube and walked up to kiss her.

'Easy, tiger, watch the lip gloss.' She offered a cheek and I duly pecked at it, but then I gave her a warm hug and she squeezed me back. 'Careful, leave some breath inside. I'm finding it hard to come by tonight. Is this it? Are we going to the Houses of Parliament?' She looked up at the St Stephen's tower (not Big Ben, that's the bell as you damned well know!). I led her by the hand towards the bridge and the south side of the Thames. 'I hope we are not trekking here, these boots are practical, but route marches will not be ideal.'

'And from where I am standing, they are worth it. You look amazing.' When I looked, I am not sure, but I swear she was blushing, but it could have been the dress reflected in her skin. 'We haven't got too far to go, about a ten-minute walk. Then the restaurant is booked for seven thirty.'

'Why so late?'

'We have a little journey to take first.'

When we arrived at the London Eye, she looked up and then looked at me.

'This is really weird, but in a wonderful way. Have you got tickets? It is one of those things that I am always saying I will go on one day, but never get around to. How cool. What do we do, queue?'

'I got us priority tickets and a glass of champagne.' It's not often you hear a girl squeal. I'm not sure if that is a good or a bad thing, but she looked very happy. We got into the very short priority queue, and just as we were about to get into the cab, a nice young lady handed us two glasses (yes, glass not plastic) of very nice cold bubbly. Have you been on the Eye? It's a bit of a weird thing. You don't really ever stop, it just moves slowly and you board as it moves past you. A very strange thing when you first do it. You then enter into a glass capsule which is egg-shaped, about sixteen feet wide and about eight feet deep. It normally takes about half an hour to do a rotation and you get to see an amazing view of the London skyline (which gets more spectacular every year). Every new Norman Foster edifice makes the night sky look more like Manhattan or LA. The capsule normally has room for about sixteen to twenty people, but for some strange reason (maybe the time of night), we were alone. We were enjoying our champagne, which with a bit of luck should last the length of the ride, but when we got to the top and started to descend, I noticed Sarah's glass was empty. I was pointing out some landmarks trying hard to impress.

'Sorry, I drank that a bit fast. It's amazing up here. The view is so cool and you would hardly know we were moving.'

'Yes, it's very smooth.' And then I noticed it. It was not so much smooth as stalled. We had for some reason stopped about a third of the way down the rotation at about two o'clock. 'We seemed to have stopped. Maybe there's a problem getting someone on, they sometimes do different things for disabled parties when they board. I'm sure it will just be a minute.' We continued to look at various buildings in our eye line, but after five more minutes, there was an announcement over the public address system; we had broken down.

'There are worse places to be stranded,' Sarah offered to be helpful.

'Yes, the view is great. I just hope they are not too long as we have a table booked.' I looked at my watch and saw that is was now seven twenty, our table would be ready in ten minutes. We sat down on one of the chairs in the middle of the cabin and she put her arm around me and her head on my shoulder.

'Thank you for this; it's such a romantic thing to do.' She turned my head and kissed me slowly.

'What about the lipstick?'

'Oh, that all went on the champagne glass. Besides, you do all this and you deserve a kiss.'

'I must try harder next time.'

'Down, boy, let's take our time.' We sat there in each other's arms watching the city change from day to night with the occasional update from the control room. It took an hour, but it seemed like just a few minutes. We did not discuss the state of world politics or sport, world hunger, or human rights, just small talk in a small place but with the biggest view on the world. By the time we got to the ground, it was eight fifteen. We walked to the Archduke, but just as I feared, the table had gone (I had phoned from the capsule, but they did not pick up). There was no way they would hold it for an hour. They were very apologetic and suggested a couple of places on the riverside. God, however, was having fun with the weather controls. The clear sky of an hour ago had been replaced by dark and brooding mess above us. What was it with this girl and storms (after the night at the Elephant Royale, I think I might have been dating Storm from the X-Men)? As we walked towards the river and the suggested places to eat, the heavens opened and it felt like the rain of a month hit us in a minute. Her hair was soaked, her feet squelched in the boots, and the dress clung to her like in a way that was far too revealing for a restaurant.

'Are you still okay to eat or do I need to get you home?'

'I am not that easy, Captain. Seriously though I am not going to sit in a restaurant soaked like this. Can you take me back to my place, I'll get dry and we can order a takeaway. This was lovely, but after being in these boots for a few hours and being soaked to the skin, I think I have had enough of dating for one night.' We began to walk in the direction of a tube station, but when I saw a cab, I hailed it and directed it to Sarah's place.

'Do you want to try it again? I really had fun tonight, ignoring the obvious issues.'

'Stop worrying, Adam. You can't control the weather or the London Eye, but you did a lovely thing with the planning. I am really touched. Of course we will do it again. We are going out, right?'

'Okay, because I wondered what you were doing at Easter?'

'Next weekend, why?'

'I wondered if you fancied coming down to meet my parents.' It went quiet in the cab for a moment. She then snuggled in to me (dripping wet).

'Adam, you have already met my mother. It would be a pleasure to meet your family.'

'Hold that thought, you might change your mind when you do!'

Chapter 35

Easter Parade
24 April 2011

Life is about compromise; I'm not sure where I first heard this, if I were an Oxford Don I would probably quote Thomas Aquinas, and if I were a theologian I might mention St Paul's letters to the Romans. In the end, it is more likely to be Burt Bacharach lyrics (I have mentioned my obsessions with these things in the past). So where was I intending to compromise? Well, you may or may not remember that the ugly subject of sex has yet to raise its head (excuse the pun) where the delightful Sarah is concerned. We have been together now for nearly a week and mates for almost five months, apart from a small Gary-based sojourn quite recently. But after every walk, drink, or date, we have always ended up in our own beds and this is not a pattern we are looking to change in a hurry (trust me, I actually like the girl and I am learning that rushing this is not a good idea).

So where, I hear you say, is the compromise in this? It comes in the form of going to see my parents for Easter. Sarah has agreed to come with me, but we have also agreed that it will just be for the day. I will pick her up early on Easter Sunday and I will drive down for lunch and to meet the folks. The other compromise is that we need to take Misty as Sarah does not like to leave her alone for too long, which I fully agree with. All I hope now is that she doesn't get car sick (yes, you have guessed it, Misty again). I said I used to have a dog when I was growing up, a lovely little mongrel called Fidget. Well Fidget could not go two hundred yards in a car before producing more vomit than I believe could possibly fit within his tiny body. I was hoping not to have to repeat this experience with Misty.

Mum sounded excited about meeting someone new, as she had not interacted with any ladies of my acquaintance since Annie (someone as you can probably guess she still has a very low opinion about). We chatted on the phone when I told her I was bringing Sarah and she seemed to know a lot more about this lady than I would have expected. I suspect my sister has been keeping her in the loop. The other thing about chatting to Mum more recently has been the transformation I can detect now that she is getting some help. It took me two weeks of calls (getting more irritated each time) in order to get her the support she needed for her and Dad through social services. They get help cleaning and a few pieces of equipment to makes dads movement easier. On the phone I can even hear it in her voice; she simply does not sound as tired and I'm looking forward to seeing how much of difference it has made in the flesh.

I arrived at Sarah's at about nine thirty (it was Easter Sunday after all) and she was just about ready. I laid a big blanket down in the back of the car for Misty and she obligingly hopped in (I hope she does not get flashbacks from the accident. Oh my, I really am losing it, aren't I?). Sarah looked lovely in jeans and a silk top. She had a little jacket over it as it was still quite nippy, but the forecast was fine for later so we should be okay. We set off towards the Thames and I took Westminster Bridge to avoid Brixton and aimed for the old Kent Road out of London; as it was still early the roads were quiet.

'So, Adam, what do I need to know about your parents?' She was sitting in the passenger seat applying a coat of something on her nails (varnish, gloss, frankly it's all a mystery to me).

'Nothing much, they are in their seventies, not rich like yours, but they are pretty nice really.'

'Oh come on, most of Mum's money comes from Dad dying. I didn't grow up loaded you know, well not that loaded.'

'It's not a big deal. You will probably be given more of a third degree by Beth if I'm honest. She knows about the Gary thing, and although she thinks I was a prat trying to stay mates for so long, she may end up being a bit protective.'

'Is her, what does she prefer to be called, lady, woman, girlfriend coming?'

'Janice, her partner, I tend to find that's a safe compromise, yes, she will be coming down too. It's going to be a bit of a shock for Mum and Dad as they are meeting you both for the first time on the same weekend.'

'Is that wise? You sure we won't give them a heart attack or something?'

'I don't think you are that frightening.'

'Oh very funny. Do they know Misty is coming?'

'Yes, as I said, I had a dog as kid, so they are used to them. I think they want to meet Misty more than they want to see me.'

'Stop exaggerating, Adam. I bet they absolutely dote over you and this is all an act.'

'Yup, you really have got a shock coming. If you think I am sarcastic, where do you imagine I got it from? Mum is a past master.'

'Are we picking up flowers?'

'Why?'

'I will rephrase that for the hard of thinking; that is you by the way. We are picking up flowers. I am trying to make an impression here.'

'Okay, flowers it is, but let me make this clear, when I turn up with you and they meet you, the right impression will have been made already. Misty also ices the cake slightly.' Sarah reached back and scratched Misty behind her ears. So far, so good; no sign of projectile vomit, yet. Sarah turned the radio on and I focused on the drive as the traffic began to build.

※

When we walked into the house, I could immediately see the difference in Mum. We are not talking fountain of youth, magic elixir stuff, but she looked like she had finally had some decent sleep and she did not seem to be in as much discomfort as I remembered from last time. She, of course, completely ignored me and went in for a hug with Sarah (how is it my mum makes my girlfriend feel more welcome than me?). Sarah was wearing high heels today and so the bending down to reach Mum was a little comic.

'It is so nice to meet you, Sarah, Adam has told us so little about you, but it's okay as his sister has kept me up to date.' Sarah was led through into the jackal's lair (sorry sitting room/lounge/front room—delete as applicable based on your underlying class) where she was met by Dad, Beth, and Janice. I followed along at a safe distance.

'I see the gang's all here.' Dad and Beth had a sherry, I guess Janice was driving as she was nursing a cup of tea. It was then that Misty bowled into the room and made her presence felt. Dad had recently acquired a stick and this may have been a red rag to a bull as far as Misty was concerned. She made a lunge for it until Sarah grabbed her and calmed her down.

'Well', Mum said, 'if you can control an animal as easily as that, we know that Adam is in good hands.' Now, I hope you are feeling the same embarrassment as me at this point. I tried to laugh along, Sarah most certainly was. Once the laughter had died down, she continued, 'We have lunch booked in the pub, shall we make a move? I liked the last place, Adam, but it was a bit rich for your father. They are just doing roasts today I think.' This was a nice way of keeping it local and keeping it cheap. It was what she wanted so who was I to disagree. 'They have an egg hunt there for the kids after lunch.'

'They are okay with dogs, right, Mum?' I was wondering if things had changed over the years.

'Yup, knowing you were coming, we checked with the landlady Ruth, all good.' My father rose again but carefully guarded his stick this time. He drained his sherry glass and addressed the assembled crowd.

'So who's ready for a real drink?' With this he set off for the coat rack at the front door.

'I guess we are off then,' said Mum as she started to shepherd us to the door (surely that was a job for Misty?).

<hr />

I needed to check, but I think that Mad Mary might have an alcohol problem, because as we walked into the pub, she was there at the bar. She saw my father walk in first and waved to him, smiled at Mum and Beth, looked confused by Janice, and finally glared at Sarah and me as we walked in with Misty. Ruth had done us proud as there was a really nice table set for six in the corner with a reserved sign on it. There was even room for Misty to lie down (Mum is showing a level of planning not normally known in our family). Once we were settled down, I went to the bar to get a round in while everyone looked at the menus (although I think Mum had already made her point about having roast very clear). Sarah came up to join me to give me a hand.

'All right, Adam, who's this then?' Mary learned across on her bar stool.

'Mary, this is Sarah. Sarah, Mary.' I tried to get Ruth's attention behind the bar, but I suspect she may have been stalling to allow the entertainment to continue (this was beginning to look like dinner and a show all over again). Finally Ruth came over and started to take the order. Mary turned round to continue her conversation with the girl she was sitting at the bar with. As we ordered the drinks, there was a bit of giggling and stage whispers between the two. Sarah took the first two drinks back to the table and as she was on her way back to the bar, three words could be heard over the top of the general noise that the two were making.

'Stuck-up bitch.' I was impressed; Sarah did not miss a beat as she walked. She simply moved in close to me at the bar and said in an equally audible voice.

'Oh, that's Mad Mary, now I see what you mean.' And there you have it, my girlfriend (oh, get over it, it's just a label), a lady who can look after herself, even without the help of Misty as backup. We wandered back to the table and got the food orders which I took back to the bar. I was now expecting round two. Sarah stayed at the table, sitting next to Mum.

'So much nicer than your last wife, Adam. At least this one likes cock.' Was that the best Mary could offer? I thought I would lower my game to her level.

'Fuck off and die, Mary,' and with that the battle of wits was over. After ordering the food, I returned to my seat bloodied but victorious.

The meal continued in a light vein. Mum was chatting with the two new ladies in the family as if they were friends of many years. Mum really does have the gentlest soul when all is said and done. I took the opportunity to catch up with Dad and checked on the state of his arthritis, his drug usage and abusage. We slipped outside after the food was consumed so he could have a quick puff before the puddings arrived. Misty had followed us out to have a nose around the garden.

'I hope that the altercation with Mary will not impact your drug supply, Dad.'

'I've found a nice little alternative with a couple of Dutch truckers who stop over every now and then. Mary is far too mad to rely on anymore, Adam. Good to see your young lady can stand on her own two feet. She seems very nice. Be a good lad and don't screw it up.'

'She is nice, Dad. It took me a while to work out quite how nice to be honest.' As he stood there and drew on his rollup, we watched Misty sniffing round the garden. I became interested as she appeared to be eating something. She kept leaping between the bushes in the pub garden, snuffling and then moving on.

'Misty, what have you got there. Come here,' I shouted across the garden. In her usual nonchalant way, she ignored me, continued chewing and snuffling in the bushes.

'Oh shit', said Dad, 'the bloody Easter egg hunt. She found the eggs.' Dad started to move in her direction, but he was not quick enough. I stopped him before he got five yards.

'Get Sarah, Dad,' I said and then bolted across the garden to where Misty was enjoying course number two or three of her lunch. She was having way too much fun to stop now and was keeping just out of my reach but continuing to chew and look around the garden for more chocolate. Dad had managed to get Sarah and she appeared at the door.

'Misty, here, now,' she screamed and Misty stopped in her tracks. She started to slink back across the garden to where Sarah was standing. All of a sudden Misty stopped and then started to convulse. She then delivered the chocolate and the foil wrapping in a very untidy brown puddle in the middle of the pub garden. The timing could have been worse, but not by much. Just as she was emptying her stomach contents, the children who were meant to be taking part in the egg hunt (and were now in tears at the sight) appeared with their parents from inside the pub where they had obviously just finished lunch. The scene was carnage, because of course there were now not going to be enough untouched Easter eggs left for discovery and the pitch had become somewhat unsavoury. I will draw a veil at the scene, but I think we shall simply say that after paying the bill, we had coffee and cake back at the house rather than dessert in the pub. My lasting memory of the afternoon was not the screaming kids or the mess left by Misty, but the smile of satisfaction on the face of Mad Mary as she rocked on her bar stool as we made our hasty exit. Her kingdom was safe, we were evicted. As I said earlier, that's just village life. Give me the city every time.

Chapter 36

To Be or Not To Be?
25 April 2011

When we arrived back at Sarah's and I moved to give a kiss before driving off, she looked at me and paused for a second.

'Aren't you going to park the car?' She smiled at me and went to get out to collect Misty from the back of the car.

'Sorry, I assumed I would just be off home now and that you would have stuff to do.'

'I thought you might like to stay for a drink. I could certainly do with one after the activities of the last few hours. It's not often I get to meet my boyfriend's parents, sister, gay partner, and disrupt an Easter egg hunt. I thought you might feel the same. Besides, it's a bank holiday tomorrow, I am sure "stuff" can wait.'

'Well yes, that would be nice, I could have one without getting into trouble with the old bill.' Sarah took Misty into the house and I found somewhere to put the car nearby. Luckily being Sunday I just had to pay for a couple of hours before the evening free period kicked in (feel lucky you don't own a car in London, they even make you pay on public holidays). When I got back to the flat, the door was open so I walked in to find Sarah. Misty was laid flat out in her bed. I think the look on her face was a mixture of discomfort and disgrace. I'm not sure she was aware of quite how incapable of eating chocolate the average dog's stomach is. Sarah was very good about it, as I thought I was going to be in trouble for not watching her precious pooch properly. Since Misty was okay (as I had stopped her early enough during her chocolate rampage), I think Sarah just put it down to a learning curve on my part. We talked about it in the car in the way back. After the accident, I knew quite how important Misty was to her, which means I needed to learn or relearn a few more things about dogs. I think I was too young when we had Fidget to be aware of the more subtle points of canine culture. I guess I needed to demonstrate that I could be trusted with Sarah's beloved mutt. As she pointed out several times, there were three of us in this relationship.

'You seem to be miles away,' Sarah offered as she came into the room. She was carrying two large glasses of red wine (don't get the idea that we are alcoholics, there are times when I drink coffee, tea, and water, it's just I'm sure you don't need to hear about them). She handed me a glass and I looked back with a face of concern. 'Well you can either drink it and leave the car here or not drink all of it. Or of course there is a third option.'

'Which is?' I was not expecting anything of this nature to have risen to today (isn't Jesus enough?), so excuse me if I am being a little slow on the uptake here.

'You could stay. I am not saying anything has to happen, but you don't have work tomorrow and we are now officially going out.'

'Yes, it's just . . .'

'It's just that you are trying not to rush me and you're being a nice guy. Adam, come on, at some point you need to take the initiative in this relationship if you want to move it on a bit.'

'I didn't want to rush you.'

'Five months, Adam! You know what happened last time you didn't take the initiative? I went out with Gary instead.'

'Okay, I get it. I'm just trying not to screw this up. I really like you as I have said a few times recently and I thought it would just develop naturally in time.

'Thank God that's all it is. I thought there was a bloody rule for a minute.' With this she was not just smiling but laughing and she leaned forward and kissed me.

'How about I cook for you, then if everything is going well, I can stay. Nothing needs to happen, just a nice evening and cuddle.'

'God knows what it takes for you to be assertive, Adam. But yes, that sounds lovely.'

'Okay, let's pop round the corner and see what you fancy me cooking. Then maybe we can watch a film or something. I have to say, I don't want to be antisocial but I have seen enough people today, so some time alone here with you sounds like just what the doctor ordered; the perfect prescription.'

'Have a look to see what I have on the shelf there might be a movie or we can pick one up at the shop, they have some on the counter.'

With this the plans for the evening were set. We walked to the shop (which was only open on Easter Sunday due to it being a petrol station), found a suitable movie that we could agree on (action in this case as she wanted me to stay awake for some bizarre reason), and I picked up some chicken to cook. When we got back, I cooked it simply with some mushrooms and a tomato and onion salad. It went down very well with the wine and we started on a second bottle while we watched the film. As advertised when the movie was finished, we went to bed and had all of the usual questions when this first happens. Who is which side, do you want water, what do you sleep in. She lit a couple of candles and put some gentle classical music in the background just to relax to. I offered to massage her shoulders and she turned to lie on her front while I started to rub some massage oil in. But for all the best-laid plans, etc. (again sorry about the pun), the massage didn't get beyond the small of her back as she turned over and pulled me on top of her and we kissed hungrily. If you think for one second I am now going to describe in lurid detail what happened next, you are very much mistaken. There was a lot more very passionate kissing and touching, but at that point just imagine I have blown the candles out and put the music on timer. Good night, see you in the morning.

The next morning I awoke to the strangest sensation. What Sarah and I shared last night was amazing, but see comments above as to the level of detail I am willing to provide on that subject. However, this morning she is doing something incredibly erotic without it being too intimate to share. I awoke to the sensation of having my feet licked and it was delightful in that half-asleep state. The light was still low and so I thought it must be about seven. I lay there and just enjoyed it for a minute or two and then I thought I had better acknowledge the fact and reciprocate.

'Sarah, you are a really naughty minx. That is heaven, but do you want me to do it to you too now?' Next to my head I could hear Sarah stirring and something of the logistics of this situation seemed to be slightly wrong.

'Adam, it's early', Sarah said drowsily, 'what are you talking about?' While she was speaking, the licking continued. Now I was thinking this girl was indeed a rare talent. Then it struck me, who can talk and lick at the same time? I looked down and to my horror Misty was licking my foot.

'Sarah, Misty is licking my foot. I thought it was you.'

'It means she wants to go out. She normally does it to me.' Sarah's hand ran up my body and stopped halfway. 'Whoa there! She doesn't normally have that effect on me. You sure you are not just after me for my dog? Misty, stop it.' Sarah got up, pulled on her dressing gown, and took Misty to the kitchen door to let her out into the garden for the call of nature. She was gone a few minutes and she returned wearing nothing more than a smile. Misty was shut outside the bedroom. 'Now, where was I,' she said. At this point, I realised that she has a much softer tongue than a German shepherd (but enough of that).

A mad panic ensued about an hour later as I remembered my car was on a meter, so I dashed out to put some more money on before I got a ticket (they even work Bank Holidays, it is almost criminal, right?). We had brunch in a lovely little café in Green Park so that Misty could get a really good walk. Sarah was now so busy during the week with her newfound source of work that she was keeping the weekdays walks a little shorter than Misty liked. Early in the afternoon I drove back to my flat. It was usually a pleasure to get home after a day away with all the noise of the family and being in other people's space, but strangely the place also felt slightly empty. I had only been in for fifteen minutes when my text went off. Sarah was checking that I had got back okay. I am not sure, but I wondered if she too was finding the silence a little much (mind you, she had Misty to entertain her). I put a wash on and started a session on the PlayStation while I listened to a little bit of 'American Idiot' on the stereo. I am not fully MP3'd at the moment; I still keep the old CDs just in case. I am one of the weird ones that still think the CDs sound better. I am the equivalent of my generation of the bearded guy who bangs on about the qualities of vinyl down the pub. Twenty minutes passed and frankly I was not getting anywhere on the level I was playing. I just could not seem to focus. The next text arrived.

>TEXT: 'What you up to? Misty is asleep after the walk. I'm bored.'
>TEXT: 'Playing a video game. Not succeeding. Missing chatting.'
>TEXT: 'Missing me?'
>TEXT: 'Are you fishing?'
>TEXT: 'Yes, missing me?'
>TEXT: 'Yes, I am. Too quiet here without you.'
>TEXT: 'You could always come back later.'
>TEXT: 'What time?'
>TEXT: 'In time for dinner. I will cook.'
>TEXT: 'Okay, see you around seven.'
>TEXT: 'Bring your toothbrush.'

I think she had made her intentions plain. I was sitting down and my head was now running over the possibilities. This was now becoming something more than nice. I was excited about going back to see her. I had better stick some clothes in a bag for work tomorrow though. In fact to make life easier, I would drop in to the office on the way over and leave a suit and shirt in the cloakroom there so as not to attract too much suspicion.

This pattern of activity began to be the norm. I had turned my new message indicator to silent on my phone as it was becoming obvious that the number of texts I was getting a day had gone from almost zero to somewhere north of fifty. I was not sure if it was at all obvious until Drew decided to make a big deal out of it.

'You got a new lady, Adam?' He produced *lady* in the way a lounge lizard might, with the emphasis on *lay*; it was rather unattractive if I am honest.

'Why do you say that, Drew?' I thought I could bluff it out and just get on with my work.

'The excessive number of texts? I'm surprised you have any phone battery left. Also, isn't that the suit I saw hanging up in the wardrobe last night?'

'I was just out for a few beers after work. Easier than getting home.'

'And the texts?'

'Just popular I guess.' And opened up a new piece of work on my screen and got on with what I was doing but I could see he was not taken in for a minute. I'm really happy with the situation with Sarah right now, but I am not up for being the latest piece of office gossip, so I don't want to enter into a debate about it with him.

'Fancy a beer after work, it being Friday? Bit of a POETS day celebration.'

'Love to but I have made other arrangements, mate, sorry.'

What I was not saying is that I was seeing Sarah later at her place. I needed to go back to mine first though as she suggested I leave more than just a toothbrush in her flat. This was getting serious, I had not got to this point in a relationship during the three years since my divorce and I was doing my best not to get too stressed about the big step of leaving my personal possessions in Sarah's flat. Also, she had not stayed at mine yet, so I thought I had better have a conversation about that too.

When I arrived, it was nearly eight thirty due to me being late leaving the office and having to go home first. Misty had already been walked so we went to have a drink in the local with the intention of picking up a takeaway later. Sarah too was exhausted from a lot of work and neither of us felt like lifting a frying pan.

'Why don't you stay at mine tomorrow? We can maybe take a drive out East on Sunday morning. Go and see a little bit of countryside.'

'Aren't you forgetting something? Madam needs to be walked and fed.'

'I know. The invitation is for the both of you.'

'You want Misty sleeping in your flat?' She looked at me with amazement. 'What about all that hygiene stuff you used to be worried about?'

'You come as a pair I thought? We can't just stay at yours. She needs to be able to stay at mine too. Besides it would be nice for Misty to see some proper countryside and not just manicured lawns and tame squirrels.'

'I am not lugging her bed all the way across town.'

'Don't worry; I will sort something out during the day tomorrow. We have a match in the afternoon and then you come with her early evening.'

'If you are sure? It sounds like a nice idea and she would love the drive into the countryside.' With this we finished our drinks and set off in the direction of the takeaway (Indian tonight, Misty has a thing for Onion Bharjis).

When Sarah told me that Misty was costing her an arm and a leg, I thought it was a mere case of exaggeration. Everyone says that, right? Well let me tell you, my visit to the local pet store was an eye and wallet opener. I thought bedding and food for humans was expensive. But the point is I wanted to show Sarah that I could be a good pet guardian (I thought dog father sounded good) as well as a good boyfriend; I knew Misty was so very important to her. I left the store with a bed, blanket, some food, and a couple of chews in an attempt to protect my furniture and shoes (we have all seen Turner and Hooch, right? I have this image of me taking Misty from room to room saying *This is not your room*).

After this I met up with Gerry and we saw another good home win so we were very happy in the pub, but I stuck to a single pint to make sure I wasn't late for Sarah.

'I guess this means you have something better to do later?' Gerry commented when I said no to a second pint.

'Sarah is coming over, but don't you dare tell Charlie. I know she does not need to borrow sugar from me or anything else on a Saturday night. I'm happy for her to meet Sarah, but give us a few more weeks to get settled first.'

'Tell Charlie, are you having a laugh. You know that Charlie talks to your mum on the phone. The whole Mad Mary and Easter egg hunt story has already been shared. You are on a clock with Charlie. You need to get this Sarah in front of her sooner rather than later if you don't want her showing up at your place.' I left Gerry ordering a second pint and headed for home.

I arrived back about twenty minutes before Sarah was due and I made sure the place was tidy. Misty's bed was now installed with pride of place in the lounge. I made sure when she lay in it she could see the room and the sofa where we would sit (maybe I have a new role as a Feng Shui consultant to canines). When Sarah arrived a few minutes late I opened the door and gave her a big kiss and a hug. Misty slipped past us into the flat. I took Sarah's bag and walked through into the lounge.

By the time we arrived, Misty was lying in her bed working hard on one of her chews.

'Very impressive, Adam. Let's see if you can get me into bed that quickly.' And with that comment, I am drawing a veil on the rest of the evening.

Chapter 37

Hanging on the Telephone
11 May 2011

Two weeks have flown by since Easter and we are seeing each other more than not. I don't mean every night as both of us still have things to do with our own lives, but whatever is going on is nice, in fact very nice. One of the other aspects about going out with me is the split Sarah made with her horizontal friend Gary. She had put up with his behaviour for a few years as he got her a fair amount of work at the agency. Now I know that sounds wrong and perhaps a little mercenary, but I don't think that was it the only reason. However when they finally split, the work really did dry up. As I have mentioned a couple of times, her move to a new agency has seen whole new world of work for her and Sarah says she has never been busier. The commissions also seem to be better paid and more consistent. One of the clients she is doing well with is a rather large three-lettered advertising agency in the West End. It has not been lost on me that now I must compete for her time a little more and this means doing my fair share of Misty activities when she is tied up (keep your mind clean, I mean with work, not to say I'm not keen to play that game with her too at some point). The upshot of this recently is that Sarah has been asked to do some work in Manchester and she needs to stay up there overnight, something she broke to me gently this evening.

'Adam, what you doing tomorrow night?' It being a Thursday, I thought I might be going to see Gerry and Charlie, but I may have jumped at the chance to see Sarah again (is this a bad sign, am I getting dependent?).

'You?' I answered smuttily.

'While that is such a lovely thought, you old gentleman you, I had something else in mind.' I snuck in close to her on the sofa and wrapped my arms around her waist and chest.

'Anything for you, my gorgeous nymph.'

'Before we go on, just a point of order, being a nymph does not imply you are a nymphomaniac that is just you being tricksy with your tongue.' I went to kiss her on the ear but she pulled away. 'No, stop it. Listen. I need you to do me a favour. Can you dog-sit Misty?

'Why, you got a big night out planned?' I pulled back and was giving her the critical eye.

'Not at all, I have to go to Manchester and they want me to stay overnight. It's going to be one of my biggest commissions yet. It's just I can't go unless someone looks after Misty. Mum can do the day but she has an event in the evening.'

'Well she can always come over to mine and then I could drop her off with your mum in the morning and just get into the office a little later.'

'Not too early. If I know my mother, she will have a hangover.'

'Well I can't take her into the office, but I suppose I could work from home on Friday. You could come and pick her up when you come back or I could bring her over to you later.'

'Adam, you are a diamond. I'm not sure what I would do without you'.

'Well I have a few suggestions of what you could do *with* me.'

'I suppose since you are being such a great help, I could see my way clear to indulging a couple of your little foibles.'

'Oi, they are not that little.' She hit me with a cushion at this point and Misty jumped out of her bed to join in with the general rough and tumble.

'That is not what I meant and you know it.'

My initial plan for Thursday evening was to go and get Misty and then come back to the flat. Maybe a takeaway and then some TV. I'm not sure what Misty likes to watch, but I am sure I could find something appropriate (maybe *K9* or *Lassie*). However, when I phoned Gerry to say I would not be over as I had to dog-sit, Charlie grabbed the phone off him.

'Adam, I have cooked enough dinner for you, why don't you bring Misty with you on your way? The kids love dogs and if I can't meet the girlfriend maybe I can vet her hound. Geddit? Vet her hound.'

'You should be on the stage, Charlie, sweeping it.'

'Oi, do you want dinner or not?'

'Actually that is a really nice idea. I am sure Sarah would be happy for Misty to meet more people. I've seen her with kids before and she is a real softy when it comes down to it.'

'Okay, then it's settled. See you later.'

I got out of the office a bit early and headed over to Sarah's place where Isobel had been sitting during the day. When I got there, I rang the doorbell and Misty started her usual greeting. I was not sure what was going on as nobody came to the door. I rang the bell again (you know you never can tell how long is polite to leave it in between rings). Finally I rang it one more time and then I saw movement inside. Isobel opened the door.

'Have you been waiting long, Adam, I had the hairdryer on.'

'What is it, industrial strength? Misty was barking her lungs out.'

'No need to be flippant, young man. Come in, I want a word with you.' I followed Isobel into the lounge and she pointed to a seat on the sofa. Both Misty and I sat down. Honestly, this woman certainly played the alpha male to a tee.

'Last time we met, you had no interest in my daughter, so what is going on now? I noticed the new toothbrush in the rack and a few items of male clothing around the place.'

'Surely Sarah told you we've become an item?' She glared at me and then broke into a smile.

'You will allow an old woman her little joke, won't you? I could see there was a spark when we had dinner, I just didn't know why you were both ignoring it. I don't exactly know what you are doing to my daughter.' I started to speak but she cut me off. 'And for God's sake, spare me the details. But you appear to be making her very happy. It has been a while since she has had a spring in her step like she has now. She is even being nice to me. Do you love her?' She stared straight into my eyes and carried on until I broke contact (I did mention alpha male, didn't I!).

'I have not discussed that with her and I am certainly not going to discuss it with you first. I'm happy to say that we have a really nice relationship and we are both doing things for each other that show we care. But we have both been burned before, so you will excuse me if I take my time getting down to words like "love".' I looked back, and although she was still staring at me, her eyes were surrounded by crow's feet as she smiled.

'Not a bad answer, young man. You seem to have your wits about you. I already like you a whole lot more than that Richard character she was engaged to. Never trusted the shifty bugger. But please don't hurt her, as if you do, I will never forgive you.'

'I will do my best.' With that I think the interview was over and I took Misty, lead, and bag of supplies and made my way in the direction of the tube to Gerry's.

<hr />

At Gerry's Misty was the hit that Misty was everywhere I took her (except for chocolate-filled pub gardens). Peter was not really into dogs, but little Ellie wanted to brush her and stroke her and cuddle her. Misty was as good as gold and I think everyone relaxed. Why is it that dogs seem to have that effect on people? (Well apart from the pit bulls you see surgically attached to skinheads). After we had eaten,

Misty woofed a good night to the kids and I took her back to the flat. By the time we got there, it was gone ten o'clock and she had done a fair amount of walking. She had a drink of water and lay down in her bed. So much for the quiet night I had expected. I put the TV on, but no sooner had I done that and the phone rang. It was then that I realised the message indicator was flashing. I wonder if Sarah had been trying already. As I picked up, the phone rang again and it was Sarah's dulcet tone.

'Where have you two been? It's nearly three hours since you picked her up from my place, I was worried.'

'I took her to dinner at Gerry's. I didn't think of mentioning to your mother, but Charlie had said earlier that she had already cooked for me. Sorry, I should have texted, but I did not think we would be that long.'

'Did she behave?'

'You know she behaves impeccably and she has given you a few weeks' grace before you have to meet Charlie now. She reckons as she has met Misty she has pretty much met you by proxy. Misty has a serious fan in little Ellie. Misty of course was playing the tart all night. She has worn herself out.'

'So I can't speak to her then?'

'Please tell me you are joking?'

'Of course I'm joking, come on!'

'Well you would need some luck with that request; can you not hear her snoring?' True enough in the dog bed in the corner of the room came a sound somewhere between and outboard motor and a chainsaw. 'So tell me about Manchester, where are you staying, is it nice? What are the people like?'

'Adam, sometimes I swear it's like talking to an excited child. You never just ask one question, do you?'

'I am just eager to know how you are getting on.'

'Okay, stand by for the download. I'm in the Hilton in Manchester City Centre. I have a lovely double room with a fairly decent view of the central plaza. This place has gone up in the world since the last time I was here, but I suppose that was about a year after the bomb so it makes sense. The people from the client and the design team are all very friendly and incredibly capable. I hope I'm up to the job.'

'Oh you will be fine. You know your stuff. Mind you, I am a little bit biased. What's that poem about my favourite poet? When asked my favourite poet, I always mention you, because you are my favourite poet and I like your poems too. Well that's how I feel about your art. It's also how I feel about you.'

'Sorry, was that you getting sloppy, Adam?'

'You know your mother wanted a chat with me?'

'Oh please don't tell me she did the *Look after my precious angel* speech again?'

'I think more the fear of God speech would be more accurate. She does care and she has noticed you are happy. So have I. I have also noticed that I am happy.' It went quiet for a minute. 'You still there?'

'Yup, just thinking. We went out for a beer and dinner tonight, it was all very tame but good fun as I said they are nice people. But you know what I wanted to do at the end of the evening?'

'If this is something rude, I am not sure I want to know.'

'Don't spoil the moment, you fool.'

'Sorry, please carry on. At the end of the evening, you wanted to do what?'

'Come and share my news with you. Come and see you and go to sleep with you. I am lying in the most fabulous king-sized bed here in a really lovely room and I am on my own. What I am trying to say is that I am missing you.'

'I'm missing you too. Misty I'm sure is missing you in her own way too.'

'Well I will be back tomorrow. I'll come to yours on the way and pick her up. I suppose I had better say good night.' Then there came the moment when one of us had to put the phone down. There was silence for a good fifteen seconds. 'You still there?'

'Yes, I am waiting for you to go.'

'And I am waiting for you.'

I could describe this in pain-staking detail, but for the sake of brevity, let's just end by saying it took nearly five minutes for us to end the call, by which time, we were both in stitches of laughter. Misty lay oblivious to this, moving from tractor to full jet engine snoring.

Chapter 38

The Key
24 May 2011

I seemed to have stopped having that dream about being chased by faceless women. I'm not sure if this is permanent or simply a hiatus since starting to see Sarah on a more permanent basis. I did however have a really odd dream last night. Inside the dream I am looking down at my clothes. I am dressed in ermine with a lot more frills than would normally be acceptable anywhere other than a costume drama or possibly during a Pearly King's event in the East End. I am holding a giant staff and there is regal music all around me, very heavy on the trumpeter section (no, I am not having a fantasy about my father being a member of the Tijuana Brass, this is something different). After a while I start to see features around me and I realise I am in the Houses of Parliament, somewhere near the door to the House of Commons. It dawns on me that I am dressed as Black Rod and this is the state opening of Parliament. But the door which I approach does not look right. It's my own front door at home (hey, don't judge, nobody ever said dreams were easy to interpret). As I approach the door and knock slowly three times, the door swings open. Inside is not the chamber I expect but another door and this time it is Sarah's. I hear knocking from the other side and the door swings towards me. Coming in the other direction is Sarah dressed as I am and carrying a similar staff. As we come together, we swap staffs and pass each other to go in the direction the other one came from. I then woke up, not so much in a pool of sweat, but more hanging out of the side of the bed about to fall to the floor. Yes, I think even I can see where this is going. We have been going out for over a month now and I am guessing my subconscious is suggesting it is high time she had a key to my place. You've got to admit though, great dream sequence. When I saw Sarah that evening, I thought I would avoid sharing the contents of the dream in case she thought I had completely lost it.

'Sarah, I wondered if you would like a key to my place. Since we seem to be sharing the occasional minding of the mutt, it would be good if you could come and go without me being there.' Sarah stopped what she was eating and glance at me suspiciously.

'My god, it has happened, Adam has taken the initiative. Of course it's a brilliant idea and I'm surprised you didn't mention it earlier. We are practically living in each other's places. Misty is now a two-flat dog. I will hunt out my spare key and you can have one for here as well. It makes sense, in fact let me find it now.' She got up and started to rummage through a dresser drawer.

'It can wait until after dinner, don't let your food get cold.' She stopped and looked at me.

'Oh, you mean you haven't got me one cut, you are just floating the idea?' With this I pulled out a set of keys to my house complete with a key fob which had her and Misty's name on it.

'I had a set cut in the Wharf at lunchtime and had the key fob engraved. Sorry if that is a bit naff, but this way you know which keys are which.' She looked at me for fully ten seconds and didn't say a word. She shut the drawer, walked over and took the keys, and then wrapped her arms around me. She held me for a little while and I could feel she was shaking. I realised she was actually crying. 'Sarah, sshhh, I'm sorry, I didn't mean to upset you.' She sniffed and rubbed her hand over her face.

'You silly man, you have not upset me. I am touched. It might seem like a little thing to you, but it is a massive thing for me. In all the time I was engaged, I never had a key to his flat. He didn't want me just dropping round. Well it became obvious why afterwards, since he was screwing my best friend. For you to show that you want me to feel free to call around whenever I want to and to already have got a set of keys made is a massive thing for me. You are so lovely. I will find you a set of keys later.' With this she sat back down and continued to eat her dinner. A couple of times when she was eating I looked up and saw her smiling at me. How was I to know it was such a big deal to her? Maybe the dream had purpose after all. Or maybe I had got a girlfriend and had suddenly grown a sense of empathy. On reflection I was doing things and thinking things I never did when I was with Annie. Maybe I was too young, immature, pick your metaphor, but I was seriously in the zone with Sarah.

Now where is all this going I guess you are wondering? Well to be honest nowhere for nearly a week. On the following Saturday I went over to help Gerry with a two-handed piece of DIY. The football season was now finished and Charlie had Gerry on a short chain when it came to household chores. Sarah had agreed to come over on Saturday night and that left Sunday for what was now a favourite thing to do, a drive out to the country. This weekend was going to be a bit of a twist as we had been invited to Isobel's for lunch (I would have to be on my best behaviour). I had not told Sarah what time I would be back and she hadn't said what time she was arriving, but with mobile phones, these things are never a problem in the modern world.

On my way back to the flat about five, I realised that it was later than I had intended to return. There was nothing on my phone from Sarah but I got to thinking. What if she is in there already? I have a mild paranoia about the place not being tidy and whether I'd left the odd cup unwashed from when I dashed out that morning (unlikely, but I still worried). I then literally stopped in my tracks and wondered what else she might find. I am not saying there was anything particularly incriminating in the house, but there were lots of things she could look at which might be slightly embarrassing such as old photos of me as a child. In the drawer by the bed, she would find some condoms, you know things like that. When I arrived she was already there but she was simply drinking a cup of coffee and watching the news on the TV while Misty was curled up in her bed.

'I had this scary thought on the way over that you would be rifling through the flat looking for dirt.'

'Adam, you are the cleanest man I have ever known, that is not likely, is it.'

'No, I meant dirt in the other sense. Gossip, scandal, embarrassing items, photos.'

'I'm not a spy, besides is there anything to find? When you say photos, you don't have anything tacky like pictures of old girlfriends, do you?'

'No, I was more concerned with you seeing pictures of me as a kid.'

'Why?'

'I was a seriously skinny, geeky kid.'

'What and you are Superman now, I suppose? At one moment Adam Cooper is just a nerd, but he enters into a photo booth and out pops Super Stud! You will believe that a man has flies.' Sarah is now simulating flying around the room and undoing an imaginary set of flies in her trousers. When she stopped and sat down eventually, her laughter died away and she looked at me. 'Did you honestly think I would be peeking into your stuff?'

'I'm just paranoid I guess. I have no secrets, but I do have photo albums here and they are not exactly flattering. Thank God that Mum didn't get around to showing you anything when we were there or Easter.'

'After all the hype, you know I am going to want to see them now, don't you?'

'Okay, look I need a shower after helping Gerry, I will fish them out and you can have a look while I am in there, but try not to laugh too much. And no taking the Michael.'

'Not even a little bit?' I took the three albums from the bookcase and handed them to her. Then I went to take a shower. However once I got to the bathroom, I realised quite how much I ached. I figured that a bath might actually be better for me. I started to run the water and put my head back into the lounge.

'I am a bit achy, you okay if I take a bath instead?' Sarah did not look up from the albums but raised her hand and waved me away as she flicked from picture to picture. She was of course laughing (I was not a photogenic child).

I immersed myself in the water and put some music on softly to allow myself to relax. I'm not a great one for baths but quarter of an hour slipped by and I did feel better for my muscles unknotting. Sarah was very quiet in the other room and I thought it was time I got out to investigate. I couldn't have her enjoying herself too much at my expense.

I pulled on my dressing gown and walked into the lounge expecting her to be laughing her head off and ready to extract a lot of pleasure at my expense. But she was sitting there silently.

'You okay, you are very quiet. I'm not sure I like quiet, it sounds suspiciously like you are up to something.' I walked around in front of her about to do something very rude by opening my dressing gown and realised immediately why she was quiet. There were tears streaming down her face. 'Sarah, what's wrong?' I knelt down and looked at her face. She had the photo album open at a shot of the family just after I had graduated. Beth was a gawky teenager, Paul was near 20, and I was in my graduation gown. Mum and Dad were either side of the group; it was the perfect family shot. I had forgotten the photo even existed. I was 21 years old.

'I saw the pictures of your family. You look so happy with your dad. I miss mine so much. We were very close, I was his little princess. He used to tell me all the time. Mother was always somehow aloof. She loved Dad's money but was always cold and critical.'

'You never said what happened, do you want to tell me or is it too painful?' I sat down on the sofa beside her and put my arm around her. She was not focusing on anything just gazing into the distance as if she was trying to recall the moment in front of her.

'Dad was helping one of the neighbours shift some fencing from their garden. That was him all over, always helping. He was not a fit man, as his job was desk-based; he was in insurance in the city. But this particular Friday he had taken the day off sick as he had felt unwell. In the afternoon he was feeling better so he went out for a walk and on the way back he bumped into Steve next door who was replacing the fence and Dad offered to help. Just as they had finished loading the stuff in the van, Dad sat down to get his breath and then went rigid with pain. His heart simply gave up, and it was such a big heart. He had overdone it and he collapsed. They called an ambulance but it was not quick enough. He was dead before he got to the hospital. Mum was a mess and I had to pick up the pieces. All the time inside I wanted to collapse myself. The funeral was the worst. I got to see all these people and hear how amazing a guy he was. Mum played the part beautifully as the grieving widow, redolent of a Hollywood heroine.' I took her hand and squeezed it. She smiled at me through her tears. 'Oh I know I shouldn't be bitter about her but she winds me up.'

'He was young then?'

'Yes, only just 60. Mother was a couple of years older than him, but she doesn't seem to age. I swear she has a picture of herself in the attic à la Dorian Grey.' With this she wiped her eyes and then started to laugh weakly.

'I used to think that about my folks, but I had a real scare when I went down and saw them in February. They are no longer spring chickens.'

'They seemed okay when I met them.'

'The home help has given them a new lease of life, but they are getting frail. I have been a bit naughty since Annie left and stayed away, now I am re-engaging. I know I won't have them forever. Maybe things will improve with your mum?'

'In all seriousness, things have improved with her since you came on the scene. She seems to think she was protecting me all this time and now maybe I don't need it anymore. I think she also likes the fact you stand up for yourself and you don't have any pretentions, not like Richard. Mother is not one for smutty humour, but although she loved his money, she disliked Richard so much she simply referred to him as Dick.' It felt like the tension had been broken. We looked on at a few more photos and then I put the albums back. I got off to go and get changed but she pulled me back to the couch.

'No way, tiger, you have made me cry, now you can kiss me better,' Sarah said as she slipped her hand inside the robe and started to rub my chest and stomach. Let's just say I hoped there was enough hot water left for another shower, possibly for two people.

Chapter 39

Walking on Sunshine
27 May 2011

After what was a very pleasant Bank Holiday weekend with the three of us (yes, including Misty) taking a trip to the coast for the day, Tuesday found me back in the office and the reality of work. After the last public holiday before August everybody seems to get either a bit down or very hyper depending on how long it is until their summer holidays. With me, I had nothing organised and so it was back to the grindstone more than anything else. In order to cheer ourselves up, Drew and a couple of the Cuffs had decided that Thursday night was party night. I had been criticised for declining these events recently. As Sarah and I had been an item for two months, I wondered if she would like to come along. When I got over to hers on Tuesday evening, I asked her while I was chopping the vegetables and she was prepping the stir-fry meat. I don't want you to think this sounds ultra-domestic, it had taken half an hour from arriving to go via the bedroom to the kitchen!

'What, drink with your banker friends? Yeah, why not, it will be laugh. Are you worried that Drew will try it on again though?'

'I think you are a big girl and you can handle yourself.'

'You calling me fat?' She giggled with mock offence.

'Hardly! I just remember the way you twatted me last time you were in the Wharf.'

'Oh yeah, sorry about that.'

'Can you come over about six? We can stay for a couple of hours and then perhaps come back to yours so that we are not back too late for Misty.'

'You can always stay on for a while and I can make it back on my own, I am a big girl you know. My boyfriend said so!'

'I'm not having you turn up and leave again. If we are together, then we are together.' And with that we got on with what we were doing.

Thursday had been uneventful except for the revelation that the contractor we had got in was more short term than we had realised and the evening event was effectively his leaving drink. To add to this, Drew had reached out to Angie, Ralph, and Bernard to see if they could join us. It turned out that Bernard was unavailable and would be for some time as his new firm had realised he had an alcohol problem and had promptly checked him into the Priory for a radical detox. All I can say is he must be very good at his job if they were willing to pay for that (not that it is uncommon in our world for people to end up there; you mostly burn out or turn to booze in this game).

When Sarah arrived, Angie said hi and Drew made a beeline towards her so he could start his usual chat-up routine.

'Hello, darlin', I didn't know you were coming.'

'No, you don't look like the type who would notice.' Not bad for a one-liner straight out of the starting gate.

'Nice', said Angie, 'I don't think we had a chance to chat last time you were here, I'm Angie. I may have been a bit tired and emotional last time.' She mimed drinking deeply. 'Adam is such a gent.'

'Yes, I know. That's why he is my boyfriend now.'

'Boyfriend, girlfriend, at your ages? How does that work?' Drew had decided to be obnoxious as his plan to pull had obviously failed. 'Surely there must be a better word for it. What about *partner*?'

'That just sounds like they are gay,' offered Ralph.

'Lady friend and gentleman friend sounds like you are in the middle of a London pea-souper with Sherlock Holmes in tow.'

'My other 'alf,' Drew offered with this thumbs in his imaginary lapels.

'I wondered how long the Cockney Tosser would take to rear his ugly head.' Drew was taken aback and looked slightly offended. 'Oh come off it, Drew, if the cap fits, then wear it.' I walked into the pub to get another drink for Sarah and myself. Unbeknown to me, Drew took this as a clear invitation to chat up Sarah. I was maybe ten minutes queuing, and when I came back out, I found Drew bent double on the floor with the women in the crowd laughing and the men wincing. Apparently Drew had laid it on with a trowel and Sarah had led him on. He ran his hand up and down her back and she slowly ran his hand down her body to his crotch. Once there she encircled his member and sack and then squeezed as hard as she could. The story afterwards is that the scream was akin to that of a locomotive letting off steam. I am hoping that will be an end of his antics as far as Sarah is concerned. I did say she was big enough to look after herself.

We didn't stay much longer than the time it took to finish the drinks I had bought. I have to say those events are fun when you are single, but a lot less fun when you have someone else you would rather be with.

※

When we left the pub, it was still before seven and I thought we might as well kill two birds with one stone.

'You fancy a detour on the way home?'

'Oh please make it as much fun as the last one. It's always nice to insult or abuse a tosser like Drew.' She went on to provide me with some of the choice lines he had used while I was in the pub getting the drinks. When she finished, I was surprised she had only squeezed his balls, not used her knee on them. I didn't think I was going to be the most popular person in his world tomorrow. 'Go on then, what did you have in mind?' she asked as we got to the tube station.

'Well as it is your night for meeting special people, you fancy meeting Gerry and Charlie?' I was already pulling up Gerry's text number to message him, but did not press send quite yet.

'Why not! I get the feeling in your world this is kill or cure, so we might as well get it over with.' With this I pressed send and we went down the escalators to the Eastern platform.

On arrival at the local tube station to Gerry's place, I got signal back and there was a message saying he would meet us in the car as it is a fifteen-minute walk. When I saw his car, we walked over and got in.

'You never bloody well pick me up! What's this about?' Gerry ignored me and focused on Sarah.

'And that is why you can't take Adam out. It's not the going out, it's the going back and apologising afterwards. I'm Gerry in case you wondered, but if you're as bright as Adam says, then I guess you didn't.' He put his hand through the back to shake her hand and then to cuff me around the ear. 'And since when do you sit in the back, I'm not a bloody chauffeur.' With this we set off and were outside Gerry's in about three minutes. I looked over at the house and saw the lounge curtain twitch.

'You joined Neighbourhood Watch, Gerry, or is Charlie unable to control herself?' We got out of the car and walked towards the front door. It was flung open when we were twenty yards away and a flock of children descended upon us. They were buzzing around Sarah all energy and questions. Sarah did her best to answer and interact but I think she was a bit shell-shocked by the time we got in the house. Charlie had chosen to hang back until this time. As we walked into the house, she came out of the kitchen drying her hands on a tea towel.

'Too late for dinner, Adam, this is not a canteen you know.'

'And good evening to you too, Charlie.' Charlie walked forward and greeted Sarah with a kiss on both cheeks.

'Wow. That's a relief,' Charlie said as she pulled back from Sarah.

'What, am I missing something?' Sarah looked confused.

'Well it has taken Adam so long to get you round here, I was expecting at least two heads. Thank God you're not ginger, one is bad enough. I was expecting a clone though.'

'What, does he have a habit of dating them?' Oh I could see how this was going, they were getting along swimmingly and I was now on the back foot.

'Two out of the last three I have met could have come from the same pod.'

'Ah, hello! I am here and I am not either deaf or disabled. Can you not talk about me like I am not here?'

'Who said that,' said Sarah and she and Charlie giggled. Gerry came in with the kids swarming around him and walked to through the kitchen to get a beer.

'Beer or wine, Adam, I think the girls can look after themselves.'

'Whiskey at this rate I think, mate. Actually wine would be great. We can only stay for one as we need to get back for the dog.'

'Don't use Misty as an excuse, Adam, she's a big girl like me'—at which Sarah smiled at me—'and can look after herself. Misty had a long walk before I came over. We can stay for a couple at least.'

'Welcome to the family, Sarah,' said Charlie as she chinked her glass.

I'm pleased to say that Charlie and Sarah did in fact get on like the proverbial house ablaze. I wonder if I was actually looking for someone in my life that Charlie approved of all along. They chatted about music and movies and what the kids were doing at school. Sarah was impressed that Charlie could hold down a part-time job and still be a full-time mum. Charlie was already angling for portraits of the kids to be drawn as presents before it was time to leave. There was a great deal of relief on my face when we walked out the door and went to catch the tube back to Pimlico.

Once we had settled into the second tube carriage for what was about a twenty-five-minute journey, Sarah snuggled in to me.

'I think that went rather well, but I do believe you have rather had it your own way today with introductions. Apart from my mum, you have not met anyone from my life. What say we go for a drink with my old agency buddies tomorrow? There is an event on, but I was not going to go. However now I think we should go together.'

'Am I likely to have to grab Gary's balls at some point the way you did Drew's tonight?' I made a squeezing and wringing motion with my hands. 'Actually that makes me feel quite sick.'

'Well, I don't know if he will be there, but I imagine he will be. Surely you are big enough to look after yourself too?'

'I am, but the trouble is when boys fall out, it is much likely to end up in fisticuffs, not a little aggressive cupping.'

'I trust you can behave yourself. Besides there are people at the agency I would like you to meet. These are people who have been important to me for a few years. Mostly we just converse through the ether so it is important that occasionally we meet up.'

'It would be my pleasure to escort you to the ball, Cinders.'

※ ※ ※

I spent the next day a little unsure and most certainly nervous of the night ahead, firstly as some 'arty' types can be a bit precious about bankers and I didn't want to spend the night defending myself. Secondly, I did not want to let Sarah down in front of her friends by getting into an argument with Gary. I am not the possessive type, but I think I could get quite territorial around Sarah. I was in danger of becoming the thing I was avoiding in my own rules, some sort of rogue aggressive male that won't let anyone near his partner. I wonder if women have their own rules and what they would be. Maybe rule 1, no overgrown schoolboys; rule 2, no blokes without a clue on personal hygiene (not something you tended to find a problem with ladies). Well anyway, this was not helping so I tried to spend the day not dwelling on what was to come, but failing miserably. Cometh the hour, cometh the man, they say and at the appointed time I met Sarah in a bar in Southfields, just on the outskirts of trendy Wimbledon where her ex-agency friends had assembled. When she saw me, she smiled and waved me over. Luckily it was very loud in there so we had to keep conversation with the people I met down to the usual small talk. It felt as if I was in a royal greeting line. If they hadn't all worked for the agency, I would have spent the evening saying *And what do you do* while shaking hands and curtsying (feel free to employ a regal female accent at this point). I can report although I am not going to repeat the details of everyone I met, they all seemed delightful people and very charming. They were quick-witted and intelligent with a real sense of the theatrical in one or two.

The evening was going very well by the time we got onto the third round but that is when Gary turned up. Apparently he had a previous engagement to attend first and so was late to arrive and already fairly well loaded. He grabbed a couple of the girls and made to dance with them, but unfortunately it was a little early in the evening for the lovable drunk routine and he was passed on like a parcel while the music played. Eventually he saw Sarah and they must have been playing a song that meant something to the pair of them as he danced over until the music brought him to a standstill at her feet. He of course did not acknowledge the fact that I was standing by her side.

'Little early for that level of being bolloxed, isn't it, Gary?'

'Ah, the high and mighty Sarah. What's cooking, sweet cheeks?' He went to slap her on the backside but his hand collided with my knee as I stuck it in the way. 'Oi, what's your game?' Gary turned to look at me.

'I have been hired for the night as close protection for Lady Sarah,' I said.

'She's no lady, I should know.' Sarah looked at me as if to say, don't make a scene.

'Well, I will take your word for that. I believe you are Gary, is that right?'

'Yeah, what of it?'

'Well I think you left something on the bar, they were looking for you a while ago, and maybe you should go and see what it is.' He looked at me through one slightly closed eye, trying to work out what was going on.

'Like what?'

'I don't know but you better be quick, you don't want someone else to claim it.' He turned, thought about it, and walked off towards the bar.

'That was actually rather impressive, Adam; I like a man who does not have to resort to violence. Shall we get out of here before he comes back?'

'You sure you are ready to go?' I looked around the room. 'The night is still young.'

'And the world is our oyster. Take me away from all this, you fool.' With this parting shot, she grabbed her coat, we waved our goodbyes, and we exited the room just as I saw Gary arguing with the barman about something that had apparently been left for him. The bemused barman was looking at the door staff and about to call them over. Game, set, and match.

Chapter 40

I Wanna Know What Love Is
10 June 2011

After the near run in with Gary at the bar in Southfields, I decided I would limit the interactions with Sarah's agency friends to smaller groups without him being present. We were now well into our third month of actual going out but in reality we had known each other for six months. We spent most of our time in and out of each other's flats, and Misty was now almost as comfortable with me most of the time as she is with Sarah. I found this out to my cost the other night when Misty stayed over at my place as Sarah had a return trip to Manchester for work. Everything seemed to be fine when I left Misty in her bed and turned in myself about eleven o'clock. Sarah and I had a brief chat before lights out, but I struggled to sleep. It was unbearably hot and so I opened the window; it felt really close. After a while I drifted off, but at about two in the morning I was awoken by a massive clap of thunder. I went to roll over once the initial shock started to subside, but before I had a chance to settle, I felt a massive weight land on the bed. I thought the ceiling had fallen in. In fact it was about sixty pounds of lean female canine now perched on my chest (I think you would agree she's a bit bigger than a Budgie). Once I realised what had happened, I reached up to give her a pat and a scratch behind the ears. I felt her body and she was shaking like a leaf and panting hard. The storm had really freaked her out. Well who was I to complain, she was such a big part of my life now with Sarah that I just calmed her down and let her stay while the thunder continued to strike. I did have the idea that since I was awake I might share this titbit with Sarah, but when I picked up my phone, I saw that she had sent a message:

TEXT: 'Massive storms due, saw on forecast. Misty may freak.'
TEXT: 'I found out. She is fine, says Woof a little shakily. Early warning is better!'

Well I thought, thanks for the prior warning. When Sarah returned the next day, I did make a point of finding out if there were any other things Misty had an issue with. She did mention one thing, but luckily it is not every day you see a clown in the street; although coulrophobia is more common than you would believe (although I don't know how common it is in dogs).

All this time spent together has made me start to think of the future. I have had longer relationships since splitting with Annie, but no longer friendships. When I first met Sarah and we went through the mates phase, one of the drivers for that was that she broke a number of the rules. The rules have been a focus of mine for some time now and I used to think they were the solution to all my problems. They were a way of not repeating the mistakes of the past and to give myself a fighting chance of a future within a meaningful and lasting relationship (excuse the soul searching, but there needs to be a point to all this after all). Now I find myself contemplating a future with Sarah, assuming we both want the same thing, and to do so means I have to a large extent break more of the rules I have set myself (I already broke the no-dogs rule and this does not sit well with my OCD fairy). The only one who needed to make her position clear (ignoring Misty, if I can) was Sarah. We needed time away from the everyday routine of life to consider our future (this is starting to sounds a little dramatic). I had a search on the internet to see if I could find a nice little place in the country that was dog friendly, where we could relax and talk about where we were going; I have always loved the New Forest and what I found was the Moorhill House Hotel just outside Burley. When Sarah and I got together than night, I decided to leave it as a surprise.

'We are free on Saturday right?' I had just got back from a long walk with Misty as Sarah had to finish up some work for her portfolio. I wanted to jump in the shower as I was hot and Misty was busily demolishing her water bowl (the temperature was still over 75 degrees at nearly eight in the evening).

'Yes, why?' Sarah put her pencil down and turned to me. We had introduced a rule when one was talking that the other stopped what they were doing and not just carrying on. It was more for her benefit than mine as I tend to multitask, but these things cut both ways. What is really weird is that this was a rule we had come up with together, something for both of us. If this was not a good sign, then I don't know what was.

'I booked a surprise getaway in the country, you okay with that?'

'Well that is so lovely of you, Adam.' She smiled but then reality caught up with her for a second. 'I will call Mother and ask her if she can sit Misty. She might not be available, but I don't trust her with anyone else. You know how it is.'

'No need. Misty is coming too.'

'Where? This sounds ominous.'

'Not at all. It will be fun. Just pack some clothes for walking and something for a nice dinner, nothing too flashy.' With this she walked out and into the bedroom. Ninety seconds later she returned wearing a dress I had not seen before. My eyes were practically popping out on sticks. It was a beautiful red dress, off the shoulder that showed a lot of leg and accentuated her curves in only the right ways. 'Does this come with a parental advisory? That is seriously sexy.'

'Why thank you, sir. Too much?'

'Just right.' I was going to be one very proud boyfriend (or whatever you want to call it) on Saturday evening when we went down to dinner.

We drove down the M3 and then onto the M27 before transferring onto the local roads. Sarah was not au fait with the area, but she and Misty were having a great time watching the ponies that walked around the roadside. I only had to stop abruptly once for a miscreant that was likely to become horse meat. We finally arrived at the hotel and pulled up on the gravel drive. It was a big old country house that had been converted to a hotel at some point, probably when the owners could no longer afford to keep it. It was all colonnades and stucco, very picturesque. We got checked in before taking our things to our room and collapsed on the bed. In the corner there was a soft bed and blanket for Misty but I had the feeling she wasn't going to accept that. This was her weekend away too and she was getting spoiled, so after a quick sniff of it, Misty leapt in one bound onto our bed and lay down between us panting and looking far too pleased with herself.

The first order of the day was to get Misty walked and to explore the surrounding countryside. We donned our walking boots, took a couple of bottles of water, and put Misty on her lead as we walked out of the hotel and into the nearby woods. The snow and rain from earlier in the year had caused a lot of flooding across the country and there was still evidence in the woods and across the heathland of very boggy conditions underfoot. I could see we were going to have to hose Misty down when we got back, especially as she had just decided to dive head first into a murky pond. She looked like she had been spray-painted with mud.

When we got back to the hotel, we found a very convenient hose outside and a bath we could use to clear her off in. I guess they were prepped for this sort of thing and it took the meaning of 'dog friendly' to a whole new level (this was definitely going on the Trip Advisor review). It took us half an hour to get her clean, and once she was, I am afraid we were not as she had transferred a lot of the filth to us. This gave me a perfect excuse for part two of my master plan. Secreted in my luggage was a bottle of champagne that I had slipped into the room fridge. For my next trick I produced a pair of champagne flutes. In the room, we stripped off and I ran the Jacuzzi bath while a now-pristine Misty fell asleep on her own bed; I think tiredness invalidated her earlier concerns over its quality. Sarah got into the bath first and soon it was filled with glorious soap bubbles. When I walked in, having at least showered the worst of the crap off me first, I was carrying an ice bucket and two glasses. I had plugged in the iPod to the room sound system and put it on a chilled playlist.

'Oh, special occasion?' She reached for a glass from me. 'Lovely, that really hits the spot. Such a luxury to have a bath with champagne. We just need candles now.' From the drawer I then took out the two candles I had hidden earlier and lit them (praying that the smoke detectors would not go off) before extinguishing the main light. I then slipped into the bath and sipped at my own drink. Sarah reached across to chink glasses. 'Cheers.'

'Cheers,' I echoed and we then lay back in the bath to enjoy the hot water easing my aching joints.

'Adam, this is all very lovely, but is it leading somewhere? You're not thinking of doing anything stupid like getting down on one knee later, are you?' She was half smiling, half frowning when she said this.

'With my knees, after that walk, I am hobbling like John Wayne.'

'Stop avoiding the question; please tell me you are not going to do anything embarrassing publicly later?'

'I want us to talk, but no, I am not planning a grand gesture, don't worry.' With this I put my champagne down and started to massage her feet. Ignoring the fact that a lot of water ended up on the floor, I am not going into what happened next.

※

When we went down to the restaurant, Sarah looked amazing. We had left Misty behind with a chew and the radio on (soft rock, don't ask, she is quite picky about music, but it does tend to soothe both the domestic and savage beast). Arriving at the front of the restaurant we were directed to a particularly nice table with a view of the forest. There was a log fire on one side of the room which was lit, although it would was not really required due to the season. There was another bottle of champagne already at the table chilling.

'Are you trying to get me drunk? If you want to try some strange sexual position, you only need to ask.'

'Behave, Sarah. How often do we get away, I wanted to make it nice.'

'Adam, I'm pulling your leg. So far today you could not have done more. I am really happy.' We took the menus from the waiter and both sipped our drinks while we worked out what we wanted to eat. Once we had handed the menus back, we were distracted by a commotion at the other end of the restaurant. A guy in his twenties was down on one knee and had a ring box open. The clapping began to circulate in the room as his dining companion nodded and they began to kiss. Sarah focused back on me. 'I repeat my previous comment, don't even think about it, Buster.' She was now wagging her finger at me. With this I pulled a small box out of my pocket. Sarah looked horrified for a moment. I handed the box over and she opened it. 'I thought for one moment there . . .' She trailed off. From the box she removed a silver chain with a small stone that matched her dress. I had taken about an hour to find a perfect match in the jeweller's having seen the dress the other night. As she put the pendant on, I decided to at least clear the air.

'Sarah, let's get this straight, I have nothing planned. I am not about to embarrass either of us, but I do want to ask you a question.'

'Go on then.'

'I want to know where you see this going.'

'Where do you see it going?'

'Okay, I'm happy to lead, since you like it when I take the initiative. When we first met, we had a bit of fun but you were not going to be someone I was looking at seriously as you broke a number of the rules. But since we have got together, I realise you are someone I care enough about that you are worth breaking the rules for. Before I get into something and get pretty badly hurt if it all goes wrong, I just wanted to know if you feel the same.' I picked up my champagne glass and downed it in one. I had not meant to be so blunt, but now I had put her on the spot I felt incredibly nervous.

'Adam, that almost sounds like an ultimatum. But I don't think you meant it that way. I agree that I was as suspicious as hell of you when we first met. Be fair, I saw you naked before I heard you speak; that normally only happens with strippers. In hindsight, I may have been a bit too quick to judge. You appear to have grown on me.'

'You make me sound like a fungus,' I said nervously.

'Quit the jokes for a minute, I'm trying to be serious for a moment.'

'Sorry.' I attempted to look as contrite as possible for my transgression.

'I'm saying that I have fallen for you too in a big way. You appear to be loyal, trustworthy, intelligent, good looking, and pretty good in the bedroom. The one thing I don't know is can you keep it up?'

'I thought you said I was good in the sack?'

'Stop being smutty, I'm still being serious.'

'I know you are, but there is still a little boy inside every man. We can't help ourselves'.

'Adam, arrggh, you can be so infuriating. I'm trying to make an important point here. I have fallen in love with you.' As she said this, she reached into her handbag and took out a box. 'The reason I didn't want you making any grand gestures tonight was that I had decided to, if you proved yourself up to it.' She opened the lid of the box and there was a man's signet ring inside. 'Will you marry me?'

Time stands still, I am in back in the dock and the judge is looking at the jury. In the public gallery are my family and my friends. Then there is a break and on the other side are Annie, Gary, Karen, and my exes. It looks like the two sides of a church during a wedding. They are all looking to the judge. He was speaking to them, but now turns to me. He is asking me what I want to do.

'So, Adam, are you ready to be a man, are you ready to be a husband? Are you ready to get it right this time?' The gallery turns to look at me and I clear my throat to speak.